THE CAMELOT CRIER

ABOUT TOWN: Newport News, Virginia

Recipe for Romance?

Camelot's most infamous playboy has developed a sweet tooth. Cord Kendrick, second son of the Kendricks of Camelot, has been seen in the company of caterer Madison O'Malley. The innocent beauty, best known for her heavenly muffins, is a departure from the models and starlets Cord is known for romancing, and Newport News is a far cry from the jet-setting bachelor's favored haunts. Although the Kendrick family has offered no comment on the simmering romance, sources say Cord has been seen spending an awful lot of time not only with Madison, but with her family, as well—a sure sign that things are heating up in any relationship. But is this sweet-as-sin chef more than Cord's latest indulgence?

Dear Reader,

We're smack in the middle of summer, which can only mean long, lazy days at the beach. And do we have some fantastic books for you to bring along! We begin this month with a new continuity, only in Special Edition, called THE PARKS EMPIRE, a tale of secrets and lies, love and revenge. And Laurie Paige opens the series with *Romancing the Enemy*. A schoolteacher who wants to avenge herself against the man who ruined her family decides to move next door to the man's son. But things don't go exactly as planned, as she finds herself falling…for the enemy.

Stella Bagwell continues her MEN OF THE WEST miniseries with *Her Texas Ranger*, in which an officer who's come home to investigate a murder fins complications in the form of the girl he loved in high school. Victoria Pade begins her NORTHBRIDGE NUPTIALS miniseries, revolving around a town famed for its weddings, with *Babies in the Bargain*. When a woman hoping to reunite with her estranged sister finds instead her widowed husband and her children, she winds up playing nanny to the whole crew. Can wife and mother be far behind? THE KENDRICKS OF CAMELOT by Christine Flynn concludes with *Prodigal Prince Charming*, in which a wealthy playboy tries to help a struggling caterer with her business and becomes much more than just her business partner in the process. Brand-new author Mary J. Forbes debuts with *A Forever Family*, featuring a single doctor dad and the woman he hires to work for him. And the men of the CHEROKEE ROSE miniseries by Janis Reams Hudson continues with *The Other Brother*, in which a woman who always contend her handsome neighbor as one of her best friends suddenly finds herself looking at him in a new light.

Happy reading! And come back next month for six new fabulous books, all from Silhouette Special Edition.

Gail Chasan
Senior Editor

Please address questions and book requests to:
Silhouette Reader Service
U.S.: 3010 Walden Ave., P.O. Box 1325, Buffalo, NY 14269
Canadian: P.O. Box 609, Fort Erie, Ont. L2A 5X3

Prodigal
Prince Charming

CHRISTINE FLYNN

SPECIAL EDITION®

Published by Silhouette Books

America's Publisher of Contemporary Romance

To Christine Rimmer, a wonderful writer and dear friend, with thanks for the title of this book!

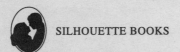 SILHOUETTE BOOKS

ISBN 0-373-24624-2

PRODIGAL PRINCE CHARMING

Copyright © 2004 by Christine Flynn

Books by Christine Flynn

CHRISTINE FLYNN

admits to being interested in just about everything, which is why she considers herself fortunate to have turned her interest in writing into a career. She feels that a writer gets to explore it all and, to her, exploring relationships—especially the intense, bittersweet or even lighthearted relationships between men and women—is fascinating.

THE KENDRICKS OF CAMELOT

William Randall Kendrick ~ Katherine Theresa Sophia of Luzandria

- Gabriel Jacob ~ Addie Lowe
- Cord Alexander ~ Madison O'Malley
- Ashley Regina ~ Matthew Callaway
  - Amelia Briana Regina
- Theresa Amelia ~ Bradley Michael Ashworth III

Chapter One

"Madison O'Malley, this here's the nicest thing anybody's done for me all week." Grinning like a young boy, the burly construction worker tipped back his hard hat and swiped a fingerful of frosting from the cupcake in his hand. The flame flickered and danced on the small candle stuck in the fluffy chocolate. "I can't believe you remembered."

"She remembers everybody's birthday," the rangy welder on his right informed him. "The cupcake she baked me for my birthday even had sprinkles on it."

"Yeah? Did she put your name on it, like she did mine here?"

The shorter man nodded at the white icing loops that spelled out Tiny.

"She sure did. Didn't you, Madison?"

"I sure did, Jake." Madison's smile came easily, her brown eyes sparkling with the pleasure it gave her to make one of her customer's day just a little special. She baked birthday cupcakes for all the customers on her route, once she got to know them, and she always put their name and a candle on the little treat. "I just didn't know if you liked chocolate or carrot cake better. If you'll tell me, I'll remember for next year."

Tiny told her that what she'd given him was just fine, and walked off, still grinning.

The welder she knew only as Jake took a cellophane-wrapped muffin from the display on the side of the gleaming silver catering truck and handed her a dollar.

"Morning, Madison." Another of the forty customers crowding toward her held out a five. "I'm taking two poppy seed and a banana."

"I have coffee and a ham-and-cheese roll here," a voice from behind him announced.

"Same here." Another worker, this one unfamiliar, took Jake's place. He handed her two five-dollar bills. "That's for me and Sid back there."

Madison glanced at the front of the newcomer's white hard hat. Buzz was written in felt pen on the strip of masking tape centered above the brim.

"Thanks, Buzz."

Having been acknowledged by name, the new guy smiled and stepped back to be swallowed by the forward surge of others wanting to make the most of their morning break.

"Hey, Madison! Do you have those carrot-cake muffins today?"

"She only does those on Tuesday and Friday," someone replied for her. "Today is zucchini and poppy seed." Another dirty hand bearing dollar bills appeared through the sea of worn denim and work shirts. "I took one of each."

A machinist with a streak of grease on his cheek held out a ten. "Same. And orange juice."

Taking the men's money, she made change from the small black pack she wore around her waist. The carefully arranged rows of muffins and cheese rolls she had baked herself that morning were quickly disappearing, along with iced cartons of juice and milk and gallons of coffee from her catering truck's built-in urn.

She didn't mind the dirt on the men's hands and clothes. Most of the welders, electricians, steelworkers and laborers at this construction site—like the stevedores and dock workers she would feed next on her route— were salt-of-the-earth, hardworking men who knew the value of even harder work. They were much like the people in the neighborhood where she'd been born, still lived and would probably die. Some were even from her neighborhood, the Ridge, as those who'd grown up in Bayridge, Virginia, called it. So were some of the guys on the dock. She was one of them. She knew the value of hard work, too. Day in and day out. She couldn't imagine living her life any other way.

"Hey, Madison." The deep, self-conscious voice came from beside her. "What are you doing this Friday night?"

Her smiled moved to the strapping steelworker who'd asked the same question three weeks running. Eddie Zwicki was tall, cute, built and probably only a year or two younger than her own twenty-eight years. "Going to bed early. I have to get up to shop and clean my truck on Saturday so I'm ready for you guys again next week."

"Don't you ever go out?"

"Not with my customers," she replied, her tone kind as she repeated the rule she'd adopted to save face and feelings. She didn't date anyone, actually. As hard as she was working to build her business, she simply didn't have the time. "But, you know what?" she asked, because he really did seem like a nice guy and there seemed to be so few single ones like that around. "I think you and Tina Deluca would get along great. I told her about you. The kindergarten teacher? Do you want her number?"

"Can she cook?"

"Your favorite oatmeal cookies are her mother's recipe."

"Yeah, but can she bake them?"

The guy was quick. "She's learning."

Someone behind Eddie gave him a shove. But even as he turned to frown at the guy who'd just passed him, he became distracted from his consideration of Tina's lack of culinary talent. As the rumble of quiet conversations around them suddenly tapered to near silence, it seemed the other men were distracted by something, too.

Madison stood near the door of her silver truck with its side popped up to serve as an awning. Moments ago she had seen nothing but the men lined four to six deep waiting to make their selections. Now, those men were shifting, booted feet shuffling in the dirt as they parted like a denim-clad Red Sea.

"Morning, Mr. Callaway," said someone from the back of the group.

"Morning, sir."

"Hey, Mr. Callaway."

"Hi, guys," came the deep and cordial reply. "How's it going this morning?"

The men's replies to the question were now accompanied by an undercurrent of murmurs. Workers who weren't talking simply remained silent and stared.

Madison immediately recognized Matt Callaway. He was the tall, commanding-looking gentleman in the suit and hard hat the others greeted with a certain deference. He owned the construction company building the enormous York Port Mall that was currently nothing more than acres of concrete slabs, rebar and steel girders.

He wasn't alone.

With a curious jolt, Madison realized she knew the man with him, too. Of him, anyway. Just as tall, even more imposing, the man earning the stares that ranged from curiosity to envy was Cord Kendrick.

She had never seen him in person before. But there was no doubt in her mind who he was. Like nearly everyone else in America, she'd seen pictures of him in *People* and *Newsweek,* on *Entertainment Tonight* and in the supermarket tabloids her grandma Nona Rossini devoured like candy. His reputation for fast women and faster living continually made the news. Even people who didn't pay attention to the lives of the rich and infamous knew of him. The entire Kendrick family was practically considered royalty by the press. His beautiful mother actually was royalty, or so Madison had heard.

She just couldn't quite remember if Cord's last scandal had been a paternity suit or a car wreck as she watched both men approach her. Certain her grandma would know, she settled her attention on the men's boss.

"Morning, Mr. Callaway," she greeted with her easy smile. "Do you want your usual?"

He was a bit of a celebrity himself, she suddenly remembered. His marriage to the oldest Kendrick daughter last year had caught half the nation off guard, since no one had even known Ashley Kendrick was dating anyone in particular. What Madison recalled most, though, was her own surprise when her grandmother had read the woman's new husband's name and Madison had recognized Matt as the very man who had given her permission to enter his site to sell to some of his workers.

The birth of his and Ashley's daughter a couple of months ago had made headlines, too. It had also resulted in paparazzi lining the chain link fence surrounding the vast construction site trying to get shots of him.

"My usual," Matt repeated, rubbing his chin. "I didn't realize I was getting that predictable."

"So you want zucchini, then? Or banana nut?"

"Surprise me."

She reached for a zucchini muffin and an empty cup for him to fill himself.

"And for you?" she asked, finally glancing toward the man she just realized would now be his brother-in-law. She had heard that the Kendrick family owned the mall project. That association alone could explain how the owner of the construction company had met Cord's sister. It would also explain Cord Kendrick's presence on the job site.

Grandma Nona was going to be terribly impressed that she'd seen them both today. But the only thing that truly impressed Madison herself was that Matt Callaway looked right at home in his silver hard hat, while the man with the admittedly gorgeous blue eyes looked more as if he were modeling his for *GQ*. The cut of his jacket was definitely designer. Italian, probably. The sweater under it looked too soft to be anything but cashmere.

His blue eyes crinkled appealingly at the corners. "I'll have his usual."

"One poppy seed. Coffee?" she asked, trying to ignore the jerk of her heart as his glance skimmed over her.

There was nothing the least bit subtle about that glance. He was checking her out, boldly, bluntly and quite thoroughly. He apparently liked what he saw, too, as his glance moved back up the length of her long, denim covered legs, over the maroon turtleneck tucked into them and up to where she'd pulled her dark hair up and back with a clip.

His beautifully sculpted mouth moved into a knee-weakening smile.

Photographs truly had not done the man justice. That expression packed enough charm to fascinate nearly anyone in a skirt.

"Cream. No sugar."

"You'll find cream down by the coffee."

"What kind is it?"

"The kind from cows."

"The coffee," he said, hitting her with that smile again. "Jamaican? French roast?"

"Folgers," she replied, politely. "That'll be a dollar and a half."

"I'll get it," Matt said.

"Already got it," Cord replied. Pulling a money clip from his front pocket, he peeled off a five-dollar bill and nodded to the logo on her driver's-side door. Mama O'Malley's Catering was stenciled in a shamrock-green arc.

"So, who's 'Mama'?" he asked.

She darted a smile past his arm as another worker took a muffin and handed over his money. "That would be me."

One appraising eyebrow shot up. "You?"

"That's right."

Cord watched the tall brunette with the long, lanky body and the face of an angel hand over a cheese roll that the man behind him couldn't reach. She wasn't being especially rude or cool to him. Her tone even held the same hints of kindness he'd heard when she addressed everyone else. She just wasn't giving him the same bright smile she'd seemed to manage for every single one of the other guys.

She didn't seem interested in conversation with him, either.

He could always get a woman talking. Young. Old. In between. Especially in between.

Hating to think he was losing his touch, Cord skimmed a glance over her once more. "You don't look anything like my idea of a Mama O'Malley," he confessed, slowly shaking his head. She didn't look like anyone's mother. She had incredible eyes, skin so smooth it begged to be touched and a mouth that made his water just looking at her. And those legs. They went on forever. "Why do you call your business that?"

"Because O'Malley is my last name and I liked the alliteration. Hi, Bob." There was the smile. All five hundred watts of it. It wasn't for him, though. It was for the guy with the belly and a welder's mask tipped back on his head. "What can I do for you?"

"Come on." Matt nudged his arm. "Let's get back to work."

Cord stepped back. "Thanks," he called to her, giving it one last shot.

"You're welcome," she replied, still polite, and turned her focus to the other men demanding her attention.

Cord felt his forehead pleat as he turned around himself, and started to walk away. Her eyes seemed to light up for everyone else when she smiled. Just not for him.

He glanced back, saw her look down as she made change from the pack around her slender waist. He wondered if they'd met before. If maybe he'd run into her at one of the local nightclubs and if he'd done something to offend her. He made it a point to never offend a woman if he could help it. He'd discovered the hard way that a woman scorned could not only be furious and hellish to deal with, but downright expensive.

The woman he'd heard the other men call Madison didn't seem at all familiar, though. He would have remembered the name. He definitely would have remembered that smile. It lit her eyes, made her seem friendly, approachable, as if she glowed warmth from within. Without it, she was just another pretty face.

"Does she come here every day?"

"Who?" Matt glanced behind them. "The gal with the snack wagon?"

"Yeah."

"We have a couple of trucks that come through here," he said, looking as if he were trying to recall the specifics of this one's owner. "I think she's been around pretty much since we broke ground." A quarter of a muffin disappeared, totally muffling his "Why?"

Cord shrugged. "Just wondered," he said, and sank his teeth into a bit of heaven that tasted of sweet butter and lemon and had him closing his eyes in pure bliss.

Madison watched the two big men in the silver hard hats walk away, devouring her muffins as they headed past a huge pile of steel beams and a bright-orange crane that sat still and silent while its operator drank coffee and smoked a cigarette. The workers only had fifteen minutes for a break. They usually cleaned out a third of her stock in five. That gave her ten minutes to pull her restock from the storage compartment at the back of the truck, fill in the gaps in the three tiers of muffins, cookies and rolls, consolidate the fruit so it didn't look picked over, and change the coffee grounds in the built-in urn so there would be two freshly brewed gallons by the time she reached her next stop on the dock twenty minutes away. She had another stop farther down the dock a half an hour after that. After a quick stop at a small tool-and-die operation, it would be back home to restock with the sandwiches and desserts she'd already made for the lunch run that started at 11:15 a.m.

Male laughter drifted toward her as she set her empty stock box in the back, flipped the switch to start the coffee and closed the stainless steel door. As she did, she consciously kept herself from looking around to see if Cord was still anywhere in sight. She hated the thought that he might catch her and think he had made any sort of impression. And he hadn't. Not really. Not in any way that mattered.

She had never before met a man anywhere near his social or economic stratosphere, or one whose presence seemed quite so…large. She was around his basic type a lot, though. The attractive irresponsible type whose sole goal was to get into a woman's pants and be gone before breakfast. She'd met plenty of them coming and going from her friend Mike's pub, since she happened to live upstairs from it and routinely borrowed his kitchen to prepare her food. And men like them, even if they were rich and famous, weren't worth the time it took to give them a second thought.

She didn't think about him, either. Not until twenty-four hours later when she found herself in the same spot she'd been twenty-four hours before, doing pretty much the same thing she did at that same time every Monday through Friday.

Cord Kendrick had so slipped her mind that she hadn't even remembered to call her grandma last night to tell her she'd met him and given the dear woman the opportunity to demand details.

The only reason she was thinking of him now was because Matt Callaway's secretary had just called her on her cell phone to order a dozen muffins of the sort she'd given Cord yesterday, along with six large coffees. She wanted them delivered to the construction trailer, which Madison could see parked a city block away toward the middle of the work site.

"I'm sorry, ma'am," Madison replied, going through the same motions she had a thousand times before as she closed the back of her truck and started to close the side. "I'm on a schedule, so I can't make individual deliveries. If you can send someone," she suggested, being as accommodating as she could, "I'll have it ready when they get here. I won't be leaving for another couple of minutes."

The harried-sounding woman asked her to hold on, which Madison did while pulling six empty cups and lids from the dispenser and popping open a cardboard tray to set them in. A half a block ahead of her the huge orange crane started up with a rumble and a roar. Break time was over.

A rustling sound came over the phone.

"I understand you don't make deliveries."

The voice on the other end of the line was suddenly much deeper, much richer and carried a faint hint of challenge. She recognized that disturbing voice in an instant. That threw her, too. She didn't want to think that anything about Cord had made an impression. She especially .didn't want anything about him messing with her heart rate.

Had the secretary come back on the line, Madison would have caved in and run the order over. It sounded as if the woman could have used a break. Since it was Cord, Madison's soft streak succumbed to self-preservation. "It would throw off my schedule."

"You don't ever make exceptions?"

"I'm not in a position to do that," she replied, pretty sure Cord Kendrick didn't eat many meals from a catering truck. If he had, he'd have some idea of how important it was to stay on time. "I have people who will be waiting for me for their break."

"What about the people here?" he asked with the ease of a man who knew exactly which buttons to push. "We need a break, too. But we're in a meeting no one can leave and we really *need* coffee. We need those muffins, too."

"Isn't there a coffeemaker in the trailer?"

"It's broken. Look," he said, having failed to elicit her sympathies, "I'll give you a fifty-dollar tip. Just bring the order. It won't take that long. Okay?"

Madison could practically feel her back stiffen as she set down the cardboard box she'd started to fill and glanced toward the long white trailer. It was as clear as the patches of blue in the early May sky that Cord Kendrick felt whatever he was doing was far more important than her schedule. It seemed just as apparent that he felt his money would get him anything he didn't want to bother getting by persuasion.

For a moment she was sorely tempted to tell him he was just going to have to go without today. As she let her more practical nature take over, she grudgingly admitted that, just this once, she could be bought.

Ever since she'd started her catering business, she had dreamed of expanding it. In the past six months, that dream had become an obsession. She wanted to cater parties. Big ones. Little ones. Maybe even weddings, where the food she presented could be elegant rather than everyday. She'd done a couple of small events already. Not that a birthday party for the McGuires' nine-year-old could be called an event, but the Lombardis' oldest daughter's engagement party had been rather nice. She desperately needed equipment, though. Having to rent serving pieces ate up all her profit. And fifty dollars could help buy the professional double chafing dish she had her eye on.

Aside from that, if she hit the lights right on Gloucester, she usually had a couple of minutes to spare.

"It'll take me at least five minutes to get there," she finally said.

"You're less than a minute away if you drive."

"It'll take me that long to close up and drive around the cordoned-off area across from where you are."

"Forget going around. Just pull up to where it's barricaded and park across from the stack of trusses. Ignore the sign."

"What sign?"

"The one that says No Admittance. And bring one of those coffees with…"

"Cream," she completed, then sighed because she rather wished she hadn't just let him know she remembered that. "Does anyone else take anything in theirs?"

She heard him ask. Then she heard him tell her they had sugar and powdered cream there before he thanked her and hung up.

She didn't know why his thanks surprised her. Maybe it was because he seemed a little impatient this morning. Maybe it was because it seemed pretty clear that he *expected* his wishes to be met so thanks weren't necessary.

Suspecting that not many people did deny him what he wanted, annoyed that she'd just done what everyone else probably did and caved in to his expectations herself, she finished boxing up the muffins and filled cups, closed the side of her truck and drove it at a crawl past girders rising from huge concrete slabs and the giant orange crane now swinging its boom toward a stack of steel beams.

Because she was always careful to park only in areas where she and her customers would be safe from traffic and heavy equipment, she was very conscious that she was going where she normally wouldn't go. She was now close enough to the actual construction to see individual sparks fly from welders' torches and feel the vibration of a back-up horn blaring as a churning cement truck edged toward massive wood forms. A forklift rolled past, carrying a large blue drum on a pallet.

Ahead of her, wooden barricades blocked vehicle access to the construction trailer. Assuming that the cars parked near the trailer had entered from the street on the other side, which she had originally thought to do herself, she looked around for the sign Cord had mentioned. She couldn't see it, but the stack of trusses that would eventually be part of a roof was impossible to miss.

Parking across from them, she shook off the niggling feeling that she shouldn't leave her truck there and slipped out, carefully balancing the box so she wouldn't tip the coffees. She would only be gone for a minute. Two max, she thought, stepping around the barrier.

It was then that she noticed the sign. The wording on the barrier faced the trailer and its parking lot. From there, the words No Admittance Without Authorization and Hard Hat Area practically screamed at her to go back.

Turning, she picked up her pace, her athletic shoes

leaving curvy little patterns in the dirt and the three wooden steps that led up to the long white trailer's door.

She didn't have to knock. The door bearing a plaque that indicated the trailer to be the construction office opened before she could even decide if she needed to.

Cord's big body filled the doorway. Yesterday's designer Italian had been replaced with designer American. Aware of the Ralph Lauren logo on the sweater pushed to his elbows, she glanced from the wall of his chest past the lean line of his jaw. She had no idea if his smile was for her or for what she carried, but he looked tired, handsome and definitely anxious to get his hands on caffeine. "Am I ever glad to see you," he murmured, and relieved her of the box. "Come on in."

He turned away, leaving her to stare at his broad back a moment before she stepped inside. As she did, Matt Callaway rose from a long blueprint-covered table where three other men gathered. All seemed to be talking at once. A middle-aged woman wearing the look of a harried den mother cradled a phone against one shoulder while she pulled incoming faxes from the machine behind her desk and fed them directly into a copy machine. The smile she gave Madison was quick and decidedly grateful.

While one of the other men retrieved the copies and passed them out, Matt reached for his wallet. "Thanks for bringing this," he said to her. "It's not a good morning for the coffee machine to be out of commission." He nodded to where Cord and the others were lifting foam cups from the box. "We have a little problem this morning and none of us can leave right now." A good-natured note entered his voice. "There are also some of us who had a late night last night and are a little more desperate for caffeine than the others."

"Hey, I was here on time," Cord defended, his tone as affable as his friend and business partner's. Lifting a cup toward the secretary to let her know it was hers, he set it on her desk. "If I'd known you wouldn't have coffee here, I'd have brought some myself." He reached into his own pocket. "I've got this," he insisted. "I owe her a tip, anyway."

Stepping in front of Madison, Cord held out a hundred-dollar bill. "Keep the change," he said.

Madison blinked at the face of Benjamin Franklin. Beside her Matt had already turned to pick up his coffee and was asking one of the men about some sort of design change. The others were peeling the lids from their cups as they looked over the pages coming from the copier and talking about variances and bearing loads. The numbers and phrases they threw around wouldn't have made any sense to her even if she hadn't been so distracted by the man watching her from an arm's length away.

She caught hint of his soap, and of aftershave lotion laced with citrus and spice. Two relatively fresh nicks on the underside of his carved jaw indicated a close and hurried encounter with his razor.

"You said fifty," she reminded him, not wanting to notice such personal things about him. It sounded as if he'd had a late date last night. Rushing to make his meeting on time could easily account for why he'd missed breakfast. "With the muffins and coffee that's only seventy-one dollars."

There were slivers of silver in his compelling blue eyes. She didn't want to notice that, either.

Someone's cell phone rang. Across the room the fax machine beeped. "Consider the difference a delivery fee."

Her voice dropped. "That's very generous."

"I'm very grateful," he said, echoing her phrasing as she took the bill and slipped it into her waist pack. "You have no idea how I've fantasized about those muffins."

His smile was all the more dangerous for the hints of fatigue that might have tugged at any other woman's sympathies. But his notorious charm was wasted on her. She'd heard too much about it. It also had nothing at all to do with the jolt that had her flattening her hand over her heart.

An echoing boom shook the trailer from ceiling to tires. Windows rattled. Conversation died. Surrounded by the vibrating cacophony of crunching metal and something heavy collapsing just beyond the trailer's walls, Madison wondered for a frantic second if they were having an earthquake. But just as suddenly as the sound hit, it stopped.

The men began speaking at once. Two engineer types headed for windows. The rest headed for the door.

Cord reached the door first, throwing it open so hard that it bounced back on its hinges. Matt was right behind him, hard hat in hand and shoving Cord's at him as soon as his feet hit the dirt.

Caught in the surge of bodies as everyone else now rushed out, Madison found herself hurrying down the steps then stepping aside so she wouldn't be in the way or get knocked over in the ministampede of foremen and the secretary coming through the doorway. Everyone else seemed to realize that whatever disaster had caused the noise was man-made rather than natural, but Madison barely had a chance to hope that no one had been hurt before she looked to where the wall of men now blocked the No Admittance sign.

They couldn't go any farther.

The crane that had been lifting long steel I-beams had lost its load. Right on her truck.

Chapter Two

Utter disbelief kept Madison rooted right where she stood. Mouth open, too stunned to speak, she stared at the pile of crisscrossed beams that had just annihilated her vehicle. Other than those twenty-foot-long, two-ton girders of tempered steel, she couldn't see anything but part of the white cab's cratered roof and a spray of glittering glass shards that had been its windows and headlights.

Her first thought as she screamed, "My truck!" and panic sent her into motion was to save what she could of her food. As she darted toward the men, her second was that she smelled gasoline.

Shoving her way past the barrier of bodies and the barricade, intent on saving what she could, it vaguely occurred to her that the gas tank had ruptured.

"Hey, lady! Stay back!"

"Somebody stop her!"

She had no idea who'd yelled at her. "That's my truck!" she cried again, only to feel something hard clamp around her arm.

That iron grip stopped her cold.

Disbelieving, distraught, she whirled to see Cord holding her back as the other men slipped past the barricade.

"What are you doing?" she screamed, struggling to break his hold.

"I'm saving your neck!" The heat of his palm burned into her, his grip as unyielding as his tone. "That claw is still swinging up there, and the beams it dropped aren't stable. If one lands on you, it'll break half the bones in your body."

Even as he spoke, a long, heavy girder slipped from the top of the pile. It slid to the dirt with the groan of metal and a resounding thud that had men jumping back as if they'd been jerked by strings. Someone yelled for someone else to put out his cigarette. Overhead, the huge black claw that had held the beams swung from its cables like the pendulum of a clock.

Madison's glance fell back to what was left of her truck and the dark pool slowly seeping from under it. With a shiver, she realized a single spark could turn the pile of collapsed metal into a bonfire.

"You're lucky you were bringing the coffee," Cord muttered above her. "If you'd been inside there, you'd have been history."

Shock turned to incredulity.

"You think my bringing you breakfast saved me from being hurt?" Adrenaline surged as her eyes collided with his. "Are you delusional? If I hadn't delivered that order, I would have been halfway to my next stop by now. That's clear over by the docks, miles away from that…that…thing," she concluded, waving her free arm at the crane.

"Hey," he soothed. "Take it easy."

Easy? "How am I supposed to do that?" she demanded, offended that he would even suggest it. "Because I did deliver that order, I'm not going to make that stop or any of my other stops. My truck has been reduced to a manhole cover, and the food I got up at three o'clock to make is mush. That truck is my livelihood, Kendrick, and the people at my stops depend on me to be there on time."

Her outstretched arm reminded her that he still had her other one shackled. Not caring at all for the patient look he had the nerve to give her, she jerked back. Hard.

Suspecting that she hadn't freed herself so much as he had let her go, not liking the idea that he held power over her in any form, she spun away, only to spin right back. He actually thought he'd *helped* her?

"I never should have listened to you," she insisted, her chin up, her voice quavering with anger and the anxiety that got a firmer grip with each passing second. "I should have stuck to my schedule and not paid any attention to anything you offered or anything you said. You're the one who told me to park there. Right there. In that very spot," she reminded him, poking her finger toward the pile. "You even told me to ignore the warning sign. So, don't you *dare* act like you've done me any favors."

She was furious. She was distraught. She clearly blamed him and him alone for what had happened.

She also looked as if she could go for his throat because she'd done what he had asked. Fearing she might do just that, anxious to avoid a scene, Cord ignored the lack-of-sleep headache brewing in the base of his skull and started to reach for her again.

She immediately stepped away. Since calming her down by touch didn't appear to be an option, he made his manner as placating as he could.

"You'll get another truck," he assured her. "I'll buy you a new one and you'll be back in business in no time."

Her eyes flashed at his attempt to appease. The bits of gold in their liquid brown depths reminded him of flame. "I need to be back in business *now*," she informed him. Her hand darted toward the pile of rubble again "Throwing your money at this isn't going to fix it. You can't replace a catering truck the way you can a car. New ones have to be ordered."

"So I'll order one."

"It took me three months to get that one! What am I supposed to do in the meantime?"

Cord opened his mouth to reply. Having no idea what to say that wouldn't just add fuel to her fire, he shut it again. Jamming his hands into his pockets, he watched her walk off. Stalk, actually, though even angry, she moved with a feminine grace that held his focus on the slender line of her back, the gentle flare of her hips, her long, long legs. She did more for cotton knit and denim than most women did for cashmere and silk. Definitely more than many of the women he'd met over the years. Especially the models. There was a softness about her curves that told him she at least had some meat on her bones.

With her luminous brown eyes and her incredible mouth, Madison O'Malley looked like pure temptation. Or would have if she hadn't gone off the deep end about who was responsible for the state of her truck.

Feeling another publicity nightmare coming on, willing to do anything to avoid it, he followed to where she'd made it past two engineers in hard hats scratching their heads over how best to move the beams. He wanted coffee. He wanted food. He wanted to finish his meetings here, get ready for the sailing race in Annapolis next week and forget he'd ever laid eyes on the spitfire now arguing with the site supervisor.

Unfortunately, what he wanted wasn't possible at the moment.

Madison wasn't arguing.

She was begging.

"Just let me see if I can get the storage door open. Please," she asked the weathered-looking man in a chambray shirt blocking her way. "I just want to salvage whatever is left of my food."

"I keep telling you, ma'am, it's too dangerous." He motioned to the driver of a forklift, far less concerned with her problems than his own. Progress had just come to a screeching halt at this section of the huge project. "You saw that beam slip a minute ago. That one there could go next," he said, pointing to one hovering at eye level. "Let us get this cleared out, then you can do what you need to do. You shouldn't be here without a hard hat, anyway."

His glance moved past her shoulder. "I told her she shouldn't be here, Mr. Kendrick," he called. "She's just not listening."

"It's okay," Cord called back, walking toward them as if he owned the place—which, she supposed, he did. "I'll take care of this."

It was as obvious as the supervisor's relief that no one was going to let her near her truck, much less inside any part she might be able to squeeze into. Realizing that, Madison looked from the crossed lengths of steel and frantically switched gears. If she couldn't save some of her inventory, then she needed to focus on transportation. She needed some way to get to her other stops and tell her customers...

Tell them what? she wondered, deliberately turning from Cord's approach. That she couldn't feed them today? That she couldn't feed them the rest of the week? The month?

Only once in her life had she failed an obligation. That had been years ago, yet she still lived with the consequences of that failure in one form or another every day of her life. She had diligently met every responsibility ever since. The thought of not meeting her commitments now added anxiety to pure distress.

She needed a vehicle. Something large. But her thoughts got no further than wondering whose vehicle she could borrow when she realized her mind was turning in aimless circles, too overwhelmed to think at all.

The staccato beep of a back-up horn joined the shouts of men and the clang of metal as she sank down on a stack of cement blocks. Not sure if she felt bewildered or simply numb, she propped her elbows on her knees and dropped her face into her hands.

She couldn't phone ahead to her next stop. There was no one in particular to call. It was simply a spot where she parked on the pier between dock 23 and 24. As soon as she arrived, some of the men who unloaded the cargo ships or tended their repairs would start swarming toward her. There were other catering trucks that serviced the area. But each had its own spot and its own loyal customers. Her customers would be waiting for her even now.

The thought that she was letting them down put a knot the size of a muffin in her stomach.

A large hand settled cautiously on her shoulder.

"Hey," Cord murmured. "Are you all right?"

Beneath his palm, he felt her slender muscles stiffen. He knew she wasn't okay. Even as insensitive as he'd been accused of being, he could see that. He just hoped she wasn't crying. He never knew what to do when a woman did that. If she was, though, he'd deal with it—simply because he couldn't let her walk off without taking care of what had happened.

His hand slipped from her shoulder. He could argue that he was no more at fault for the present condition of her truck than she was. After all, she had made the decision to accept the order and deliver it. And she was the one who'd made the final decision about where to park her vehicle.

He could also point out that the true culprit here was the crane or its operator, both of which belonged to Callaway Construction. As upset as she seemed, he doubted that she'd care about that logic, though. As for himself, all he cared about was avoiding headlines. The last thing he needed was more bad publicity. He especially did not need another woman suing him. His father would disown him for sure.

"Here." Tugging at the knees of his slacks, he crouched in front of her. Relief hit when she glanced up. Her golden-brown eyes were blessedly clear. Not a tear in sight. As he pulled off his hard hat and pushed his fingers through his hair, he thought she looked awfully pale, though. And more than a little upset. Not that he could blame her. Her truck was scrap metal. "You need to wear this."

Lifting the silver metal hat, he sat it on her head, tipping it back so he could see her eyes. "It's the only way Matt will let you stay in this area."

"What about you now?"

He shrugged. Following rules had never been his strong suit.

"Look." He clasped his hands between his spread knees. "We can work this out. I'm going to make sure everything is all right. Okay?"

She said nothing. She just stared at him as if he were speaking some language she didn't comprehend, while someone shouted for the laborers who'd wandered over to get back to work.

The way her delicate brow finally pinched made him think she might ask how he was going make everything right again. She didn't seem the type to accept a man's word on blind faith. His word, anyway.

Instead she asked, "What kind of car do you have?"

"Car?"

"What do you drive?" she clarified.

He nodded toward the closest of the vehicles on the other side of the barricade. "That Lamborghini over there."

Madison glanced at the squat silver car. As low and flat as it was, it looked as if something heavy had landed on it, too. "Of course," she murmured.

Taking a deep breath, she shook her head as if willing it to clear. Her fingers trembled as she lifted her hand to her forehead and nudged back the hat's hard plastic inner band. "I need something bigger." Curling her fingers into her palm, she lowered her hand to hide the shaking. If she was going to fall apart, it wasn't going to be where anyone could see it. "I have my lunch restock at the pub. If I can get a van or something of that size and some ice chests, I can get my customers their lunch today and let them know I won't be there for them tomorrow.''

''A van,'' he repeated.

''Your insurance should cover the cost of renting one. I can't turn this in on my policy.'' She'd already had two minor fender-benders. ''My premiums are high enough as it is. Something like this will send them through the ceiling.''

Cord held out his hand to quiet her. He needed to keep her calm. He also wanted very much to keep settlement as simple as possible. ''Your insurance won't have to pay a cent,'' he assured her, not bothering to add that he would be writing the checks himself to make sure of that.

He wanted to keep insurance companies out of this completely. Hers, Callaway Construction's and especially Kendrick Investment's. If insurance carriers were involved, that would mean they would need her statement. There was no reason for his name to appear on the incident report Matt would have to file to satisfy site and government safety regulations. But if she mentioned in a claim statement that hc'd told her where to park—and to ignore the warning signs, to boot—that would be all it would take for his name to leak out somehow and for the press to start dragging it through the mud again.

He could see the headlines now.

Prodigal Prince of Camelot Destroys Working Girl's Livelihood.

There were times when he couldn't win for losing. All he'd wanted was breakfast.

''Just tell me what you need and I'll see that you get it. How many ice chests?''

''Enough to hold two hundred sandwiches, a hundred cans of soda, and two hundred cartons of milk and juices.'' Doing a quick mental inventory of her normal lunch run, Madison decided she'd have to forget coffee. She had no way to make it. "I can put desserts and fruit in boxes."

"How soon do you need it?"

Ten minutes ago, she thought. "An hour and a half," she replied, because that's when she normally would start her lunch run.

She thought for certain that the man crouched in front of her would tell her there was no way that would happen. At the very least, she expected him to point out that the paperwork alone could take that long. Yet, he gave no indication at all that he expected her needs to be a problem.

Looking very much like a man who never expected needs of any sort to be a problem, he rose with an easy, athletic grace and offered her his hand.

She had no idea why the gentlemanly gesture caught her so off guard.

"Consider it done," he replied, taking her hand when she didn't move. He tugged her up, promptly let her go. "An hour and a half," he agreed. "Where do you want the van delivered?"

She couldn't believe he was being so cooperative. She didn't believe, either, that he could pull off such a miracle. "Mike's Pub on Lexington and Hancock in Bayridge," she said, wondering if Mike Shannahan could be bribed into letting her borrow his pickup. Mike loved his truck. He polished and pampered it as if the thing had a soul. Maybe if she promised to cook him dinner every night for a month, he'd let her use it. "It's about five miles southeast of here," she added, on the outside chance that miracles actually did happen.

Reaching into the front pocket if his khakis, Cord pulled out his money clip and slipped out a twenty-dollar bill. "Have Suzanne in the construction office call you a cab," he said, as she stared at the money.

"What about my truck?"

"I'll take care of it. You just do what you need to do with the van. Hey, Matt," he called, and left her staring at the hat dent in the back of his golden hair as he walked away.

It took nearly an hour for a cab to arrive. Madison spent most of that time pacing between the trailer and the barricade and trying to reach Mike on her cell phone. Mike had been four years ahead of her all through school, so she'd actually known his sisters better when they were all younger, but Mike had always been like a big brother to her. Since she rented the apartment above the pub from him and used the pub's kitchen to prepare her food, he was also her landlord.

She couldn't reach him, though. The pub didn't open until noon and he wasn't answering his home phone.

When the cab arrived, she was trying to think of who else had a truck and wouldn't be at work that time of day. Twenty minutes later she had concluded that even if she did locate a truck, it would take forever to borrow the ice chests she needed. Still refusing to give up, because giving up simply wasn't something she did, she decided to rent ice chests and was mentally calculating how long it would take her do that when the cab rolled to a stop.

Mike's Pub, with its familiar green awnings, leaded-glass windows and angled, corner door, sat on a narrow street that reflected the very essence of the Ridge's roots. There wasn't a building or business in the Ridge that hadn't been there for as long as Madison could remember. Corollis' Deli sat next door to the pub. Next to the deli, the beauty shop still turned out women with perms and blue hair, but had recently updated to add weaves. Across the street, below two stories of apartments, Reilly Brothers' Produce anchored one corner, the Bayridge Bookstore the other. In between were sandwiched the pharmacy and an Italian bakery that had been run by three generations of Balduccis.

Surrounding them all was the neighborhood, with its tree-lined streets, tidy houses, cracked sidewalks and bicycles lying on neat lawns.

All Madison noticed after she paid her driver was the white van parked near the corner mailbox.

A young man in a blue mechanic's uniform met her as she stepped from the cab. After confirming that she was Madison O'Malley, he handed her the van's keys, told her there were ice chests and ice inside it, and left in a beige SUV that had been waiting nearby to give him a lift back to wherever it was he'd come from.

As she stared at the keys in her hand, it took her a moment to realize she could stop worrying about how she was going to make her lunch stops. Cord had actually done what he'd said he'd do. And with time to spare.

Madison had even more time to spare a few hours later. And spare time wasn't something she usually had.

She usually finished her lunch route by 12:40 and returned to the pub near 4:00 p.m. With her normal routine seriously shot, she found herself back an hour early because she had no truck to gas up and clean, no leftovers to drop off at the seniors' center and no idea how she was going to salvage her business.

As she pulled up behind the silver Lamborghini parked at the curb, she also had no idea why the fates had seen fit to throw Cord Kendrick into her path.

Three animated preteen boys hung around the racy car in front of her. Only one seemed able to tear his glance from all that horsepower when she walked over to see what they were up to. Sean Bower's focus, however, had already turned back to the wide black tires when he spoke.

"Isn't this way cool, Madison? It must go a hundred miles an hour!"

"Way cool, Sean," she replied, unable to help smiling at the wide-eyed awe behind his little glasses. The Ridge was a Ford-and-Chevy sort of neighborhood. A car that probably cost more than any of their homes necessarily drew attention. Particularly the attention of the juvenile male variety. Personally, she still thought the thing looked as if something heavy had sat on it. "And I'm sure it does." She ducked her head to see Sean's face. "You might want to back up so you don't get drool on that fender."

Backing up herself, she glanced toward the ten-year-old Balducci twins. She'd never been able to tell them apart. It didn't help that they both always wore blue navy SEAL baseball caps. "You boys all keep your hands off the car. Okay?"

The one on the right, Joey, she thought, put his hands behind his back. "We didn't touch anything."

"Yes, you did, Jason," his brother insisted, proving that she'd gotten them wrong again. "You breathed on the rearview mirror and made your nose print on it."

"Did not!"

"Did, too!"

"Boys?" Madison called, stopping with her hand on the pub door's ancient brass handle. "Wipe the print off. Okay, Jason? And keep your hands to yourself."

She didn't wait to see if the boys would comply. Had

Cord's car been parked a couple of miles farther south, she would have reason to be concerned about the safety of his hubcaps. The kids from this neighborhood, though, rarely caused real trouble. When everyone knew who you were, knew where you lived, who your parents were or who your teacher was, it took considerable creativity to stray too far from the straight and narrow.

When she walked through the door, the sounds of the boys' animated voices gave way to the voice of a sports announcer coming from the wall-mounted television above the bar. Rumor had it that, except for the TV, the neon beer signs and a new mirror behind the bar, Mike's Pub hadn't changed much since the first Michael Patrick Shannahan had opened it a hundred years ago. Four generations and four Michael Patricks later, lace curtains still hung over the front windows, dark wood booths still lined the walls, a dozen scarred wooden bar stools still lined the long, brass-railed bar, and pints of beer still flowed from the taps along with the bartender's sympathy for whatever injustice or woe a patron had suffered that day.

Her eyes were still adjusting to the dimmer light when the men sitting at the bar ahead of her turned to see who'd joined them. Usually when she arrived home, the place was packed with dock workers who worked the seven-thirty to three shift and stopped for a cold beer and conversation on their way home. Since she was a little early, only Ernie Jackson and Tom Farrell were there.

"Hi, Madison." The craggy-faced Ernie gave her a toothless smile. "Finish up early today?"

"How's it going, Ernie?" she asked automatically.

"Can't complain," he said, and turned back to the beer he'd probably been nursing since noon.

Tom, newly retired from the docks, lifted his coffee mug to her. Madison suspected he was there escaping

Mrs. Farrell. According to Grandma Nona, Tom's wife of forty-three years had drawn up a "honey-do" list a mile long and had harped on him since his first day off to get started on it.

From behind the bar, Mike caught her eye and tipped his head toward a booth near the front door. With his deep auburn hair, green eyes and infectious smile Michael Patrick V was Irish to the core. His smile was missing, though. All she saw in the big man's freckled features was curiosity.

"You have someone waiting for you," he said.

She already knew that. "Thanks," she murmured, and glanced behind her.

Had she not seen Cord's car, she would have taken the outside staircase to her upstairs apartment as she usually did and, alone and in private, faced the panic clawing at her stomach. Given that she had an audience, she staved off that panic as best she could and walked over to the large and faintly cautious-looking man rising from the booth next to the last.

The way Cord stood at her approach spoke of manners that were more automatic than practiced.

It was a fair indication of how upset she was that something that might have impressed her barely registered. She was too busy thinking that Cord Kendrick looked as out of place in the working-class establishment as his car did out on the street—and wishing she had never laid eyes on his too-handsome face. She structured her entire life around the work that kept her running sixteen hours a day, six days a week. The thought of any part of that structure collapsing had her stomach in knots.

Assuming he wanted the van back, she held out the keys. "Thank you. Very much."

Rather than taking the keys, he asked, "Did the van work out?"

"It got me where I needed to go."

"Then, keep it until a new truck can be delivered. That's what I want to talk to you about," he said, motioning for her to sit down. "I have no idea what it is you'll want, so we need to arrange for you to order it yourself."

Preferring the isolation of the high-backed booth to being the day's entertainment for the guys at the bar, she slid onto the green Naugahyde bench seat. Cord slid in across from her, his long legs bumping hers.

"Sorry," he murmured.

As if hoping to coax a smile from her, he smiled himself. It was sort of a half smile really, an expression that held a hint of contrition and male appeal that would have had the hearts of most women melting.

In no frame of mind to be charmed, definitely in no mood to smile, she simply watched him push aside the beer he'd ordered and hadn't touched.

"So what do you want me to do?"

"Tell me where you want to order the truck from." Leaning forward, he clasped his hands on the dark and scarred wood, his voice low enough that the men gave up trying to listen and turned their attention back to ESPN. "I'll get a letter of credit to the dealer. I also need to settle up with you for the food you lost this morning and your lost profits for the day. They took your truck to a salvage yard a few miles from here. I told the owner of the yard not to do anything to it until he heard from you. I don't know what you had in there that might be of personal value to you, so you might want to check it out. All I was able to get were these."

He pulled her sunglasses from the inside pocket of his

beautifully styled leather jacket, along with his check-book. The pen he also withdrew looked suspiciously like real gold.

"Thank you," she murmured, taking the glasses. Considering how flat the cab of her truck had been, it amazed her that they were still intact. He amazed her a little, too. A few hours ago she hadn't been inclined to give him the benefit of the doubt about much of anything. She had to admit now, that the man seemed to be doing whatever he could.

"I appreciate what you're trying to do," she said, voice calm, insides knotted. "And I appreciate the use of the van. But I'm going to lose more than just today's profits. There are state laws regulating businesses like mine. I can't meet the refrigeration and sanitation requirements with the van, and I'm not going to risk having my food preparation license pulled. All I'll be able to sell now is baked goods, fruit and soda," she told him. "I can't even sell coffee because I don't have enough thermoses, and I wouldn't have any way of filling them on the road. That's only a third of my business."

"Coffee is?"

"Baked goods and sodas."

His broad shoulders lifted in a dismissing shrug. "Then, I'll pay you the other two-thirds for every day you're without the right kind of truck."

He clearly didn't see a problem. He also seemed to think that all he had to do was open his checkbook and her little crisis would be solved.

Wondering if life was always that easy for him, and suspecting it must be, considering who he was, she forced patience upon her growing unease. "This isn't just about money. Money isn't going to feed my customers or get me my work back," she explained, needing him to understand that dollars couldn't begin to replace the structure of her carefully ordered life. "I get up at three o'clock in the morning to do my baking and make sandwiches. At eight-twenty I load my truck and leave for my first stop. I finish my breakfast-and-break run, come back for lunch restock and finish the lunch run by twelve-forty. After that, I gas up my truck, drop off leftovers at the seniors' center, stop at the produce market and come back here so I can clean up the truck, refill the dispensers and get my dry ingredients mixed up for the next morning's baking.

"All I'm going to be able to do now is a breakfast-and-break run," she continued, only now allowing herself to consider what tomorrow would bring. With all she'd had to deal with that day, she had managed to avoid that prospect so far. With her sense of anxiety growing, she truly wished she could avoid it now. "That means I won't have to bake nearly as many cookies and I won't make sandwiches at all. And I won't have my lunch run to make, or my truck to take care of when I get back, so that means I won't have nearly as much to do when I get back in the afternoon."

She shook her head, wondering how many hours that left unfilled. Not wanting to know, self-recrimination lowered her voice to a mutter. "If I hadn't wanted the money for that stupid chafing dish, everything would be fine."

Cord watched the pretty, sable-haired woman across the booth from him rub her forehead. Her short, neat nails were unpolished, her slender fingers ringless, her dark and shining hair pulled back and clipped casually at her nape. Her lush mouth was unadorned, free of the shiny sticky gloss worn by so many of the women he knew. There was a freshness about Madison O'Malley that wasn't terribly familiar to him, a lack of studied polish that spoke of interests beyond the hours he knew some women—his own mother and sisters included—spent being manicured, pedicured, highlighted, waxed, masked and massaged. On the other hand, it didn't sound as if she had time for such fussing. From what he'd just heard of her schedule, she barely had time to sleep.

That she also now seemed as upset with herself as she was with him wasn't lost on him, either.

Overlooking the fact that anyone else would be grateful for the break, and hoping to cash in on the blame she seemed to be feeling toward herself, he focused on the chafing dish she'd just mentioned. He had no idea how it figured into what had happened, but he'd buy a gross of them for her if it would help fix this little mess.

"This chafing dish," he said, ducking his head to see her eyes. "Is it something you need for your business?"

"It's one of a lot of things." Absently pulling a napkin from the holder, she lifted her head. "I'm trying to expand my catering business, but I don't have the equipment and serving pieces I need for parties. If I'd had a couple of good double chafers I wouldn't have had to turn down Suzie Donnatelli's wedding last week. Not that she asked," she admitted, sounding as if she were talking more to herself than to him as she rolled the napkin's edges, "but I know she would have if I'd told her I could do it.

"That's why I took the coffee and muffins to the trailer," she hurried on, her racing thoughts leaving him in the conversational dust. "It wasn't worth being off schedule for twenty dollars worth of coffee and food, but a fifty-dollar tip would make a serious contribution to my equipment fund. As it was, the tip you gave me would almost buy the blasted thing, but it wound up costing me my truck.''

For a moment Cord said nothing. He just sat there wanting very much to keep her away from her last thought.

''Okay,'' he said, buying himself a few seconds while he weighed the new information she'd more or less given him. If he read this woman correctly, she was actually more upset about having time on her hands than she was her loss of income. She also had something more she wanted to do, but hadn't been able to because she hadn't had the extra income to do it with.

''If I get you equipment and catering jobs, would that help?''

Madison opened her mouth, blinked and closed it again.

''I can buy you whatever you need,'' he said, thinking that anything he had to pay would be a bargain compared to what it would cost him if he couldn't make her happy enough to stay away from insurance companies and lawyers. ''And I know lots of people who entertain. You can work on that end of your business until your new truck gets here.''

His expression mirrored hers when her eyebrows pinched.

''What?'' he asked, needing to stay up with her, if not one step ahead.

''It's not just the equipment I lack. Not exactly,'' she confessed, sounding as if one set of concerns had just given way to another. ''It's the experience. I've done a few small parties,'' she explained. ''I've just never done anything of any size that wasn't just hors d'oeuvres.'' Suddenly looking a little self-conscious, she dropped her voice another notch. "I'm sort of still in the planning stages."

Cord drew a slow, deep breath. When he'd walked in, he had thought that he could write out a couple of checks, make sure she got an even better truck than the one she'd had so she would have no cause for complaint, and hope that would be the end of it. There was also the little matter of getting her to sign a release of claim for Callaway Construction, but there were details to iron out first.

"You can practice on me," he concluded, tightening his grasp on the only negotiating tool he'd been able to find. "I'm having a few people in this weekend. Saturday night. Nothing formal," he assured her, since that seemed to be a concern. "I'm not a formal kind of guy." That was his family's forte. He could hold his own with a wine list, and he enjoyed the finer things as much as the next man. He just didn't like having to put on a tux to do it. "I thought I'd call a restaurant and have them deliver, but the job is yours if you want it."

When Madison felt excited, nervous or uncertain, she needed to move. Needing to move now, she slid from the booth, took a step away, then turned back.

"You want to hire me?" she asked, looking incredulous, sounding doubtful.

"It works for me, if it works for you."

Madison promptly started to pace. Three steps one way, three steps back. Cord Kendrick had connections in circles it would take a miracle for her to enter on her own. And there he was, his impossibly blue eyes following her every move while he waited for her to accept or decline the offer of her lifetime.

His mother had been royalty.

His older brother was the governor of the state.

His father was related to the Carnegies or the Mellons. Or maybe it was the Vanderbilts. All she knew was that he'd come from old money that had made tons more.

Granted, from what she'd read, the Kendrick family had little to do with Cord himself, but the circle he reputedly ran in wasn't that shabby, either: Grand Prix racers, supermodels, platinum recording artists. Owners of large, multimillion-dollar construction companies.

"I don't know," she murmured, pacing away from him. "I'd planned to practice more on my friends first." It was one thing to help them out with their parties. She knew what it took to please them. But catering was all about referrals. "What if your dinner is a disaster? If I'm really not ready, I could end my career before I even get started."

Because she kept turning away, and because her voice was still low, Cord was having trouble catching what she said. Wishing she would stand still, he levered his long frame out of the booth and caught up with her two empty booths down.

"You'll be fine," he assured her.

"How do you know?"

"I've tasted your cooking."

Her tone went flat. "You had a muffin," she reminded him over the scream of race cars on a motor oil commercial. "That's not exactly chicken Florentine.

"Can you make chicken Florentine?" he asked as she paced the other way.

"I can make lots of things." She tried out new recipes and new twists on old ones on her family all the time. "There are just some things I've never made for more than four people."

"This will only be for seven or eight. And Florentine

would be great. Throw in some pasta, a salad and something for dessert and you're home free.''

Her uncertainty remained as she turned back. ''What kind of pasta?''

He shrugged, took a step closer. One dinner party disaster would hardly be the end of the world for him. But if it wasn't a disaster and he could help her get more business, he would have made up for the loss of work she was so upset about now. ''Something northern Italian. White sauce, not red.''

She started pacing the other way. Grabbing her arm, he turned her right back. ''Will you stand still?''

Her faint frown met his. ''I think better when I'm moving.''

''Well, you're making me dizzy.''

''Hey, Madison. Everything okay over there?''

Apparently grabbing her hadn't been the wisest thing to do. Dropping his hand, Cord turned to see the burly bartender scowling at him from the other side of the bar. The two men bellied up to it weren't looking too friendly toward him, either.

''Everything is fine,'' Madison assured the man. ''We're just talking.''

''You sure?''

''Positive.''

The ledge of Mike's brow lowered with the glance he gave Cord before looking back to her. ''You just let me know if you need anything.''

''Honest, Mike. Everything's okay.'' A smile smoothed some of the strain from her delicate features as she glanced toward the other men. ''Thanks, guys.''

Cord watched the customers turn back to the mirror, where they could keep an eye on his and Madison's reflections. As if to be sure she truly wasn't being harassed, the guy she'd called Mike kept a more direct focus on them. At least, he did until the ring of the phone demanded his attention.

The quick concern of the men for her had seemed almost brotherly. As if they regarded her as…family. He'd had that same impression from some of the men around her truck at the construction site, too.

Cord hadn't had a lot of experience with the sort of protectiveness he sensed here. And certainly not within his own family. Not that he could identify, anyway. But he had friends. More than he could count. There just weren't many he truly trusted, and of those not a single one was female.

He had discovered long ago that women only wanted two things from him: a good time and his money. He'd never been opposed to a good time himself, and as long a woman was willing to play by his rules and keep her mouth shut around the press, he'd take her along for the ride. But this woman was nothing like anyone he'd ever met. She had *workaholic* written all over her, and she didn't seem interested in his money at all. At least not beyond what it would take to replace her truck.

The thought of the press had him heading back to their booth and picking up his pen. After writing out a check, he used her curled-up napkin to write his address on.

"My home and cell numbers are on that, too," he said, handing the napkin and check to her. "The check is for whatever food you have to buy for the dinner. You can give me a bill later for whatever you want to charge for your time.

"I have to go, but there's something I need you to do for me," he continued, his back to the bar as he glanced from his watch to the confusion in her expression. He hated to rush, but he had already bailed on Matt to take care of Madison, and he needed to get back to their meeting. Callaway Construction's next construction draw hinged on the reports he had to review and sign. He tended to blow off responsibilities others imposed on him, simply because they were someone else's idea of what he should do and not his own. The responsibilities he chose himself, however, he took quite seriously. He wasn't about leave his best friend to cover paychecks and costs for materials from his own pocket.

Three other customers walked in, men coming in for a beer after work, from the looks of their grease-streaked clothes. They didn't seem to notice him and Madison. Not yet, anyway. They were too busy bantering about the Lamborghini outside as they headed for the bar, and speculating about who it belonged to. It wouldn't be long before they did notice them though. And the fewer people who recognized him, the better.

His voice dropped. "I need you to keep any conversation we have just between us." He was going to take a chance that she was exactly what she seemed. A woman who just wanted her business back. She hadn't said or done a thing that would lead him to believe that she was looking for a quick million dollars the way others had when they thought they had something on him. And she definitely didn't appear to be interested in acquiring his money by showing any interest in him personally.

That part actually stung a little.

"Just between you and me," he continued, pocketing his checkbook before the newcomers could glimpse much more than his profile, "I have a real knack for drawing bad publicity. It will be a lot easier for both of us if you don't mention my name to anyone. Especially to the press. Just tell your friends that everything is being handled by Callaway Construction and that I'm its representative. Things are only going to get complicated if we don't keep the details just between us." He held out his hand. "Okay?"

Madison glanced from his hand to the odd intensity in his eyes. Despite his casually confiding tone, she couldn't help feeling that her agreement meant far more to him than anything else they'd discussed.

Living in the Ridge, she knew how crazy things could get when other people started poking their noses into someone else's business. She had never considered it before, but she supposed that poking its figurative nose in people's business was exactly what the press did every time something went into print. It occurred to her that he routinely faced the nosiness of the Ridge on a global scale.

"Okay," she said. Considering all he was willing to do for her, and having no desire to sabotage any of it, she took his hand. "Just between us."

His grip tightened. "Thank you."

Her heart did an odd bump against her ribs at his relieved smile. Not sure what to make of the little tug of sympathy she felt toward him, she slowly withdrew her hand.

"You have my number," he continued, once more relaxed. "Call me with the name of the dealership for your truck and to set up a time for you to come to my place Saturday. I'd like dinner around eight."

It occurred to her as she watched him give her a nod, go to the door, then hold it so two other customers could walk in before he walked out, that she hadn't actually agreed to do his party. They'd only been in the discussion stages, and the last she remembered, she'd been balking because she truly didn't feel ready. Yet somehow in the course of their conversation he had managed to let her know what he wanted, for how many and when, and walked out the door as if there had never been any question about whether or not she would take the job.

"Hey, Madison," Mike called as, insides shaky, she headed for the door at the back of the bar. "Who was that guy? He looks familiar."

"Just someone who's going to help me replace my truck," she replied, too excited about the opportunity Cord offered to feel railroaded, too apprehensive about it to overlook his knack for talking her into what he wanted.

Unfastening her fanny pack from around her waist, she took out the key to her apartment. She really didn't want to go into details with Mike now, but she couldn't leave him with only that. "It got totaled on a construction site."

A dozen heads turned toward her. "You all right, girl?" old Tom asked.

"Oh, I'm fine," she assured, pushing open the door to the kitchen. "I wasn't anywhere near it when it happened. I just have to order another one now."

Mike set the glass he'd just dried on the shelf behind him. "What about your route?"

"I have a van for the breakfast and break runs. I'll tell you about it when I come back to make dough."

She would mix up dough for her cookies and dry ingredients for her muffins after she dumped the ice chests, swept out the inside of the van and came up with a way to provide her customers with coffee. It relieved her to have those things to do. Being occupied kept her from thinking about things she didn't want to think about. And right now what she didn't want to think about was the man who had totally wrecked what had started out to be a perfectly pleasant day.

Unfortunately, her reprieve was short-lived. Word was already out about her truck.

Chapter Three

News of Madison's misfortune spread through the Ridge at roughly the speed of light. By the time she left for her modified route the next morning, she had heard from no less than a half-dozen people, her mother included, who felt she should sue Callaway Construction, the crane operator, the company that had made the crane and anyone else a good attorney could come up with to see that she got a decent settlement. After all, she could have been in that truck. Emotional distress was worth a fortune in court these days.

One of the Donnatelli boys, the one with the law degree, even volunteered his services. She found his message on her answering machine when she returned that afternoon.

A few hours later she ended the constant flow of advice, along with the fun everyone was having spending her imaginary money, when she told her grandmother, who told Mavis Reilly, who told everyone else, that she wasn't going to sue anyone because she had parked where she shouldn't. She had even seen, and ignored, a warning sign.

She didn't mention who had told her to park there. Aside from the fact that she'd agreed to keep Cord's name to herself, she had finally calmed down enough to remember that she'd had a feeling she shouldn't have parked where she had. Since she'd done it, anyway, part of the blame was hers. Once everyone realized that she wasn't merely a victim and that her truck was being replaced, the juice went out of the gossip—and she was no longer the topic du jour on the local grapevine.

That relieved her enormously. Though there were those around her who thrived on others' problems and seemed to think it their duty to dissect, discuss and decide how best to handle them, Madison preferred to handle her life on her own. She had carved out a neat little niche for herself with her work and her family, and as long as her days were full and she took care of those who counted on her, she had nothing to complain about.

She just couldn't stand to be idle. And with her work load cut, she would have been desperate to fill the time she now had on her hands had it not been for Cord's dinner party. She could whip up batches of muffins and cookies practically in her sleep. She could chop, slice and dice the makings for chicken salad and tuna sandwiches while shuttling cookies from oven to cooling racks and wrapping muffins in between. On Sundays, when she cooked for her family, she breezily pinched and dashed her way through marinaras, braises, paellas and pastas. Her favorite bedtime reading was a good cookbook. *Bon Appetit* and *Gourmet* magazines formed little towers on her coffee table and nightstand.

If there was anywhere she possessed confidence, it was in the kitchen. At least, she'd once possessed it there. The need to impress Cord's guests resulted in three long afternoons of experimenting and tweaking. Yet, by the time Saturday rolled around, she still wasn't convinced that what she planned to serve was absolutely, totally right.

The need to impress Cord himself only magnified the anxiety she was trying to hide when she pulled into his driveway twenty minutes early.

The directions the secretary from Callaway Construction had given her had been complicated. She had even been told that the house was apparently easy to miss. Afraid of being late, Madison had given herself an extra half an hour to get there. She was glad she had. She'd passed the single-story cedar-and-shake structure twice, secluded as it was in the forest of bushes and trees edging Chesapeake Bay.

Wanting everything to be as close to perfect as she could make it, she quickly checked to make sure her seat belt hadn't wrinkled her white blouse and black slacks too badly before she pulled a cooler with the components of her appetizers and main course from the back of the van. Leaving the cooler by the front door, she returned for a box of utensils. She made a third trip for the large bag of fresh ingredients she'd shopped for that morning and the dessert it had taken her three attempts to get just like the picture in *Cuisine*.

Balancing the bag in one arm and her chocolate raspberry mousse torte in the other, she rang the doorbell with her elbow and drew a deep breath.

Thirty seconds later the breath came out, and she rang the doorbell again.

When no one answered after nearly a full minute, the anxiety she felt turned to a different form of unease.

Wondering if Cord was even home, she peered through the wavering lines of stained glass that framed the large door to see if she could detect any movement inside.

She hadn't talked to Cord directly at all in the four days since the demise of her truck. He hadn't answered his home phone when she'd called to give him the name of the dealer she'd ordered her first truck from, so she'd left the message on his answering machine. Within two hours, he'd left a message on her answering machine indicating that he was out of town, and telling her that Matt Callaway's secretary would take care of everything in his absence. The next morning she'd received a call from the dealer, who told her he had a letter of credit in hand that would cover the cost of any truck in his fleet and to discuss the sort of vehicle she wanted.

When she'd called Cord the second time to thank him and finalize the menu and time for his dinner, she got his voice mail again. The message he left in reply while she was on her route said only that what they had discussed was fine and that he'd see her at six o'clock.

She saw no movement inside. Wondering if something had happened and that he hadn't returned from wherever he'd been, she pulled back.

She'd taken two steps away when the latch clicked, the door swung wide and her heart bumped her breastbone.

Cord filled the doorway. He had one hand on the knob. The other secured the end of a black towel slung low on his lean hips. Another towel was looped around his neck.

She swallowed, opened her mouth to speak and found herself taking a deep breath instead. His broad shoulders, chest and arms looked damp and as hard and as sculpted as hammered bronze. Below the dark terry cloth around his hips, his powerful calves gleamed with droplets of water he'd missed in his hurried attempt to dry off.

Suddenly aware that she was staring, her glance jerked to the carved lines of his recently shaved face. He had rubbed the towel around his neck over his wet hair. The short strands stood up in spikes several shades darker than its usual sun-bleached wheat.

"You're early," he said, seeming totally unconcerned about his state of undress. Glancing from the flush coloring her cheeks, he nodded to the items she carried. "Give me those."

Stepping past the threshold, he reached for the bag in her arms and the plastic cake carrier balanced against her hip. The back of his hand brushed her breast beneath the bag. As his other brushed her side, her lungs filled with the clean scents of soap, shampoo and the minty smell of toothpaste.

"Got 'em," he said, his face inches from hers. Stepping back, he tipped his head toward the open door. "Come on in."

Her box of supplies sat on top of the cooler. Wanting badly to match his ease, she grabbed the cooler by its side handles, determinedly ignored the odd tingling sensations where his hands had so casually brushed her body, and followed him into a wide foyer. The space opened to a wall of floor-to-ceiling windows with a view of the bay that went on forever.

"Where did you go?" she called.

"To your right," came the deep reply.

Peering around the box balanced high on the cooler, she glimpsed huge abstract paintings on the high walls, overstuffed leather furniture, lacquered tables and marble sculptures all perfectly placed. Beyond it all was that end-less view of the bay.

Her glance had just settled on the mast of a sailing sloop moored at the edge of that view when she heard the quiet slap of bare feet on gleaming hardwood floor.

The box that had blocked part of her view suddenly disappeared. ''The kitchen is this way,'' he said, and left her to follow him once more.

''Did you get your truck ordered?'' he asked as he slid the box onto a long slab of black granite counter. The built-in double refrigerator was stainless steel. So were the state-of-the-art appliances built into the counter that overlooked the living room and the water. A high, goose-necked faucet stretched over a stainless steel triple sink behind her.

''Yesterday,'' she replied, looking around for a spot to set the cooler. She was almost afraid to touch anything. The closest she'd come to a kitchen like his—a house like his, for that matter—was pictures in magazines. ''They have a used one they can refurbish with a propane coffee maker and cold section dividers like I had. It'll only take about three or four weeks to get it.''

From where he turned to lean against the counter, Cord watched her set her cooler down by the pantry door. He had forgotten how pretty she was, he thought, watching her rise and brush back a strand of dark hair with her forearm. Or maybe when he'd seen her before, she just hadn't been wearing the makeup that made her dark eyes look so sultry, her mouth so shiny and ripe. Dressed as she was in a crisp white blouse and slim black slacks, and with her dark hair swept up and away from her face, there was a natural elegance about her that hadn't been quite so obvious in the cotton and denim.

He hadn't noticed the hint of innocence about her before, either. For a few moments there, it seemed she'd actually blushed when she'd first seen him.

Watching her pull out pans and utensils from the box, he wondered now if the high color in her cheeks wasn't there just because she was hurrying.

"Order a new one," he told her.

"That'll take longer."

"Then rent the refurbished one to use until the new one comes in."

"The beams didn't land on a new one," she pointed out over the dull clunk of a metal pan on granite. "I'm fine with the one I picked out. It's the same model and year as my old one and I'll have the same equipment."

It seemed that she had no intention of taking more than she felt entitled to. She pulled a pristine white apron from the box. Turning from him, she looped it over her head and tied it around her narrow waist. "Do you have a cutting board?"

"I have no idea," he admitted, not ready to drop the subject. He could see where the shorter turn-around on a used truck would hold a certain appeal. Getting back to her full route as soon as possible was important to her. He knew that. He just didn't know another living soul who would refuse what he was offering her.

She glanced up. Deliberately avoiding looking anywhere but straight into his eyes, she murmured, "Excuse me?"

"I have no idea," he repeated. He wiped at a drip running down his neck. "Except for the basics, I really don't know what's in this room. The designer I hired pulled this place together for me."

The dark wing of her eyebrow slowly arched. "You don't know what's in your own home?"

"I'm hardly ever in this one. I bought it last year so

I'd have a place to dock my boat while we're building the mall. Most of the time, I live in Annapolis or Manhattan." He wasn't in those places much, either. The condo on the York River and the apartment across from Central Park were investments that happened to be handy places to crash when he came back from whatever challenge his restlessness drove him to conquer. There wasn't any one place that he actually called home. Except, maybe, the family estate in Camelot. But that huge sprawling mansion with its private lake, tennis courts and riding stable had never felt like a place he belonged, either.

He didn't care at all for the direction of his thoughts. Cutting them off with the ease of a man accustomed to burying what truly bothered him, he pushed himself from the counter.

"Tell you what," he said, not totally sure why she looked so puzzled. "Help yourself to whatever you can find. Since the weather's good, I thought we'd have hors d'oeuvres on the lower deck and dinner on the upper one. I had the housekeeper set up the bar and take the dishes out before she left, but you might want to check out everything first. I'm going to get dressed."

Madison didn't get a chance to do much more than nod before he lifted the towel from his neck and walked out, drying his hair. Staring at the muscles rippling in his naked back, grateful that the towel around his lean hips hadn't slipped, she let out a breath of pure unadulterated relief.

She didn't know which had been more unnerving. Trying to carry on a conversation while pretending to ignore all that beautiful muscle, or suspecting he knew how all that beautiful muscle rattled her.

She had seen men's bodies before. In magazine ads for

underwear that barely covered the essentials. On the beach, slicked with oil. She had just never been so close to one wearing nothing but terry cloth and a smile. And she mostly definitely had never been close to one who had turned her insides liquid at little more than the contact of his shower-damp skin when he'd relieved her of her load at the door.

She could hold her own with the men she knew. She could banter easily with the best of them. But her experience where men were concerned was limited pretty much to the intellectual and the verbal. When it came to actual physical contact, other than for a few less-than-memorable kisses with Tommy Webster under the bleachers in high school, she couldn't claim more than the occasional brotherly hug.

She was twenty-eight years old, more talk than action, and she still clung to the idea that when she made love with a man, she would be hopelessly in love with him. The fact that a man with the reputation of an alley cat made her nerves flutter was simply a quirk of fate she would overlook. He had hired her to do a job. Considering that his guests were due to arrive in a little over an hour, she needed to focus on doing it.

Feeling a nervous need to move, anyway, she turned to the lovely cherry wood cupboards and cabinets. She had never in her life cooked in a kitchen as beautiful as the one she moved through now. Yet, as she started searching for a cutting board, her focus wasn't on the overtly expensive and upscale surroundings, or on how intimidated she actually felt in them. Her attention was on what Cord had said about this house.

He had bought a house most people could only dream about simply to have somewhere to park his boat.

She assumed that the boat he'd referred to was the

sailboat she could see moored at the dock beyond his multitiered deck when she hurriedly slipped out the glass dining room door five minutes later to check the deck's layout. From her vantage point above the water, she could see scuba gear on one of the benches inside the long, high-masted sloop. A bright yellow canoe rested upside down on the wooden dock next to it.

It appeared that Cord was drawn to the water and what lay beneath its surface. She'd heard that he flew his own plane, too, and that he liked fast cars. He won and lost small fortunes gambling. He gambled his own life climbing mountains with names like McKinley and Everest.

Judging by his toys and his rumored pursuits, he was a man who thrived on thrills and adventure. He obviously possessed the considerable skills those pursuits required to have survived them for so long. But she figured he also had to have nerves of steel and lack any sense of fear to actually enjoy the reckless pursuits and behavior that earned him his headlines.

Or maybe what he lacked, she thought as she mentally worked through the placement of the dinner buffet, was common sense. She was a creature of habit. She thrived on routine and needed stability the way she craved air. She couldn't begin to comprehend the need for such excitement, much less the need to deliberately seek it.

"Did she forget anything?"

Madison turned from the long blue-tiled serving area beside the built-in barbecue. Cord stood in the doorway, one shoulder against the doorjamb, his hands in the pockets of his casual beige slacks. His collarless blue pullover turned his eyes the color of a crystalline sea.

"She?" she asked, grateful to see him covered with more than a towel.

"My housekeeper."

"No. No," Madison repeated, unable to think of a thing the woman had overlooked. Silverware had been rolled in crisp burgundy napkins and secured with brass rings. Blue pottery dinner plates sat stacked beside their smaller version for dessert. "I'll set the hors d'oeuvres down by the bar before your guests arrive." She glanced at her watch, winced at the time. "While you're having drinks down there, I'll set out the buffet. I didn't ask before," she continued, slipping past him to turn on the oven so it would be ready for her first tray of shrimp-stuffed mushrooms. "Do you want me to stay after to clean up out here, too?"

"Irene will do that," Cord said, turning to follow a little more slowly.

Rounding the corner into the kitchen, he opened the glass door on his refrigerator-size wine grotto.

"Irene?"

"My housekeeper. She comes in once a week, and whenever else I need her." Selecting a bottle of wine, he headed for a drawer and a corkscrew. A beautifully arranged basket of breads now sat farther down on the counter, ready to be taken outside. Beside it, Madison had arranged water biscuits and sugared pecans around a generous wedge of Roquefort cheese. Nestled against the wedge were three yellow and orange nasturtiums.

Considering what little he truly knew of her, but knowing the clientele she usually served, he had expected her fare to be good, but a little more basic. More home-style than gourmet.

Impressed by how appealing the plate looked, he used the small spreader she'd positioned in the wedge to put a bit of the buttery, blue-veined cheese on a crusted pecan and absently popped it into his mouth.

The flavorful combination of sweet and salty impressed him, too.

"How does it taste?" she asked from behind him.

"Good. Very good," he conceded, surprised by how hesitant she sounded.

He turned to see if that same hesitation might be in her expression, but she'd already looked away. If he caught anything at all in her profile, it was relief.

A little surprised by her uncertainty, he opened the wine. After pouring two glasses, he offered one to her on her way back from the double ovens. With nothing else to do until his guests arrived, he figured he might as well entertain himself by watching her cook.

She traded him the goblet for a bulb of garlic on her way to the sink. Sniffing the wine, she gave an approving nod. "Thanks," she murmured, setting it down. "I'll use it in the sauce for the chicken. Peel a clove of that garlic for me while I get the rest of this stuffing mixed up, will you? Then, you can julienne the jicama."

Cord glanced from the small beige bulb she'd handed him to where she now ran water over a colander filled with large peeled shrimp. "Do what?"

"Julienne the jicama," she repeated, turning off the water and giving the colander a shake. She moved to the stovetop in the center island. Turning on the burner under her large sauté pan, she dropped in a stick of butter and nodded to a large, rather wicked-looking knife on the cutting board she'd found. "You can break the skin on the garlic with that."

He knew what jicama was. He'd had the white-fleshed and crunchy root in salads. He also knew it was spelled with a *j* that was pronounced like an *h*. It was achieving the julienne part that had him feeling slightly stumped as he set his wine on the counter and the garlic on the cutting board.

He was a little lost on what to do with the garlic, too. He had never cooked anything in his life that didn't simply require reheating or a couple of turns on a grill. As a child, the family cook had chased him from the kitchen. As an adult, he'd lost all curiosity about what went on in one.

"I had the timing on everything all worked out," she said, looking preoccupied as she quickly wiped her hands on her apron before reaching into the box by the pantry. She turned with jars of herbs and a plastic bag of what looked like bread crumbs. "But it's taking me longer because I changed my mind about the appetizers. I thought about making both of them ahead of time, but the stuffing for the mushrooms is better fresh."

Since he'd yet to do much more than frown at the garlic, she reached past him to peel it herself. With a few quick motions, she'd set a clove on the cutting board, smacked the flat side of a knife against it with her hand, slipped off the cracked skin and started chopping.

"I told you I didn't think I was really ready to do anything like this," she pointed out, scooping minced garlic on the knife and adding it to the butter melting the pan. "I'm used to preparing things ahead of time and just delivering them. Cooking on-site is totally new. Since this was your idea," she reminded him, sounding somewhere between nervous and grateful for the opportunity, "I'd appreciate it if you'd help me out so I can have everything ready on time."

The entrée of chicken breasts stuffed with spinach and seasonings sat in the cooler ready to be popped into the oven. The ingredients for her fettuccini and the raspberry vinaigrette for the jicama, arugula and pear salad was in there, too. All she had to do was finish the main appetizer.

She had mushrooms cleaned and shallots rinsed and waiting. Grabbing the latter, she started furiously chopping, reducing the bunch by half in mere seconds.

Afraid she'd cut herself if she didn't slow down, wondering at the worried furrows in her brow, Cord calmly reached over and covered her hand with his. Beneath his palm, he felt her stiffen.

"Relax, will you? You're feeding seven of my friends. Not my grandmother. No one's going to care if things aren't ready the instant they arrive."

It was Madison's intention to tell him that she would care. This was her first catering job that didn't involve dropping off trays of cupcakes or finger sandwiches. More unsettled by him and her surroundings than she wanted to admit, she was also desperate to prove she could handle it. Her words, however, died in her throat.

The heat of his hand seeped into hers, snaked inside her, brushing unfamiliar nerves along the way. She didn't know how it was possible, but with just the touch of his hand to hers, he had managed to alter her heart rate, her breathing and render her silent.

Realizing that she'd also gone as still as Lot's wife, she glanced up to find him staring at her mouth.

Her heart gave an odd little jerk as she looked away. Slipping her hand from beneath his, disturbed by his effect on her when she wanted him to have no effect at all, she reached into the sink.

"What do you mean about your grandmother?"

His broad shoulders lifted in an indifferent shrug. "Just that she can be pretty picky about what's put on her plate."

She handed him the jicama. "Some older people get that way."

"I suppose," he conceded, thinking she suddenly seemed a little self-conscious as he took the peeler she handed him, too. "But she's always been demanding. If food isn't presented the way she thinks it should be, she sends it back to the kitchen. I remember her sending a plate back once because the chef forgot a garnish."

"With the prices some restaurants charge, I suppose a person should get everything she's paying for."

"This was her own chef," he clarified. "And the plate was mine. I couldn't have cared less if there'd been a mint leaf with my peas, but she insisted that was the sort of detail that changed the experience of eating from mere sustenance to dining. And when she ate, she 'dined.' We all did."

Back to chopping, Madison arched an eyebrow. "She sounds quite formal."

"I figure it's an occupational hazard. She's a queen," he explained, drawing the peeler over the large bulb-shaped vegetable in his hand. The peeler slid across the skin. The skin stayed on. "She lives and breathes formality," he admitted, only to become aware of Madison's knife suddenly moving more slowly. Sensing a change in her attention, he backed off the subject. "But I'm not that way unless I have to be," he assured her, and took another swipe with the peeler.

He hadn't intended to bring up his heritage. The woman working beside him had made it clear from the beginning that she wasn't terribly impressed with him or his money. As impersonal as she seemed to want to keep their dealings, he was certain she would be even less impressed if he went throwing his relationships around. Not that he ever did. The last thing he wanted to do was remind anyone of who he was. He spent as much time living down his heritage as he did living with it.

Her arm brushed his, the clean citrusy scent of her hair suddenly masking the aroma of sautéing garlic as she reached in front of him. "You need to hold the peeler at an angle," she said, taking what he held. "Like this."

All he could see was the top of her dark head and her hands as she showed him how to position the blade against the vegetable. Before he could do much more than think about how silky her hair looked, how good she smelled, she took his hand to position it herself and pulled back to let him try it on his own.

He deftly removed a paper-thin layer of peel.

"So," she said, stepping back to scrape chopped shallots into the pan, "what else is she picky about when it comes to food?"

Apparently it wasn't what he'd said that had slowed her down. She'd merely been distracted by his lack of progress.

The only thing distracting him was her. He'd only intended to watch. Not participate.

"Using the proper fork. Eating at least a taste of everything on the plate. Wadding peas up in your napkin."

A faint smile brightened her eyes. Warmth, or maybe it was amusement, lit the flecks of gold. "You would have been how old? Six? Seven?"

"And ten and eleven. By then I couldn't see any point in the one-taste rule. I'd had peas before and I was pretty sure mint wasn't going to mask the taste."

"What did she do?"

With her smile turned away, he went back to his task. Now that he had the hang of it, peels flew.

"She pointed out that none of my siblings appeared to have a problem with what they were served. Then she would have the butler bring me a fresh serving. I had to do the one-bite thing before I could be excused.''

"How long did you hold out before you caved in?''

She seemed to know that he hadn't given in easily. Not sure what to make of that, deciding it just made her easier to talk to, he gave her a rueful smile of his own.

"I fell asleep in the chair.'' The smile faded. "I'm still not sure why she would do that,'' he confided over the comfortable sounds of metal on the cutting board and sizzling in the pan. "She knew I didn't like peas, but she'd have them served every time we went there.''

"How often did you go?''

"Every summer. Dad stayed in Richmond and we spent a month in Luzandria.''

"Maybe she thought they'd grow on you.''

"It was more like she just forgot that I hated them,'' he concluded, now that he thought about it. "But she never served what my brother and sisters didn't like,'' he admitted, surprised that he could still feel slighted by something so trivial. "Gabe would turn white at broccoli, and Ashley and Tess would starve before they would touch venison or rabbit. They reminded them of some movie, or some story characters or something.''

"Bambi and Thumper.''

"Who?''

"Bambi and Thumper,'' Madison repeated, stirring. "They're the deer and bunny your sisters were probably thinking about.''

"Maybe I should have come up with a character for peas,'' he muttered, slicing.

"It might have saved you a few nights alone at the table after everyone else had finished.''

"Might have,'' he agreed. "Better yet, I could have

had something I liked in its place the way Gabe and my sisters did when she served something they didn't like.''

Seeing that he'd finished, she showed him how to get the proper thinness of julienne cut—which turned out to be nothing more than slicing the crisp, radish-textured vegetable into slender strips.

"Gabe is the oldest?" she asked, when it was clear that he had the hang of it. "Right?"

"Right."

"Are your sisters younger or older than you?"

"Both younger."

"Did you ever ask your mom to remind your grandma about what you didn't like?"

He shook his head, aware of her moving about behind him as he focused on his task. "I don't think so." It had been so long ago that he really didn't remember. "I probably didn't want her to hear that I was being difficult or ungrateful. Besides, I don't remember seeing my mom much except at meals. She was always busy with grandma and the girls or going to Gabe's matches.''

"Matches?"

"Polo."

"Did you play polo, too?"

Cord hadn't thought about those summers in ages. Frowning at the growing pile of slender shreds, he didn't much care for how he felt thinking about them now. "I found my own things to do," he muttered.

He hadn't cared for polo. He loved the horses. Loved their speed. But he'd hated all the time he'd spent waiting on the sidelines to play. So he'd ditched polo and spent his afternoons roaming the woods catching things he got into trouble for bringing into the castle. Then, the summer he turned fifteen, he'd tired of the time alone and ignored the standing family rule of leaving either the estate in Camelot or the palace grounds without a body-guard or an escort.

He and his siblings had all grown up knowing that any member of the Kendrick family was a lucrative kidnapping target. The public rarely thought about the existence of groups or individuals who saw holding a hostage for ransom as their ticket to financing themselves or their causes. Yet that reality had followed him wherever he'd gone. But in Luzandria, he'd figured the chances of being snatched off the street were pretty remote, since no one had known he'd be on the streets to begin with. So he started spending his afternoons in the beautiful Mediterranean city below the castle. That was where he'd learned to play craps with the hotel and casino employees who hung around the back doors of the world-class gambling establishments on their smoke breaks.

Those forays had led to his first scandalous headlines. He hadn't been taken for ransom, but he'd been caught, nonetheless. He hadn't counted on the paparazzi with their telephoto lenses who flocked to Luzandria to cash in on celebrities who came to see and be seen.

That had been the first time he'd publicly embarrassed his family and his royal grandmother. On an international level, anyway.

He hadn't been looking for trouble. He'd just been trying to make some friends to hang out with during those long, boring summers. And he had made friends. Lots of them. They just hadn't been friends his family had approved of.

He picked up his wine, took a preoccupied sip.

It was about that time that the press had dubbed him the prodigal prince of Camelot.

He had been born too late to get the preferential treatment of his older brother. Yet, his parents had still held him to the same exacting standards of behavior. Cord had known early on that even exceeding those standards wouldn't matter because he could never be the firstborn son, number one, the heir apparent. It wouldn't matter what he accomplished, because Gabe, being two years older, would have achieved it first.

He had been totally overshadowed by the brother he'd been compared to nearly every step of the way. But while he'd resented the comparisons, he honestly hadn't envied Gabe. He hadn't wanted the demands placed on him, the overwhelming responsibility of always doing everything right. And the very last thing he'd wanted to do was spend his day hanging around with his brother and the sons of other moneyed men being groomed for greatness. With Gabe and Gabe's friends, he'd always just been the kid brother, tagging along, getting in the way, wishing he were somewhere else.

There had been different expectations for his sisters, but even there, their roles had been clear. As the oldest daughter, Ashley had been molded to be a perfect lady like their mother. Tess, it seemed, had been born simply to be the rather spoiled baby of the family.

He hadn't been sure where he'd fit in at all. So, he'd made a place were he did fit, where he chose his responsibilities, competed on his terms. The person he competed with most was himself. He climbed mountains just to prove to himself that he could. He raced the wind on the ocean because he loved the freedom he felt when it whipped through his hair, the control he felt harnessing it to make it take him where he wanted to go. He was drawn to people who made their own rules, who bucked convention, who weren't afraid to have a good time. Life was too short to worry about using the proper fork or watching everything a person did or said. He'd had to go outside the privileged circle confining him to make his own life, but he had found people there who liked to play as hard as he did. They accepted him.

They accepted his money, anyway. Yet now, as then, he found that no matter where he was, he often wished he were somewhere, anywhere, else.

The memories he had buried long ago brought feelings he thought he'd buried, too. Loath to acknowledge the quiet resentment and doubt he'd worked so hard to escape, he dried his hands, preparing to leave the preparations to the woman quietly watching him.

"I'm sorry," she said.

His eyebrows merged. "For what?"

"You didn't look too happy thinking about those things you found to do." A thoughtful smile touched her mouth. "It's not easy, is it? Being a middle child, I mean."

She poked at the shrimp sizzling in their seasonings.

"I'm one, too. The second of five," she told him, her tone strangely sympathetic. She looked up again, that same empathy in her eyes. "How long did it take you to find your place in the hierarchy?"

Moments ago the disquiet he'd felt had to do only with him. Now, with her looking at him as if she knew how rootless he'd once felt, feeling oddly exposed because of it, the ease he'd felt with her disappeared like the steam rising from his stove.

"I still haven't," he admitted, and tossed the towel aside.

"Tell you what." He had no idea why he'd told her what he had, why he'd even let himself think about the rest of it. His childhood and the intimate workings of his wealthy, high-powered and high-profile family weren't something he discussed with anyone. "People will be here pretty soon. I'm going to take wine down to the bar and load some CDs into the stereo.''

Feeling as if she'd crossed some invisible line, Madison watched him go. She had no way of knowing what had so suddenly triggered his need to escape, what thoughts had slowly robbed him of his easy manner with her. But she didn't doubt for a moment they had to do with his family. She'd just never expected what she had sensed in him in the moments before he'd withdrawn and walked away.

There had been something lonely and protective about him. Or, maybe it was simply something...lost. She couldn't define exactly what it was. Yet it seemed to remain with him even as he smiled and laughed with the small contingent of beautiful people who arrived at his dock twenty minutes later with the blast of a sailboat's horn.

Chapter Four

Cord's date for the evening was petite, tanned and a dozen shades of blond. Except for models in magazines, Madison had never actually seen a woman whose blinding-white teeth were perfect, whose body was perfect, whose clothes, definitely designer and definitely expensive, were perfect. But that was how the woman she heard someone call Tawny looked to her as she slipped behind the knot of people on the lower deck to set out the hors d'oeuvres. In a word, Tawny-whoever-she-was looked stunning.

So did the three other gorgeous ladies who had arrived with three very successful-looking men Cord apparently often sailed with in races. Madison caught that much from remarks she overheard before she quietly moved back inside. While setting out dinner and, later, clearing the table after everyone had left it, she also learned that Cord had just returned from three days of diving off the coast of Cape Hatteras. Now, drying her last pan and wiping down the counters, all she could hear over the music that had been turned up too loud to hear actual conversation was laughter and giggling.

Not that she had been eavesdropping. She had consciously avoided concentrating on what was being said. Partly because it would have been rude to overtly listen. Mostly because she just wanted to hurry up and get out of there. She could see Cord through the open door laughing with his guests. Surrounded by beautiful people, beautiful himself, he epitomized the glamorous life she had heard and read about and seen on TV. A life she never would have imagined she would personally witness, even in a professional capacity. Yet, even though he was very much part of his party, very much the generous host, he seemed oddly apart from it somehow.

She jerked her glance from his profile, quickly rinsed the sponge. She didn't want to be curious about him. She especially didn't want to wonder why he had looked so lost before when he'd spoken of his family. Or why, even surrounded by his friends, he seemed so restless now.

She told herself she was imagining things and put the sponge away. The man had it all. Wealth, women and a seemingly endless supply of friends. Even more people had arrived, many presumably by boat, too, since only three more had come through the front door.

A model-thin redhead in skin-hugging white pants, a cropped silver top and a navel ring swung through the doorway from the deck, a martini glass in one hand, a tiny purse shaped like a butterfly in the other. Seeing Madison across the counter that divided living room from kitchen, she gave her a brilliant smile.

"Can you point me to a bathroom?" she asked.

"I believe it's that way," Madison replied, indicating

the direction she'd seen others go over the course of the evening.

Over the heavy beat of heavy metal, a laughing female screech drifted in from the deck.

The redhead turned back to the door, her fabulous hair flying. "What're you doing out there?" she hollered, clearly not wanting to be left out.

A female voice called back, "Ron's trying to throw Tawny in the hot tub!"

Another screech. "He'll ruin my Ferragamos!"

More laughter.

Madison turned away. It was none of her business if Tawny wasn't smart enough to kick off her shoes before someone dumped her in the water. It was none of her business that Cord's idea of a dinner party was more wild than hers. She had done what she'd been hired to do. With the dishes cleared and cleaned and dessert set out, there was no reason for her to stay any longer.

"You don't need to rush off."

Madison glanced up as she set her box of utensils on the closed cooler. Cord stood in the doorway, one corner of his mouth tipped in a smile. The hand that she'd last noticed holding a goblet of wine at dinner now held a can of cola.

"There's nothing more for me to do," she murmured.

The overhead lights picked out strands of gold in his sun-bleached hair as he nodded toward the party. "Then, come on out with us."

She blinked at his easy smile. "You mean, join you?"

"Why not? It's still early," he pointed out. "We're barely getting started."

It was after nine o'clock. More than an hour past her weekday bedtime. It was the weekend, though.

She glanced down at her black slacks and plain white

blouse. She had taken her cue from her two semesters of culinary school and dressed to serve. Yet, it wasn't the thought of how servantlike and ordinary she looked compared to the sleek and stylish set filling the decks outside that had her backing away from his unexpected invitation. It was how totally she knew she did not belong in that glittering group.

"Thank you," she murmured, certain he was just being polite. All he had to do was look at her to know she didn't belong. "But I'm afraid I wouldn't fit in very well with your friends. I wouldn't have any idea what to talk about."

"You can talk about anything. Movies. Travels."

"The only places I've been outside of Virginia are Washington, D.C., and Disney World." Washington was just across the state line, so that barely counted. The other had been her high school senior class trip. They hardly qualified her as a member of the jet set.

"Seriously?"

Wishing he didn't looked quite so astonished, wishing she hadn't been quite so honest, she untied her apron and dropped it over the frying pan in the box. "Seriously," she replied, and moved back to business.

"I was going to go look for you in minute. To tell you I'm going," she explained, "and that I'm afraid there isn't going to be enough dessert out there for everyone. I didn't know you were expecting more company."

"I wasn't. They just saw us and stopped." He hesitated. "Are you sure you want to go?"

"I have to," she replied, thinking how unfazed he sounded at having his party crashed. Between the twenty-some-odd uninvited guests and his invitation for her to stay, it seemed he truly believed the more, the merrier.

She turned to the cooler.

"I'll get that." With a faint clink, his soft drink hit the counter. "Just get the door for me."

"I can do it."

She bent for the cooler as he did.

With his face inches from hers, he arched one eyebrow. "Just get the door?"

At a distance he was merely compelling. Up close, she could practically feel the quiet tension radiating from him.

Madison drew back. It wasn't until she straightened that she noticed how the muscles in his jaw had tightened. Noticing it now, it occurred to her that maybe he wasn't just being considerate. Maybe he was looking for a few moments' escape.

Certain now that she hadn't just imagined his discontent most of the evening, she took another step back just as a balding jock-type walked in to announce that they were out of beer.

Another screech accompanied a splash.

"In the fridge, Ben," Cord said, hefting cooler and box. "Help yourself."

The redhead walked back through, wearing a thong bikini she must have had on under her clothes or in her microscopic purse. The guy after the beer didn't move. It seemed he totally forgot what he'd come in for as he stared at the white strings that kept the woman's backside from being completely naked.

Cord didn't even seem to notice.

Feeling more out of place by the second, Madison followed him into the wide entry hall and pulled open the door. Music and laughter were muffled moments later when she closed it behind them.

Low lights illuminated the curved walkway. Post

lamps cast a golden glow over the wide drive. With the muted sounds drifting from the back of the house, she pulled her keys from her purse and unlocked the back door of the van. A black Mercedes had parked beside her.

"Thank you," she murmured when Cord set her things inside .

"You, too," he replied. "You really surprised me."

"I did?"

"Actually, yeah. You did," he admitted, sounding as if there wasn't much that truly did surprise him anymore. "You're even better than I thought you'd be."

He closed the door with a thud. Towering over her in the pale light, he ran a considering glance over her face. "You've either worked in some good restaurants or gone to culinary school."

Her eyes shied from his. "I did a few months of each." With him watching her so closely, she didn't feel comfortable mentioning that even with a partial scholarship, she hadn't been able to afford the housing to stay in school. Or that her minimum-wage stint at the posh Gregory's Bistro outside Williamsburg only lasted three months because she'd had to split her tips with the busboy and the sommelier, and the forty-mile round trip cost her a fortune in gas. His guests were drinking hundred-dollar bottles of champagne. It wasn't likely he'd understand the concept of pinching pennies.

"And thank you," she repeated, because she was truly pleased, and relieved, by his compliment. "I hope everyone liked dinner."

"Amber Johnson certainly did. And if Amber likes you, you're in." He chuckled, the quiet sound rich, deep and surprisingly relaxed. "According to her husband, nothing pleases her. She wants your business card."

Madison blinked up at him. "She does?"

He chuckled again. "Yeah. She does," he confirmed, looking as if he didn't know why she seemed so surprised. "Do you have one?"

Surprise turned to a barely contained smile. Amber Johnson had cornered Madison when she'd set out dessert a while ago. The attractive brunette had appeared to be in her late thirties, more polished than her bubbly counterparts and extremely interested to know how she had prepared her caper sauce.

Almost afraid to believe that she might actually have earned herself another job so soon, Madison reached back into her purse and pulled out a small white card.

In the pale light, she watched Cord frown at what she'd just handed him.

Her smile died. "What's the matter?"

"You need a different name."

"What's wrong with Madison O'Malley?"

"For your company," he muttered, eyeing her evenly. "Mama O'Malley's is fine for your construction route, but it doesn't sound like anything a woman like Amber would call to cater a dinner or theater party. The food you served tonight doesn't match the name, either."

He considered her once more. In the shadows her skin looked as smooth as marble. "If you really want to do this, you need to do it right. And if you do," he said, pulling his focus back to possibilities, "I don't think it will be long before you can give up the construction truck and do this full time."

She was good. She was actually better than good. It wasn't just her cooking that impressed him, either. It was her way with people. All evening, he had been aware of how easily she'd slipped among his guests, setting out dishes, sweeping them away. Though she'd seemed oddly uncomfortable with the idea of actually joining the party, she had appeared as at ease among his acquaintances as she had the workers who'd surrounded her truck, totally comfortable in her role of serving what she had prepared. And her smile. Every time he saw it, he was drawn to it. Drawn to her.

He wasn't sure why that was, or what he saw in her smile that he didn't seem to notice in anyone else's. All he cared about at the moment was how her personality could add to her business potential. Aside from wanting to keep her occupied and happy with him while she waited for her truck to be delivered, there wasn't much that excited him more than taking the kernel of a money-making idea and seeing it to fruition. Usually, he dealt in real estate. The bigger the project the better. And when he felt passionate about a project, he worked as hard as he played—which was probably the only reason his father hadn't kicked him off the board of Kendrick Investments. His knack for spotting sure things had made his family millions.

"Give up my truck?" he heard her ask over the spinning of his mental wheels. "I'm not going to do that. I want to do both."

"Both?"

"Sure," she said, clearly puzzled by why he would think otherwise. "I never intended to give up my route for event catering. I just figured I'd do my route during the week and cater parties on the weekends. That's when people entertain, anyway, so it would be perfect." The evening breeze tugged a strand of hair from its clip. Impatiently shoving it back, she searched his face. "What kind of name do I need?"

She was excited about his assessment of her potential. He could see that excitement glittering in her beautiful dark eyes, hear it in her animated voice. She was also a tad manic, he decided. She had to be, to want to work herself into the ground the way she so apparently did.

"Who is your market?"

"What do you mean?"

"Who are you trying to sell yourself to? And what image do you want? Are you after homey or elegant? Trendy or classic? Do you want upscale? Do you want—"

"Yes."

His eyebrows merged. "Yes, what?"

"Yes, all of it. I'll make whatever the client needs. But mostly elegant and upscale. I've been doing 'homey' all my life."

"Then if you want upscale, you need an upscale name. Just use your own."

Excitement melded with tolerance. "You just said I need something different."

"I mean use your first name. Call it Madison's." It's simple. It has class. Put that on the first line. Under it, print Catering of Distinction."

Madison blinked at the card he handed back to her. She didn't know which pleased her more; that he thought her name had class, or the simple elegance of his suggestion for the new branch of her company. The realization that she felt flattered by what he thought had barely registered when he glanced over her shoulder. She turned to see his date moving toward them.

Disappointment shot through her. She would have loved to hear whatever other advice he had to offer. "Your girlfriend is missing you." She turned back. Ducking her head, suddenly feeling invisible compared to all that golden hair and skin, she shoved the card in her purse. Since Cord had given it back, it was apparent he felt Amber should be left with her original impression. He could give Amber her phone number. "I'd better let you get back to your guests."

"She's not my girlfriend. She's just someone I met at a club last week."

"Oh. Well," she murmured, thinking that might explain why the woman hadn't seemed to mind that the redhead had been hanging all over him when Madison had taken out the salad. Cord hadn't seemed to mind Red's attention. But then, he hadn't seemed to encourage her, either. "You should still get back to your guests." She gave him a quiet smile. "Thanks for your help."

Cord didn't want her to go. What he wanted was to stand there in the relative quiet watching the intriguing play of excitement and uncertainty in the delicate lines of her face while they talked about getting her new enterprise up and running. He wanted to encourage that smile.

The blonde waved at him. "Cord? Are you coming back in?"

"I'll be right there," he called back, seriously considering blowing his own party.

"Barry just wants to know where to put somebody who passed out."

Madison stepped back. "It sounds as if you might have some overnight guests tonight."

He was sure he would. When he entertained, he almost always did. And he entertained a lot—when he wasn't out somewhere himself. He liked to have people around, liked the noise, the energy. The distractions.

He didn't much care for being alone.

He shook off the thought, started to ask her to wait. But Tawny was still headed for him, and Madison had disappeared around the driver's side of the van.

"You need a marketing plan," he called after her. "I'll see what I can come up with and talk to you in a couple of days. How about Monday?"

"Monday's fine." With her key in the lock, she looked to where Cord had just been joined by the exquisite blonde. It didn't matter that he said the woman wasn't anyone special to him. They looked beautiful together.

She pulled open the door. "About three?"

The music grew louder as the front door opened again. Others were coming out, their laughter and voices crowding into the space between her and Cord.

"Where?" he asked, stepping closer.

In my world, she thought, as a guy she could have sworn she'd seen on *Entertainment Tonight* appeared with his arm draped over a clone of Britney Spears. She'd be so much more comfortable there. "Come to the back door of Mike's Pub."

Chapter Five

Cord had planned for months to leave Monday morning for the qualifying rounds of the annual Annapolis-to-Hamptons yacht race. Sailing was in his blood, his bones, and except for the thrill of conquering a massive mountain, there was nothing he loved more.

It was a fair indication of how intent he was on preserving Madison's business interests that his crew had left that morning without him.

The balmy spring breeze taunted him, ruffling his hair, teasing him with the feel of what he was missing. Instead of being on the deck of a sloop, he was in an alley twenty feet down from a Dumpster, knocking below a faded sign that read Mike's Pub Main Entrance around Front and carrying a business plan it had taken him hours to compile.

"Hi."

The door ahead of him remained closed. The one that

had opened was at the top of the slanting wooden staircase he stood beneath. Backing up, he saw Madison leaning over the railing of the tiny landing at the top of it.

An instant later she disappeared, wood squeaking as she quickly descended.

Turning as soon as she hit the ground, she headed for him. "I heard you through my window," she said. "You're right on time."

She wore her dark hair up, the ends poking from the back of her head in little spikes. Restraining it this time was a yellow clip that matched the simple yellow T-shirt tucked into her denim capris. Just once, he thought, he'd like to see her hair down.

The thought of how all that silk would look tumbling over her slender shoulders had his fingers tightening on the file. He already knew how it smelled. The fresh scent of her shampoo had reminded him of sensuous breezes and warm tropical nights. He didn't doubt for a moment that her shining hair would feel incredible in his hands.

"You live here?"

"Up there."

He took another step back when she pointed up to the landing. Beside the bright-blue door above them, an open window allowed lace curtains to flutter in the late-spring breeze. Below the window, a red window box overflowed with lush green herbs.

Over the past century, the once-red brick building had aged to dingy shades of black and gray. Paint peeled off the eaves. Utility lines draped from eaves to power poles. As he turned to the woman whose smile reminded him of sunshine, Cord couldn't decide if the bright spots of color and thriving vegetation simply added vibrancy to something slowly dying, or if they looked totally out of place.

Wondering the same thing about Madison—how vibrant and how out of place she seemed here—he watched her unlock the faded and chipped door to the pub and push it open.

"I moved here after I started using Mike's kitchen and his old tenant moved out," she explained, looking a little self-conscious about her decidedly working-class surroundings as she held the door for him to follow. "It was easier than trying to sleep at home while everyone was still up, and trying not to wake everyone when I had to get up so early in the morning. It was time to move out, anyway," she admitted, on her way through a utility room lined floor-to-ceiling with empty metal beer kegs. "I think I was the only female around here over the age of twenty still living at home."

The storage room opened to a small industrial kitchen lined with old double ovens, an older commercial refrigerator and an ancient grill. A dented stainless-steel-topped island dominated the middle of the black-and-white-tiled floor. At the far end of the room, an open pass-through exposed a neon beer sign by a barroom basketball game.

"I'm here, Mike. Hi, guys," Madison called through the swinging door a few feet from the pass-through.

The greetings of a half-dozen male voices overrode the background noise of a television tuned to a sports network and the ping of a video game.

Pulling back with a smile, she let the door swing closed.

Curious, confused, Cord watched her head for a pair of deep commercial sinks to wash her hands. "What are we doing here?" he asked, scanning the room that hadn't seen an update in at least fifty years. Like the building itself, the bloom of youth had long faded from the kitchen. It did, however, seem clean. Any surface that could shine, did, and the air held a hint of lemon disinfectant.

"I have to make cookie dough and muffin mix to bake in the morning. Hand me the baking soda and salt from that shelf over there, would you, please? And the vanilla?"

He didn't know baking soda from a bread hook. He thought about telling her that, too. He also considered pointing out that his only sous-chef experience was what he'd earned helping her with the jicama, in case she planned on pressing him into service again. But the way she bustled about, opening drawers, setting measuring cups on the island, spoke of the preoccupation he'd seen when she'd taken over his kitchen. Minus the uncertainty. It seemed easier, and more interesting, just to do as she'd asked.

He found the words Baking Soda printed on a large gold-colored box. Setting the file he carried on a tall wooden stool, he started the rest of his search. "How long will this take?"

"About an hour and a half," she replied, holding a bowl big enough to hold a beach ball.

His eyebrows formed a single slash. "I thought we were going to discuss your business plan."

"We can talk while I work." Focused on her task, she didn't even glance at him as the bowl met the metal-topped island with a solid clunk. The sound had barely faded before she began pulling down bags of chocolate chips, nuts and oatmeal from another row of shelves. "I have to be finished and cleaned up by four-thirty. That's when Erma gets here."

"Who's Erma?"

"Erma Wickowski. Mike's weeknight cook," she said

on her way to the refrigerator. "The grill opens at five. It's not usually busy on a Monday, except during football season, but they're starting a dart tournament tonight and this place will be packed. I don't want to be in her way."

"If you knew you had to do this, why did you say to meet at three?"

"Because I wanted to hear your plan, and this is the first chance I had to talk. After I finished my route, I had to go to the produce market for fruit and clean the ice chests and the van."

Removing a flat of eggs, she set them on the island and returned for butter. In between, she grabbed a clean apron from a drawer beneath the island and closed the drawer with her hip.

Cord glanced at his watch, looked up to frown at her back. He doubted she'd been in the kitchen two full minutes when she dumped a few pounds of butter into the bowl of a huge mixer at the end of the island and turned on the machine

The low drone of the mixer muffled the faint squeak of her sneakers.

There was no denying her efficiency. There was also no denying that the woman was even more obsessed than he'd thought. The day she'd lost her truck, she had mentioned getting up at the totally insane hour of 3:00 a.m. to prepare her food. He couldn't recall exactly what time she said she finished her route. Somewhere around 1:00, he thought. But he remembered her saying she did something afterward, too. It just hadn't registered that, after putting in nearly ten hours, there would be so much more she had to do. Especially with her route cut in half.

From what little he knew of her life, it had already sounded far too regimented for him. Watching her now, he began to suspect she had it scheduled practically to the minute.

As a man who had a healthy respect for spontaneity and scheduled only what he wanted or had to, he couldn't begin to imagine living that way.

"What do you do when you finish this?"

"Sometimes I grab a hamburger here and eat out front at the bar. Sometimes I get takeout or a pizza and eat upstairs. It depends on what I recorded from television the night before. Everything I like is on too late to watch when it's actually on."

"Too late?" he asked, watching her crack all two dozen eggs into the whipping butter.

"I'm usually in bed by seven-thirty on Sundays and weeknights," she explained. "All the good stuff comes on after that."

She glanced over her shoulder, a self-effacing smile curving her lush mouth. "But you didn't come all this way to talk about my day." Anticipation lit her eyes as she nodded toward the file on the stool. "Do you really have a plan for me?"

He most certainly did. And his first suggestion should be that she get herself a life. Where was the fun? The distractions? The adventure? There was no room in her day for surprise or spontaneity. No impulsiveness. All the woman seemed to do was work.

"Yeah," he murmured, at a loss as to why she wanted to tie herself down even more. He'd spent his life escaping structure and regimentation. If his work wasn't a game to him, he'd find something else to do. Yet she seemed bent on working herself twenty-four seven.

"I've outlined an advertising campaign," he told her, "and defined a marketing area in the upscale communities within an hour's drive of here. I came up with a couple of logos for you to consider, too.

"But before I forget," he continued, as she buzzed by with the empty egg carton, "a climbing buddy in the Hamptons has a lunch meeting every Friday in his boardroom. I told him about you and he wants you this week. I'll leave you his card so you can call his secretary to make arrangements."

"This Friday?"

"Is that a problem?"

"Of course not," she replied, sounding determined. "It's just that I'll have to do some juggling. Amber Johnson asked me to do hors d'oeuvres for a cocktail party for her this Friday. Thank you for that, by the way." Her mouth curved. "Your party already got me my first referral."

The pleasure he felt at her news was totally unexpected. What surprised him more was the reason the unusual feeling was there. It wasn't because his original idea to keep her employed was already working, but because what he'd done had made her smile.

"Just part of the plan," he said, liking the way her expression made him feel. Her smile was as soft as spring rain, gentle, renewing—and gone before he could consider just how badly he craved renewal himself.

"I have my construction route to do first," she murmured, wiping her hands on her apron. "So I could do the prep work for both before I do dough. Or maybe I should do dough, then the prep work for the lunch and do her hors d'oeuvres when I get back from my route."

Looking as if she were madly calculating how to pull off that day, she turned up the speed on the mixer. The louder whir drowned the sounds of ESPN filtering in from the bar.

"Hire help," he finally said, suggesting the obvious.

Her brow pinched. "I don't want help. I'll do it myself."

His expression mirrored hers. "What are you going to do when you have more work than you can handle?"

"Sleep less."

"It doesn't sound like you sleep now."

"Of course I do. I get seven hours a night." A knowing look entered her eyes. "That's more than you get, I bet."

That was true. Some nights. The fact that she'd first met him after one such sleep-deprived night, then been at his house on a night when turning in early hadn't been an option, pretty much confirmed her conclusion, too. He had never sensed disapproval of his lifestyle from her. But after the way she'd refused to stay the other night, she clearly wasn't comfortable with it, either.

Before he could figure out why her comfort with it even mattered, she'd turned to the bowl on the island and started measuring out flour.

She absently rubbed an itch on her jaw with the back of her hand. "What kind of logos did you design?" she asked, bluntly changing the subject.

"When was the last time you took a vacation?" he returned, changing it right back.

"What does that have to do with why you're here?"

With anyone else, he would have let the matter go. The woman now sporting a smudge of flour near her chin wanted to get down to business, and that was what he should do, too. The sooner they discussed his plan, the sooner he could get on a plane and catch up with his crew. But there had been something about her from the beginning that made him feel there was more to her drive than a desire to succeed. Success was usually measured in dollars or size. At least, it was in the only circles he knew. Yet money still didn't seem to be her goal, and she would never achieve any size with either branch of her business if she tried to do everything alone.

Having eliminated the normal motivators, he was left with the feeling that she somehow *needed* to push herself as hard as she did. No one enjoyed work that much.

"Just humor me," he muttered. "Everyone needs a break once in a while. I just want to know the last time you took one."

"I don't remember," she said, sounding as if it had been far longer than she cared to admit. "And I don't need one now, if that's what you're getting at."

"I wasn't suggesting you take one now. What do you do on weekends?"

"The things people normally do on weekends," she said, only to realize that what constituted normal for her wouldn't be anywhere near usual for him. The man had a housekeeper who apparently did everything for him but tuck him in at night. For all Madison knew, she might even do that, too. But the possibility of him changing sheets, pushing a vacuum cleaner or standing in line with a crowd at a meat counter seemed as likely as her attending a royal ball.

"I borrow Mom's car and do my bulk shopping for the week at a warehouse store," she explained, obliging him. "And I take my truck...the van," she corrected, "to the car wash and do my books and my laundry and clean my apartment and cook dinner for my family."

"That's it?"

The look she gave him seemed to asked what else he expected. "That's all I have time for. By then it's Sunday night."

"My point, exactly."

"What point?"

"That you don't leave any time for anything but work. You didn't mention a single thing that didn't sound like a responsibility or a chore. When was the last time you spent the day at the beach or played tennis or golf?"

She eyed him evenly. "We don't play a lot of tennis or golf around here."

"Then, what about spending a day on the water, or skiing?"

"I don't know anyone with a boat. And I don't ski."

"I meant snow skiing."

"Me, too."

"How about movies? When did you last go to one?" he pressed. "Or for a walk on the beach? Do you ever step out the door over there to watch the sunrise?"

The cool blue of his eyes moved over her face, quietly searching, quietly invading. Before he'd made his way down to movies and walks, she'd halfway expected him to ask about the theater, the symphony or flying to Las Vegas or London for dinner. Those would be the sorts of diversions he would be accustomed to himself. Except maybe for the symphony. She had never been to one, but with his penchant for action and the faint air of restlessness she'd often sensed in him, he didn't seem at all like the type who would sit still for two hours of orchestra.

That gave them even less in common. Two hours of music sounded like a lovely escape to her.

Reminding herself of how very different were their worlds, uneasy with how clearly he must see that as he studied her so closely, she turned away. With her dry ingredients blended, she scooped the batter off the blades and dumped the flour and leavening into the bowl.

"Why won't you let yourself relax, Madison?"

"You wouldn't understand," she murmured, and

started mixing the whole mess with a long wooden spoon. Motion suddenly seemed necessary. Vital, actually. Even if it hadn't, she'd learned that cookies tasted better when she mixed in the flour by hand.

"Try me."

"It's not a big deal. Okay?"

"If it's not a big deal, then it shouldn't bother you to tell me."

"I thought you were here to help me build more business."

"I am," he said easily enough. "And we'll talk about that as soon as you stop stalling and answer me."

The hand expertly wielding the spoon suddenly stilled. With a glance that hinted heavily at tolerance, she picked up the entire bowl, set it on the island and pulled out a stack of cookie sheets.

Cord leaned against the island all the while, his arms and ankles casually crossed, patiently watching her.

"Madison."

"What?"

"I mean it. We're not discussing anything until you tell me."

"Okay. Fine," she conceded, over the clatter of metal. "I work so I don't have a lot of time to think."

Reaching back under the island, she pulled out a box of disposable food service gloves and an ice cream scoop, and braced herself for him to ask what it was she didn't want to think about.

Thinking he couldn't ask anything if she made enough noise, she lined up the sheets, butting them side to side, slipped on gloves and started to scoop.

She was desperately hoping he would simply let the matter go when he reached over and curved his fingers on the underside of her jaw. Her breath caught at his touch, her heart jerking wildly as he tipped her face toward him.

"I had the feeling it might be something like that," he finally said, his tone oddly quiet. His thumb moved over her chin, his glance following the motion a moment before returning to her eyes. "How long do you figure you can keep blocking your mind before you burn out?"

Understanding was the last thing she ever would have expected from him. Torn between being drawn by that empathy and feeling totally exposed by it, she felt his thumb brush her skin once more.

She slowly lowered her head, felt his compelling touch drift away. "I don't want to think about it."

He gave a mirthless chuckle. "I hear you there," he muttered. "I've got a ton of things I'd rather not think about, myself."

Reaching for a pair of gloves, he dipped his golden head toward the scoop in her hand. "Do you have another one of those?"

Disarmed by what he'd done, by what he'd said, she handed him hers and bent to get another utensil for herself. When she straightened, he was scooping dough, checking her pan so he could space lumps on a sheet just as she had.

She didn't know if he simply needed something to do, or if he was intentionally helping her. Either way, he'd just exposed something of himself, too.

"I imagine there are," she quietly said. "Things you'd rather not think about, I mean."

Cord felt himself hesitate. Beyond the incident with her truck and a party that turned a bit wild, she could only know whatever she had read about him. Wondering what she must think of the tabloid headlines that haunted him, wondering what she must think of him because of them, he slowly shook his head.

"I'd hardly know where to start," he admitted, packing dough into the rounded utensil. "Actually, yeah, I do," he said, changing his mind. "I'd start by forgetting the lawsuit over that brawl in Vegas. I had nothing to do with starting it, but I was the one with the money and the reputation so my name was in the headlines. Once that happened, everyone who'd been there started hiring lawyers and going after me."

Beside him, Madison moved a sheet aside, started another. "But didn't you pay settlements?" she asked, as if such payment admitted guilt.

"It cost less than going to trial," he explained. "And settling early cut down on publicity. That's all my parents wanted. To get it settled and get me out of the papers."

Rule number one when you were a Kendrick was to keep the family name out of the press unless the press was positive. The publicity generated by charities, property acquisitions and certain social events was acceptable, even desirable. Since he only participated in one out of three, his chances for favorable press were already limited.

"The guys who sued me knew they wouldn't get squat if it did go in front of a jury," he continued, filling her in on one of the finer points of legal negotiation. "So their lawyers told them to take the money and run.

"I'd also like to forget about the street race between me and that race car driver in Monte Carlo a few years back," he went on, now that he was thinking about things he wished he could avoid considering. "We might have both been killed if we hadn't been arrested first. And I most definitely would like to forget the paternity suit that idiot model brought a couple of years ago."

On a roll, he snapped out another raw cookie. "That thing didn't get settled until DNA tests proved I couldn't possibly be the father. I'd only known her for a couple of months and slept with her twice before she started talking marriage. Both times I used protection with her. I've used protection with every woman I've ever slept with,'' he insisted, digging into the dough again. ''It hasn't been anywhere *near* the number who've claimed they've been with me, either, but I'd have to be crazy not to be careful.'' Adamant, still talking, he glanced toward the woman beside him. ''Turns out she thought she could make me marry her. Do you have any idea how it feels to be set up like that?''

He didn't expect an answer. He was just venting, something he never did. It felt good, and he was preparing to continue when he noticed the faint blush of color on Madison's cheek. Her focus remained resolutely fixed on the island as she slowly continued her task.

He couldn't believe what he'd just said to her. Having her know he practiced safe sex was hardly the worst thing she could know about him. Letting her know he wasn't as indiscriminate as the press made him sound wasn't a bad thing, either. Still, he couldn't help but wonder at some of the things he tended to blindly admit to her. He also couldn't help but wonder what she must be thinking now.

''I imagine it made you feel used,'' she said quietly. She remembered those headlines, and the sensationalism surrounding them. ''What other people say about you and what other people do must make your life...difficult.'' She truly couldn't imagine what it must be like for him. To be watched constantly, knowing people were just waiting for him to mess up. To be taken advantage of. To never know if people truly cared about him or if they were only after whatever they could get out of him.

The thoughts squeezed hard at her heart, adding another layer of sympathy to what she already felt. "But those things weren't what I meant."

When she'd agreed that, like her, there were things he probably didn't want to think about, she truly hadn't been thinking of those well-publicized situations at all.

"I meant what you told me last week. About your family," she murmured. "It's hard when a person doesn't feel as if he belongs. Especially with the people who are supposed to be the first to accept him. I just figured that was one of those things you tried not to think about, too."

Cord had never told anyone about the alienation he felt with his family, the depth of it, the sense of isolation that kept him from feeling a part of the five other people who shared his genes. It was as if he'd been born a changeling, the one Kendrick who didn't care about conforming to standards others decided made him acceptable. His interests were simply different from theirs. What appealed to him appalled them. Yet, twice now, the forthcoming and slightly baffling woman beside him had alluded to that sense of separation as if she knew exactly how he felt.

Before he could decide just how disturbed he was by her uncanny perception, she smiled.

"I'm glad you mentioned the lawsuits, though." As nice as he was being about helping her expand her business, as easy as he was to talk to, she could practically feel him slipping past her normal guard. Especially with the empathy tugging at her even now. His reminders kept her safe. "I did wonder why you would settle the one about the fight if you weren't guilty," she admitted, understanding now. "There's something else I'd like to know, though."

He might be innocent of fathering a child, and she

didn't doubt that he had been used by his accusers in the brawl, but she needed to remember what had led to those situations to begin with. She doubted that anyone had dragged him into the lounge in Vegas, the race car in Monte Carlo or into that model's bed. There was a side of him that definitely liked to live fast and wild.

She couldn't help wondering why that was.

"What's it like to bungee jump off a cliff in Hawaii?"

He'd expected her to ask for clarification of another transgression. She felt certain of that from the hint of relief in his expression as he took another scoop from the bowl.

"The bungee jumps were in Oregon. The only thing I do in Hawaii is surf and hang glide."

She tipped her head, considering him. "But why do you like doing those things? And climbing mountains," she added, because that seemed even more dangerous somehow.

Cord could have told her it was because he was addicted to the adrenaline rush. He loved that edge of the unknown, and the surge of power he felt when he'd conquered it. He could have told her he did it for the same reasons she wanted to work herself into the ground. When a person's heart was racing and his mind occupied with survival, it was difficult to think about much of anything else.

He almost did tell her, too. As he stood watching the quiet interest in her eyes, he realized that he actually wanted her to know all that about him. He wanted her to understand it the way she seemed to understand how he felt being the odd man out in his family.

The realization had no sooner struck than he took a mental step back.

He was there to discuss the plan that would turn her

business into a catering phenomenon, and thus keep her thoughts from lawyers and lawsuits. Not to bare his sorry soul to a woman who subtly withdrew from him every time he touched her. It wasn't as if she would jerk away or act at all offended. Her retreat was more subtle. More like an uneasiness with the idea of getting physical.

Thinking it might be easier to keep his own thoughts from straying in that direction if she didn't look and smell so good, he retreated himself. Never would he have expected the combination of herbal shampoo and vanilla to be so erotic.

"Because they're there," he replied, offering nothing more than he would have to anyone else.

The swinging door swung open.

Cord's glance jerked up at the same time as Madison's. The rust-haired owner of the pub stood with one hand holding open the door, a Guinness beer T-shirt stretched over his massive chest. The guy he'd heard referred to as Mike seemed like a regular sort of guy to Cord, and particularly watchful of the long-legged brunette smiling at him.

He was also built like a bouncer.

"I thought I heard you talking to someone back here," he said to Madison. He nodded to Cord. "How's it going?"

"Good. Thanks," Cord replied, peeling off the clear gloves.

Curiosity slashed the man's ruddy features. "You're the guy helping Madison settle her truck claim."

Cord glanced away. If pressed for his name, he wouldn't lie. But he'd just as soon not have to mention it, either. "That I am."

"Then you're with an insurance company?"

Cord gave a shrug that could have been interpreted as

just about anything. "Actually, I'm more with Callaway Construction."

"But you haven't always worked with them." Mike's eyes narrowed in concentration, his forehead furrowing. "I told Madison the other day that you looked familiar to me. You still do," he insisted, looking intent on identification. "Did you ever play for the Oilers?"

"The only football I played was in college."

"What about the PGA?"

"I'm afraid my golf game isn't anywhere near that good."

"Huh," Mike grunted, hands on hips. "I could swear I've seen your face before."

"Everybody looks familiar to you," Madison helpfully interrupted. "You're the one who told me everyone has a twin somewhere. He probably just reminds you of some sports personality you've seen."

Unable to place the man at her side, Madison watched the big Irishman give up and turn his attention to her. If Cord looked familiar to him, she was certain it was only because he'd seen his face at the supermarket checkouts. Mike didn't follow celebrity gossip. But he lived, ate and breathed sports. To his way of thinking, when it came to the rich and famous, if a person didn't own a team, coach or play on one, he wasn't a celebrity at all.

"Erma just called," he told her, getting to his reason for coming in. "Her daughter had her baby and she needs to stay with her other kids."

Concern flashed in Madison's eyes. "Amy had her baby already? She's not due for three weeks."

"I guess nobody told the kid that. Erma says they're both doing fine. It's another girl. Six pounds something," he replied, sounding as if he knew that would be her next question. "Any chance you can help me out tonight? And maybe the rest of the week? Jackson was going to cover for her," he said, speaking of his Friday night and weekend cook, "but Erma wasn't supposed to be gone until the end of the month and he's got his day job. I figure you've got the time since your route got cut short and you don't have to go to bed quite so early."

Madison didn't hesitate. "No problem."

"Thanks. With the tournament starting tonight, this place will be packed."

Looking as relieved as he sounded, he pushed back through the doorway, the door swinging behind him.

Cord frowned at the top of her head. "Do you always do that?

"Do what?"

"Take on whatever anyone asks when you already have other plans?"

Looking puzzled, she reached for the cellophane to cover the sheets they'd filled so she could put them in the fridge. "Mike's a friend," she said, as if that somehow explained everything. "And what plans?"

"The business plan we're supposed to discuss?"

"We can talk while I work."

"We haven't so far."

"Only because you said you wouldn't until I told why I like to stay busy," she pointed out, ever so reasonably. "If it hadn't been for that, we could have been talking about the advertising campaign and logos you mentioned for the past ten minutes."

"Hey, Madison," Mike called through the pass-through. "Any chance you can boil some eggs? The pickled egg jar out here's low, and we'll need 'em for tonight."

"Sure, Mike," she called back.

"You know what?" Cord nudged his full sheet toward her. "I think it'll work better if I just catch you later."

Not liking that idea at all, she glanced up to see that his gaze had moved to her jaw. "But I want to hear your plan."

"And I want to tell you about it," he said, catching her chin once more. With the pad of his thumb, he brushed away the tiny smudge of flour he'd missed before. "I just want your full attention when I do."

She could have told him he had her attention. He had every cell in her brain and her body totally focused on him every time he touched her. But he'd already dropped his hand and turned away, and now Mike wanted to know if she could whip up her special nachos to serve as the night's special when she finished her dough.

"Since you'll be doing this the rest of the week," Cord said, picking up his file on his way to the back door, "I'm going to head up to Annapolis. I'll see you when I get back."

"When will that be?"

"That depends on whether or not my team qualifies for Saturday's race."

Madison never minded helping Mike. There wasn't much she enjoyed more than cooking, especially when the people who ate what she prepared seemed to enjoy it. The people who crowded into Mike's to play darts, watch a ball game or just socialize with their friends were also her friends. She'd either grown up with them or with their children, and when there was a crowd, it felt almost like a party.

That was never how it felt at her grandmother's house, though. And her grandma's house was where she went the following Sunday, as she did every week, to take the latest fashion magazines to her little sister, Jamie, to catch up on neighborhood gossip with her Grandma Nona and listen to her mom insist that she really didn't need to spend her only day off with them.

Her mom never came right out and said that. She just hinted around it until grandma picked up the ball and ran with it—which, eventually, was what the spry, outspoken septuagenarian did when she asked Madison how she thought she would ever get a man if she spent her only day off cooped up in the house with three women.

Madison knew that her grandmother just wanted to see her married. She wasn't so sure what her mom wanted from her, though. When Nona started in on the husband thing, Beth O'Malley would just quietly say, "Mom, please. Leave the girl alone."

That's exactly what she'd said, again, two seconds ago.

"I'll leave her alone when she stops spending her Saturday nights doing her laundry and her bookkeeping. She's twenty-eight, Beth. She's a beautiful girl. Heaven knows she can cook," she proclaimed, waving to where Madison stood at the stove. "She gets that from our side of the family, you know. It's a gift.

"Anyway," she continued, refusing to sidetrack herself, which happened on occasion, "it won't be long before she's thirty. According to *Cosmo*, a woman who hasn't had a serious relationship by then will find it even harder to find a man. With the pickings around here growing slimmer every day, then what's she going to do?"

Beth O'Malley looked up from where she sat paying bills at the yellow Formica kitchen table in the cozy, white-and-yellow kitchen she'd learned to cook in herself as a child. At fifty-two, she was still an attractive woman, despite the gray she refused to dye from her short, dark hair and the fatigue in her eyes that came from being on her feet all day at the Pay-N-Pac. She had been a checker there for eleven years—which was about how long it had been since Michael O'Malley had walked out on her and all five of his kids and she'd moved in with her widowed mother.

Removing her reading glasses, she narrowed her eyes at the woman she would probably look just like in another twenty years. "When did you start buying *Cosmo*?"

Grandma Nona sat on the opposite side of the table going through the coupon section of the Sunday paper. Scissors in hand, she kept clipping. "I didn't buy it. Madison did. She brought a copy for Jamie last week."

Beth's voice fell as she turned to her second oldest daughter. "What are you doing buying a magazine like that for your sister? Jamie is just a child."

"She's sixteen," Madison reminded her, as much in defense of herself as her admittedly sheltered sibling. Jamie was disabled. And fiercely protected by them all.

She lowered her voice even more, though she truly doubted Jamie could overhear. Her youngest sister was on the couch in the living room with her headphones on far louder than was sensible, blissfully scanning the new *Seventeen* magazine Madison had just brought her.

"You know how into the prom all the girls are right now, Mom. Jamie heard some of her friends at school talking about a hairstyle article and she wanted a copy. She didn't get to see the one Caitlin O'Connor brought."

Disapproval faded to a different sort of concern. "Weren't they sharing with her?"

"Apparently, one of the nuns confiscated it before they could."

"Did you hear that Amy Flaherty had her baby?" Grandma asked.

Madison and her mom both turned to where the small woman with the head full of tight silver curls sat in her hot-pink jogging suit, scissors still in hand.

Beth, dressed in the navy slacks and blouse she'd worn to church, gave her a look of total incomprehension. "What does that have to do with appropriate reading material for Jamie?"

"Not a thing. But we were talking about Madison before you changed the subject and I was just thinking that babies are another reason she needs to find a husband."

Light suddenly glinted behind her silver-framed bifocals as she glanced to where Madison opened the oven door.

"You know what that means, don't you, Madison? That means there will be a christening," she continued, clearly pleased with the prospect. "Maybe her brother-in-law will come for it. The one who's the insurance agent in Baltimore? Mavis said she heard from Erma that he broke up with the girl he was going out with. That's a good thing, too," she confided, "because according to Mavis, the girl was as spoiled as week-old fish and Erma really didn't want her for a daughter-in-law.

"Anyway," she continued, liking her idea more by the second, "I'll ask Erma if he's coming and if he is, I can volunteer you to pick him up from the airport." She smiled as Madison stuck a fork into a pan of scalloped potatoes. "What do you think?"

"I think Theresa Shannahan would never speak to me again," she replied, deciding the potatoes needed a few more minutes. "She's had a thing for Don Flaherty since high school. If he's available, you should let her know."

"Little Theresa Shannahan?" her mother asked her.

"She's not that little," Grandma Nona muttered. "Last I saw her…"

"She's a nice girl, Grandma."

"Well, it's you I'm worried about. Not her. And that's another thing. You're always fixing up your friends with men you meet out there on your route. Like Tina Deluca," she said, over the two-tone chime of the doorbell. "It's time you keep one for yourself."

"Somebody want to get the door?" Jamie called from the living room.

"I've got it," Madison announced, and closed the door on her pork roast, the potatoes and the debate about her future.

"It's probably the paper boy." Flipping through the bills she'd been paying, Beth pulled out a check. "Give him this."

"And tell him to stop throwing the paper into the rosebushes," Nona insisted. "He does it one more time I'm going to make him go in after it." Paper rustled as she gathered up her clipped coupons. "How long before dinner?"

Madison glanced at the clock on the white enamel stove. It read 1:50. "Ten minutes," she replied, taking the check on her way from the room.

Her mom's voice followed her. "I'll set the dining room table."

They'd had dinner at 2:00 p.m. on Sunday afternoon for as long as Madison could remember. And for as long as she could remember, they'd eaten the meal at the old mahogany dining room table with the "good" china and a linen tablecloth it had to take her grandmother an hour to iron. Even now that her older sister and both brothers had moved away and there were only four of them at home—and despite the fact that her mother routinely claimed there was no need to go to all the trouble—Grandma insisted that Sunday dinner needed to be properly served. The rule was inviolate, rather like Cord's grandmother's insistence that a plate needed to be properly garnished.

The thought that her grandmother actually had something in common with a queen gave Madison pause. It might also have made her smile had she not then wondered if Cord's grandmother had ever tried to fix him up with the local princesses, or whoever it was Her Highness would consider a suitable match.

Wondering how Cord would handle such well-meaning interference, thinking she might just ask, she hurried through the living room, holding up five fingers on the way to let Jamie know how long she had before she needed to start getting herself up and to the table.

She reached for the knob, frowning a little to think of how often thoughts of him would creep into her consciousness. Even more disturbing was the anticipation she felt at the thought of hearing from him again.

Wanting to believe that whatever anticipation she felt was there only because of his ideas for her business, reassuring herself that she didn't need to worry about it right now, she blew a strand of hair from her face and opened the door.

She had expected to see the neighborhood's short, skinny newspaper boy in his usual battered baseball cap. Instead, she found her view blocked by six feet of tall, powerfully lean and decidedly handsome male wearing a black polo shirt, beige slacks and an easy smile.

Chapter Six

Madison's heart skipped a beat before it sank. Cord was the last person she wanted to see on her grandma's porch. He was definitely the last person she would want inside her house. "What are you doing here?"

As greetings went, she suspected hers wasn't the most cordial. Cord, looking faintly preoccupied, didn't seem to notice.

"I told you I'd catch up with you when I got back," he said, sounding as if she shouldn't look so surprised to see him. "I went to your place, but the kids playing in the puddle on the corner said you were over here. By the way, you might tell the skinny little guy with the freckles that this is the third house on the right, not the second. The guy next door wasn't too happy with me getting him out from under his sink. He was fixing a clogged drain."

"Why didn't Mrs. Petruski answer the door?" she asked, referring to cranky old Mr. Petruski's wife.

"I didn't ask."

Tipping his head, he ran a glance from the knot of hair anchored on her head to the pale blue hoodie that met the low waist of her jeans.

Aware of his scrutiny, more mindful of the commotion his presence could cause simply because his car would draw so much attention, she darted a glance to the shower-dampened street.

The obscenely expensive silver vehicle he drove was nowhere in sight. The only unfamiliar automobile on the block was the shiny black Ford SUV parked at the curb. "Where's your car?"

"At the house. I drive the Explorer sometimes because it's less obvious and I don't get followed so much."

"By the police?" she asked, thinking of his penchant for speed and how fast the Lamborghini must go.

"By photographers. How long will you be here?" he asked, his reference to the press sounding like nothing more than something that was always in the back of his mind. "I know you have Sundays off, so I thought we could discuss what we didn't get around to talking about the other night."

"Now isn't…" *a good time.*

Madison muttered the mental conclusion as the door was pulled from her hand. Grandma Nona appeared at her elbow, her perfectly penciled eyebrows lowered in curiosity.

"I heard a man's voice and couldn't figure out who you were talking to out here," she said, speaking to Madison, looking at Cord.

Curiosity moved to a smile, then, with a start, back to curiosity again. "You're a friend of Madison's?"

Cord's smile eased into place as he took in all five feet

three inches of the brightly dressed lady staring up at him. "I hope so."

"Well then, invite the young man in," she admonished her granddaughter. "What are you doing leaving him standing on the porch?"

"You know who you look like?" she asked, reaching out to take his elbow herself. "You look just like the youngest Kendrick son. The one who's always getting himself into one mess or another. Anyone ever tell you that?"

It seemed to Madison that her grandmother was prepared to drag the man in if need be. Fearing she might, Madison stepped out of the way to keep from getting herself knocked over and watched, helpless, while Cord stepped into the room that suddenly seemed dated rather than merely familiar, a little shabby rather than just comfortable.

The fact that Cord seemed totally at ease being hauled into her world only made her more aware of how totally *un*easy she felt in the moments before her grandmother closed the door to resume her scrutiny.

Cord held out his hand. "Cord Kendrick, ma'am."

"That's right," her grandmother said, returning his handshake. "That's the one."

"I mean, that's who I am." He could get away with evading Mike's curiosity. He seemed to know that here, with her family, an introduction was unavoidable. "The one who finds himself in those messes."

"Cord," Madison said, wondering why there was never a convenient hole around when a girl needed one, "this is my grandmother, Nona Rossini."

"The pleasure is mine," he said, and lifted the elderly woman's weathered hand to kiss the back of it.

With anyone else, the courtly gesture would have

seemed ridiculously old-fashioned. Knowing that he'd probably been taught such manners with older women because he had, in fact, been at court, only added a note of unreality to a situation that was already beginning to feel a little surreal.

"I hope I'm not interrupting anything," he murmured, straightening.

"Oh. Oh, my." Her grandmother's bespectacled glance darted to Madison, then back to Cord as he released his hold. "No, of course you're not. We're just…" Her eyes narrowed to slits. "You *are* him," she announced.

Madison would bet her new truck that she knew exactly what her grandmother would say next. She would want to know what on earth he was doing in the Ridge, in her living room, and with her granddaughter. Wanting to stave off the interrogation to come, and seeing that Cord's attention had moved to her sister, anyway, she motioned him past the overstuffed chairs with crocheted doilies on their arms to the old green sofa with a colorful afghan covering its back.

A minute ago, brown-haired, hazel-eyed Jamie had sat slouched on the sofa, one leg moving in time to the music blasting in her ears, the other immobile in the brace hidden beneath her long skirt and her nose still buried in a magazine. Having sensed something unusual going on, she'd lowered the magazine and now stared, mouth open, at the man who'd just stepped over her crutches.

He held out his hand. "Hi."

"Jamie, this is Cord. Cord, my sister, Jamie."

"How are you doing?" he asked the pretty young girl blinking back at him. Jamie clearly recognized him, too. But then, his face was right there on the cluttered coffee table. His photo was in the lower left corner of a *People* magazine, along with those of a half dozen other celebrities who'd recently attended a Johnny Depp movie premiere.

With one hand, Jamie pulled off her headphones. The other disappeared into his. She didn't say a word. She just watched him smile at her, then started breathing again when he let go of her hand. Only then did she say, ''Hi'' herself.

''Madison, I turned the heat down on your chutney.'' Her mom crossed from the kitchen to the little dining room holding a stack of dinner and salad plates with both hands. ''You might want to check it. And the timer just went off on whatever you'd—''

Whatever else she'd intended to say was forgotten. Clearly startled to find a large, unfamiliar male dominating the living room, Beth O'Malley stood at a dead stop six feet from her destination. She appeared even more stunned when she happened to recognize him.

She also seemed about to lose her grip on the china.

''Let me get those.'' Cord stepped into the space that separated the dining and living rooms. An instant later he had the dishes.

Beth's hand promptly flattened on her chest.

''I'm sorry,'' she murmured, apparently aware of how close she'd come to losing her mother's Lenox. ''I didn't realize we had company.''

''You must be Madison's older sister.'' Dishes rattled as he set them on the linen-draped table. ''I just met Jamie, and I know she has one more.''

Madison couldn't believe it. Her totally no-nonsense, unflappable and slightly careworn mother actually blushed. Her high cheekbones turned a truly flattering shade of ripe peach. As if her mom couldn't believe it herself, her hand flew from her chest to her cheek to feel for heat a moment before Madison walked over to introduce Cord to her and explain that she was actually her mom. Her older sister, Taylor, lived in Maryland. Her brothers were in Maine.

Gathering her usual composure, Beth accepted his handshake, said she was pleased to meet him, then looked to her daughter. Questions and a healthy dose of disbelief filled the brown eyes so like Madison's own.

"I see I came at a bad time. You're getting ready to eat." Pushing his hands into his pockets, Cord looked from her mother's open curiosity to where Madison stood an arm's length away. "How about I go now and call you later…"

She didn't get a chance to tell him she thought that might be a really good idea.

"No!" three female voices simultaneously insisted.

"There's no reason for you to leave," her mother said, more quietly.

"Madison has made plenty of food." Grandma's silver hair gleamed with the decisive nod of her head. "You can join us. Do you like pork roast?"

Cord's eyebrows shot up. "Madison did the cooking?"

"All of it," Grandma said, proudly. "There's no better cook in the Ridge, either. Any man…"

"You are welcome to stay," Beth cut in, sparing them all her mother's well-meaning endorsement.

It was impossible for Madison to tell what was going on behind Cord's guarded blue eyes as he glanced from the two older women to the youngest one trying not to gawk at him from the sofa. She could only hope that he was looking for a courteous way to decline the embarrassingly enthusiastic invitation.

"Thanks. I'd love to," he said, instead. "Especially if

Madison prepared the meal. I'd never pass up a chance to eat her cooking.

"I've had it before," he said, apparently realizing that his comment, and his presence, required a bit of further explanation. "I had muffins from her catering truck and liked them so much that we got to talking about her business and how she wanted to expand it. She catered a dinner for me," he continued, wildly oversimplifying. "Since then we've been trying to get together to talk about a business plan."

The man definitely got points for being glib, Madison thought. But, then, she reminded herself, because she needed such reminders to keep her perspective about him, he was notorious for his smooth talk and charm.

Even now, his bare-bones explanation had both older women raising their chins in acknowledgment. They were hanging on his every word. She couldn't see Jamie, because her back was to her, but she felt fairly certain her little sister was hanging right with them.

"So do you two want to talk and we can eat later?" her mother asked.

"No. No," Madison repeated. What she wanted was for him to go. Now. She didn't want him charming her mom, her grandma or her sister the way he so apparently charmed everyone else. She most especially did not want him in the home she'd practically grown up in. She wasn't ashamed of it by any means. It was as nice a home as any in the Ridge. It was just that his being there invaded a part of her she hadn't been prepared to share with him.

Unfortunately, the situation was out of her hands.

"They can't talk now, Beth," her grandma muttered. "It's two o'clock. Dinner's ready. So, Mr. Kendrick—"

"Cord," he corrected.

"Cord," she repeated, looking pleased to be on a first-name basis with someone so famous, "if you'd like to wash up, the bathroom is right down that hall. Second door on the left. We'll have the meal on the table in no time." She patted the chair next to where Madison always sat. "You can sit right here."

He thanked her, took a step back and turned to where Madison stood rubbing her forehead. As her mom and grandmother hurried back to the kitchen, her mom for another place setting, her grandmother undoubtedly to grill her on what to make of Cord's presence, he took a step closer.

His voice dropped like a rock in a well. "Are you okay with this?"

The man had no idea what he'd set her up for. Or himself for that matter.

"Would it make a difference if I said no?" she asked, smiling gamely as she dropped her hand.

"What would you like to drink, Cord?" Her grandmother poked her head around the door, her eyes darting between the two of them as if to be sure she didn't miss anything. "We have iced tea or milk. And we have a bottle of Manischewitz we keep for special occasions."

"Milk would be great."

Grandma beamed and disappeared.

"I'm a special occasion." A teasing light entered his eyes. "I'm honored."

She could steel herself against the smile. It was the hint of apology there, too, that got her. "Don't let it go to your head," she murmured back. "You're a male. You're breathing."

"Madison? Do you want me to take out the potatoes?"

"Yes, Mom," she called back. "Go wash," she said

to him, sounding just like her mother. She cringed, started to apologize. But they were in the Ridge, and telling everybody to wash up before a meal was simply what they always did.

"Yes, ma'am," he replied, that light still in his eyes. His glance darted over her shoulder, settled on the crutches, then on Jamie who had yet to say another word.

"Do you need any help over there?"

Jamie's eyes went wide again. "Oh, no. No. I'm good. I'm…thanks."

"Just holler if you do." He hitched his thumb toward the hall, held up both hands. "I'm going to go do what you sister said."

"Madison O'Malley," her grandmother whispered the moment Madison set foot in the kitchen, "why in heaven's name didn't you tell us you knew that man."

"It slipped my mind."

"Slipped your mind!"

"Mom, please." Beth's voice was a whisper, too. "We can talk later. He's right in the other room, for Pete's sake."

"He's in the bathroom. I can hear the water running."

"It's still not polite to talk about someone while he's right here in the house. Do you need help there, Madison?"

"I have it, Mom. If you'll just put the chutney in a bowl and grab the salad, I think we're ready."

"Bread." Grandma headed for the pantry. "We should have baked some. All we have is store bought."

"Store bought is fine, Grandma." With the roast on a platter and the potatoes ready to be carried out, Madison started making gravy. With every movement, she prayed desperately that her dear, good-hearted maternal grandmother would, just once, not be quite so much her usual outspoken self. It was hard to anticipate what Nona would say.

In some ways Nona Rossini bore an uncanny resemblance to Her Majesty, Queen Sophia Regina Amelia Renaldi of Luzandria. Not physically, Cord thought, as the woman with the tight silver curls passed him the gravy, explaining as she did that no one made better gravy than Madison. His eighty-year-old grandmother had eyes of sharp, clear blue, not the warm brown that had been passed on to Madison. Her skin was pale, not Nona's light olive. And while they were both fairly small and gray-haired, his very regal grandmother wouldn't have been caught dead in such a neon-bright shade of pink, much less in a jogging suit with flowers appliquéd to it. Their demeanor wasn't even all that similar, given that Madison's grandmother in no way expected to be waited on, where his own had been born to expect deference. They both, however, seemed highly opinionated, liked things done a certain way and wouldn't take no for an answer.

"Take another slice of meat," Nona insisted, from her chair at the foot of the table.

"Really, this is fine," he replied, looking down at the white china plate he'd just filled.

As if he hadn't spoken at all, she speared another succulent slice from the platter in the middle of table. It landed atop the one nestled between creamy scalloped potatoes and chutney thick with raisins, onions and apples.

"Thanks," he murmured.

"You're welcome. No need for you to take such a small portion.

"So," she continued, now that grace had been said and plates filled to her liking, "why don't you tell us just how the two of you got together?"

Madison sat on his left, two feet from his elbow. Even with that space separating them, he swore he could feel her go still. He also thought he heard her sigh.

"We're not together, Grandma. He's just helping me with my business."

"We met at the construction site for the York Port Mall," he said, thinking it easier to give the woman what she wanted than to evade it. He sliced off a bite of roasted pork. "I told you how impressed I was with her cooking. So after I heard about her truck getting wrecked, I tracked her down and she told me about how she'd wanted to expand her business. I'm always looking for projects that can't miss and I don't think this one can."

Madison's sister sat across from her. Madison's rather sedate mom sat across from Cord. While grandma chewed, he watched Beth give him a faint smile. Taking a bite himself, he prepared to change the subject before he had to bend any more of the truth.

His glance settled on the teenager. Jamie had the same dark and shining hair as her sister, only she wore hers long and fringed around her pretty face. A certain shyness kept golden brown eyes on her plate.

"What year are you, Jamie?" he asked.

Startled, her glance jerked up. "A junior."

"At St. Mary's," Madison added helpfully when she said nothing more.

"Is that all girls?"

Jamie shook her head. "It's coed."

"I got stuck in an all-boys school," he confided, wondering if her smile was anything like her sister's. "It was pretty boring." Except for when he and Matt would pick fights or hot-wire cars in the parking lot, he thought. He didn't mention that, though. Nearly getting kicked out of school was one of those things he'd just as soon forget. "Except for the games. Going to games was pretty good. Do you go to yours?"

"Once in a while," she replied, looking a little more at ease as she reached for her milk. "But sports are all over for the year. There's nothing going on now."

"There's prom," her mother prompted.

"Yeah. Except I'm not going."

Cord swallowed, went back for more. "Why not?"

"Because I don't have a date."

"There's still plenty of time," her mother assured her. "It's nearly three weeks away."

"What about the Balducci boy?" Madison's grandmother reached for the butter knife. "The one with the twin brothers. You like him, don't you?"

"The one with the nose ring?" Madison stared across the salad bowl at her little sister. "You said you'd never go out with a guy who pierced anything other than his ear."

"And even that's disgusting," Grandma muttered, buttering bread.

Jamie gave her sister a look that seemed to say "Get real." "The one with the nose ring is a cousin. Grandma means Steve. And it's not like I really *like* him," she clarified, "so don't go saying I do, okay, Grandma? I'd die if he thought I did."

Grandma Nona looked bewildered. "Then, how's he going to know to ask you to the prom?"

"He isn't going to. No one's going to ask me," she added, her tone awfully philosophical for someone so young. "I can't dance."

Remembering her crutches, Cord nodded toward where

they leaned against the doily-and-dish-covered buffet behind her. "Because you're on those?"

Lifting her glass to her lips, Jamie nodded.

"But you know the moves. Right?" As encouraging as everyone else was being of her, he couldn't figure out why she seemed so resigned herself. Assuming her use of the crutches to be temporary, he saw no reason for such defeat. She was a pretty girl. She would be even more so when she gained the maturity of her sister. Guys probably flocked after her in droves. "You might not be able to dance fast, but you can lean on the guy for the slow ones."

"I never learned how to dance fast or slow. I've been on crutches forever."

Not defeat, he realized. What he sensed in her was merely acceptance.

Silverware clinked against china as he sent her a thoughtful glance. The breeziness of her reply, encouraged his quick, "What happened?"

For a moment the only sound he heard was the rhythmic tick of the grandfather clock at the end of the hall and the shouts of the kids playing in the street.

Madison's mom glanced toward the elderly woman in pink. Madison's interest seemed to have turned to her plate.

Only Jamie didn't appear uncomfortable with the question. "I was in an accident when I was a kid," she replied, piling chutney on pork and forking it into her mouth. She chewed, gulped. "But I would love to know how to dance. Even if a guy did ask me to the prom and I could balance against him for the slow ones, I don't know any of the dip stuff. Or that thing where you turn under the guy's arm. That's what looks like fun."

Her dancing didn't seem like such a problem to him. "Have you ever thought of taking lessons?"

Even as she mumbled that she hadn't, Madison lifted her head. The sudden disquiet he'd sensed in her had already vanished.

"Would you want them?" Madison asked, looking as expectant as she sounded. "I'll pay for them if you do."

Jamie's eyes lit up at the prospect. But it was her mother, sounding terribly practical, who replied.

"That's a lovely offer, Madison. But if someone like Cord thinks your catering business has potential, then you need to be saving your money for that."

Beth turned her soft smile to her youngest daughter. "You can go to the prom whether or not you can dance," she assured her. "Any boy who wouldn't take you just because you can't isn't worth your time, anyway."

"Absolutely," Grandma agreed. "Which reminds me," she announced, eyeing Cord. "Did you really date Cindy Crawford?"

Cord's eyebrows rose.

Beside him Madison stifled a groan.

He couldn't imagine what thread of logic had pulled the woman from a date for a prom to tabloid headlines. Considering the baffled way her own daughter was looking at her, he didn't even try. "Actually, she was married when I met her. Despite what the press claims, I never date married women."

Grandma raised her chin. "I always wondered about that. About just how much you can believe of what's printed these days, I mean."

"I'd say about half."

"Well, Mavis Reilly thinks anything in print is gospel. Now, I can tell her I have it from the horse's mouth that it's not."

The woman's smiling proclamation was accompanied by the bowl of chutney she handed him, since she could see his was gone.

Rather than helping himself to more, which he normally would have done because it tasted incredible with the meat, Cord slowly set down the bowl along with his fork.

He wasn't quite sure what had been going on when he'd asked Jamie about her leg, but even in that admittedly awkward moment he hadn't felt at all out of place in this modest, amazingly welcoming home.

He felt out of place now, though, and suddenly quite separate from the generous ladies allowing him to share their meal.

"Mrs. Rossini," he began, not totally sure how to say what he had to say without sounding vain, presumptuous or egotistical. His life bore little resemblance to what he'd experienced with Madison and the people she knew. Compared to what he'd grown up with, the way he lived now, her life and the lives of those at the table were all blissfully private. "If you don't mind, I'd really appreciate it if you didn't say anything to anyone about me being here. I'm not asking you to lie if someone asks something specific. Just please don't volunteer anything.

"I'm used to having people poke around in my life," he admitted, keeping the resentment he felt at that from his tone. "But Madison isn't. Not with the press, I mean. All it would take is for a reporter to find out that we're working together and they'd be asking a thousand questions and trying to dig up information about her. It won't matter that we're just doing business. She's a beautiful woman," he admitted candidly, "and I can guarantee that there would be assumptions. I can't imagine how the press could create any sort of scandal around her, but I can somehow get bad publicity just by breathing. It would be best if nothing is said until we have her business plan in place and she has the event end of her business up and running. By then I'll be out of the picture and any story will dead end.''

He glanced toward Madison, then to her mom. ''As hard as she works, I'd hate for speculation about her association with me to cause her problems.''

He hadn't considered Madison at all when he'd first asked her to keep their business just between them. He'd been thinking only of doing what he had to do to keep her away from insurance companies and lawyers. That was still his goal. But it didn't seem right to subject the unsuspecting and good-hearted woman beside him to the exploitation of the media. Or her family for that matter. They had a nice life here.

Grandma Nona's frown added a few more pleats to her forehead. Disappointment at having to keep news of his presence to herself seemed to being doing battle with approval for his willingness to protect her granddaughter. ''I'd never thought of that,'' she finally conceded. ''But I see your point.''

''You mean I can't tell anybody?'' Jamie asked, crestfallen.

''As he said,'' Beth quietly reminded her, ''it would be better for Madison if we didn't.''

''What about after he's helped her?''

''After that, talk all you want,'' Cord replied. ''Then, she can use whatever publicity she gets to focus on Madison's, Catering of Distinction.''

''Oh,'' her mom said. ''I like the sound of that.''

Grandma Nona repeated the name aloud. She then repeated it again. She liked it, too. Or so she proclaimed before she announced that she'd always known Madison's skills in the kitchen were far from ordinary, which allowed him to shift the focus of the conversation and ask where Madison had inherited her culinary talent.

Madison knew what her grandmother would say even before the animated woman began to recount how her own mother, who'd been born in Italy, had been famous for miles for her cheeses and pastas. Madison barely heard what she said, though. She paid little attention, too, to the stories she and her sister had heard before about the old village their great-grandmother had come from, which ultimately lead to mention of Palermo, which somehow led to mention of Pamplona, Spain, and how Cord had once run there with the bulls. She was far more aware of the concern he had seemed to feel for her reputation, his desire to protect her from publicity until it would serve her—and that he thought she was beautiful. He'd actually said that. Right there in front of her family.

More drawn to him than she knew was wise, and having inherited her mother's driving sense of practicality, she made herself remember something else he'd said, too.

He'd just made it clear to them all that he wouldn't be around for long.

She reminded herself to remember that as she eventually started clearing the table, just as she always did, and prepared to help do the dishes, just as she always did, too. But this particular Sunday, both her mom and her grandmother insisted they could take care of everything. Neither would hear of Cord helping, either, even after he told them that he really didn't mind helping in the kitchen.

The remark brought a curious glance from her and a shrug and smile from him that made her heart feel strangely full. But she didn't have time to consider why that was. Her grandmother had already led him back to the table where Jamie dished up the dessert of bread pudding, which her mom had made and Cord helped himself to twice.

Not long after that both her mom and grandma told him he was welcome there anytime, promised that he didn't have to worry about them talking about him to the neighbors, though it clearly killed her grandma to keep such news to herself, and more or less pushed the two of them out the door so he could talk to her about his plan.

His plan for her business was the last thing on Cord's mind, however. They had no sooner darted through the raindrops and climbed into his SUV so he could take her home—since she'd walked the ten blocks from her place—than he asked what had happened to her sister.

Chapter Seven

A familiar disquiet sank over Madison as she settled into the soft camel-colored leather seat of Cord's black SUV, breathing in the new-car smell and staring at the dash controls for the stereo system and a DVD for the back seat. It occurred to her, fleetingly, how ironic it was that the vehicle Cord used so he wouldn't be noticed was nicer than the ones most people in the Ridge drove every single day.

He had asked about her sister.

She would much rather think about his car.

Actually, given a choice, she would rather consider anything else. Even things she would ordinarily find totally disconcerting. Such as how his big body seemed to be even larger in the confines of the plush interior. Or how embarrassing it had been when her grandmother had casually remarked about what an attractive couple they made. Grandma Nona had stopped short of saying she was sure they'd make beautiful babies together, but Madison felt fairly certain that's what the matchmaking matriarch of her family had been thinking before Jamie, bless her, had changed the subject.

To his credit, Cord had handled the afternoon beautifully. Madison just couldn't help but think, however, that he had to feel as grateful as she did to have finally escaped.

"Madison?" he prompted.

"She was hit by a car," she replied, knowing no way to avoid the explanation. "It's been hard for her, but she's getting along really well now." As well as she could, she mentally qualified, having to live with her leg in a brace that ran from heel to thigh.

The engine started with a low roar. A couple of quick motions and Cord had his seat belt on and the windshield wipers clearing the blurry view. Now that it had started to shower again, the kids had deserted the car and tree-lined street.

"I'm glad to hear that. She seems like a great kid."

"She is." Madison felt her shoulders relax as she locked her own seat belt into place and he pulled away from the curb. "She got a late start in school, but she's made up for most of it. She even got on the yearbook committee for next year."

"So what's the rest of it?"

She glanced toward Cord, caught his strong profile, his easy grip on the wheel.

"There's more to it than she was just in an accident," he said. "Everyone but your sister got quiet when I asked what had happened."

It seemed she'd relaxed too soon.

Madison's first thought was to remind him that they were supposed to be talking about his plan for her busi-

Get FREE BOOKS and a FREE GIFT when you play the...

LAS VEGAS
GAME

Just scratch off the gold box with a coin. Then check below to see the gifts you get!

YES!
I have scratched off the gold Box. Please send me my **2 FREE BOOKS** and **gift for which I qualify**. I understand that I am under no obligation to purchase any books as explained on the back of this card.

▼ DETACH AND MAIL CARD TODAY! ▼

335 SDL DZ9S   235 SDL DZ97

FIRST NAME	LAST NAME

ADDRESS

APT.#	CITY

STATE/PROV.	ZIP/POSTAL CODE

(S-SE-07/04)

7	**7**	**7**	Worth TWO FREE BOOKS plus a BONUS Mystery Gift!
🍒	🍒	🍒	Worth TWO FREE BOOKS!
🔔	🔔	♣	TRY AGAIN!

www.eHarlequin.com

Offer limited to one per household and not valid to current Silhouette Special Edition® subscribers. All orders subject to approval.

ness. That was why he'd tracked her to her grandma's house, after all. But she had come to recognize a sense of determination in him that she suspected few people beyond his own inner circle knew he possessed. That sense of purpose was what had driven him to push his team to first place in the race she'd finally been able to ask about. It was also what had made him refuse to back off when she hadn't wanted to admit why she pushed herself so hard.

When he wanted something, he invariably got it. And right now he wanted to know about her sister.

They came to the stop sign at the end of the street, her silence drawing his glance. But instead of prodding her as she thought he would do, the nature of his interest underwent a subtle shift.

"Is this one of those things you don't want to think about?" he quietly asked.

It was *the* thing.

Her glance fell to her lap.

"It was my fault."

Evasion was pointless. It seemed easier just to say it. Just to get it out. Get it over with.

"Your fault?" Sounding as if he couldn't imagine how such a thing could be possible, he turned to take them down another narrow neighborhood street. "Jamie said she'd been a kid when it happened. How old were you?"

"She was four. I was fifteen."

"You weren't much more than a kid yourself."

"But I was supposed to be watching her," she explained, touched by his quick defense. "I don't remember where mom and dad had gone, but Taylor was spending the weekend at a friend's house." Cord had seen photos of Taylor. Grandma had pointed her out, along with Taylor's husband and children and both of their younger brothers in the family album. "That left me to watch the boys, too. I can't remember which one of them got the chain saw, but they'd decided a limb was in the way of their tree house and they were going to cut it down."

She'd heard the saw start up, she told him, and had run into the backyard imagining all sorts of bloody mayhem since the saw was big and the boys were not. She'd thought Jamie was right behind her. But she'd just taken the saw from Russ and Scott when she heard car tires screech out front.

Jamie hadn't been with her. Instead, while Madison had been yelling at her brothers, the little girl had followed their cat into the street.

"She was in a coma for days," Madison murmured.

With her head still down, she absently curled the long blue drawstring from the hood of her top around her index finger. She unwound it just as slowly, focusing on the methodical motion while rain ticked on the roof, the wet road hummed under the tires and the wipers slipped back and forth across the window.

She was barely conscious of the lulling sounds. As she always did when something forced her to remember why her sister now struggled with body-image issues that went beyond a normal teenage girl's desire to fit in with her peers, or when boys passed her sister over in favor of physically unchallenged girls, she went through the familiar litany of what she could have done, what she *should* have done, differently.

Instead of letting go of her sister's hand at the front door when she'd run from the porch through the house and assuming the little girl was behind her, she should have kept hauling her with her. Better yet, she should have picked her up, carried her into the backyard, then gone after the saw. Or maybe she shouldn't have had her sister on the porch with her when she'd gone out to sweep it, because she'd been assigned that task, too. If she had kept Jamie inside the house, if she had even kept the *cat* inside the house, the accident would never have happened. All it would have taken was for her to do any one of those things, and everything would have been so very different for Jamie.

Everything would have been different for all of them.

The rain continued to drum against the roof. The wipers continued their rhythmic slap and slide across the windshield. Still systematically winding and unwinding the blue string, she thought of what Jamie had gone through. She thought of all that she had missed because of her.

She had just started to consider all that Jamie seemed to be missing now, when she realized they had come to a stop.

She looked up to see that Cord had pulled in behind the white van she had parked in the deserted alley behind the pub.

Aware of him studying her profile, her glance fell back to her hands.

"I tried to explain what had happened," she said, because, at the time, she hadn't known what else she could have done. "But my father wouldn't listen to me. He just kept yelling over and over that something like that would never have happened if I had been more responsible, and if Taylor had been in charge.

"I'm sure it wouldn't have happened if Taylor had been there, either. She always knew what to do," she conceded, her faint smile strained. "She still does. She has this amazing ability to always say and do the right thing. Grandma says it's a gift."

Fabric rustled as Cord shifted in his seat. From the

corner of her eye, she caught his motions as he flicked open the latch of his seat belt and draped one wrist over the steering wheel. "What about your mom? She didn't blame you, too, did she?"

"She never said she did. But at the time she barely spoke to me. She didn't really talk to any of us," she told him, wanting him to know that she wasn't the only one who'd been denied her mom's presence. "She was at the hospital so much that we didn't see her for days at a time.

"Even after Jamie's life was no longer in danger," she continued, "there had been all those surgeries to face. She had five or six in the first two years alone." Her mom had been nearly distraught with worry with every one of them, too. Though, over the years Madison had managed to block much of that awful time, she remembered that clearly enough. All of her mom's energy had gone to the child who had needed her most. And she'd had none left for anyone else. When her mother had come home it had been only to clean up and catch a few hours of sleep. "Mom was at Jamie's side nearly every minute."

Cord listened to the subdued tones of Madison's voice as she spoke, wondering what she was omitting. She clearly didn't want to go into what it had been like for her at home during that time. And he wasn't about to push her to find out. With a father who would burden his daughter with such guilt, a father who compared her to her perfect sibling rather than offering the comfort and reassurance she would have needed at that time herself, he could well imagine how totally alienated and unwanted she must have felt.

He knew exactly how it felt to be compared to an older, more "responsible" sibling. He knew how damaging it could be, too. But his family had never blamed him unfairly when it had come to something he had done. Not the way Madison's father had.

Cord couldn't remember ever feeling anger for an injustice imposed on someone else. There had been occasions when he'd thought something unwarranted or unreasonable on another's behalf, but he'd never felt for anyone else the kind of anger that came when an injustice had been aimed directly at him.

He felt it now, tightening his jaw, his gut.

He also made himself ignore it. Going into how shamefully Madison had been treated would only take her deeper into a place he knew she wouldn't want to go. So he simply waited, giving her the time she needed to tell him whatever else she cared to trust him with.

"Our family was never the same after that," she finally said, letting the drawstring unwind again. "Our parents fought constantly, and Dad eventually left. Since Mom couldn't take care of Jamie, work and raise the rest of us alone, we moved in with Grandma.

"With everyone else grown and gone now," she continued, finally looking up, "it's just Mom, my sister and Grandma there."

"And you go every Sunday to fix dinner, do Jamie's nails and take her magazines."

Jamie had told him that. "Mom works six days a week, and Grandma does all the cooking and helps Jamie with her therapy, so I figure they could use a break. And Jamie is really into the magazines right now because of the prom," she said, as if to justify what she did—or maybe to justify her presence there. "She pretends she's okay with not going," she confided, finally smiling for real, "but I know she really wants to."

For a moment Cord said nothing. He just considered

the way her smile relieved the strain that had quietly slipped over her, and how grateful he was to see it again.

"Do you think she could dance if she did have lessons?"

"The doctors once said she'd never be out of a wheelchair. But she's been up and on crutches for over five years." A hopeful note entered her voice. "I suppose anything is possible."

He understood now why she'd jumped to pay for lessons when he'd mentioned them. She did anything she could for her sister.

He cut the engine but made no move to open his door. He could also now see how she had so easily recognized the distance he felt with his family. She felt a certain distance with her own. Yet, what struck him most as he watched her unlatch her seat belt was that her family didn't seem to feel that distance with her.

"I really like the idea of lessons," she confided. Sounding as if she hadn't written off the idea nearly as quickly as her mother had, she gave him a small smile. "Thanks for the suggestion. And thanks for being such a good sport about this afternoon. I don't know too many men who wouldn't have run screaming when Grandma brought out the photo album."

Her glance shied from his. "I need to apologize for that. And for the way she kept going on about my cooking. And for her not-so-subtle hints about what a good wife I'd make. You have to understand that she's nowhere near as modern as she thinks she is. In her eyes, a woman is an old maid at twenty-five."

"Your grandmother is great, Madison. She just says what's on her mind. And you don't owe me any apologies. I had a great time."

"Liar," she murmured.

"I mean it." He reached over, tipped up her chin. "I honestly can't remember the last time I enjoyed myself as much as I did this afternoon." A faint smile curved one corner of his mouth. "And I liked seeing your pictures. You were kind of cute without front teeth."

Outside, the rain continued to fall. Inside the vehicle, their breath had already begun to fog the windows.

Madison swallowed past the pulse beating a little too rapidly at his touch. "I can't believe you weren't embarrassed to death."

"I can't believe that you were," he murmured, quietly studying her face. "Those people really care about you." His glance fell to her mouth. "And I meant it when I said you were beautiful, Madison. You were a beautiful child, too."

Dangerous, she thought, feeling something warm gather low in her stomach. The man was definitely dangerous—and so far out of her league that she had no idea how to play his game. She didn't even know what the rules were. She had no experience with smooth, sophisticated men. She had no real experience period. But she would die before she'd let him know that.

"You don't need to try charming me," she quietly warned, fearing he already had. "It won't work."

"I know." His hand slipped along her jaw until his fingers curved at the back of her neck. He leaned closer with the movement, close enough for her to see the tiny chips of silver in his smiling blue eyes. "That's what I like about you."

Her breath caught an instant before his lips touched hers. Her heart slammed against her breastbone. As hard and carved as his mouth looked, she wasn't prepared for how soft it felt. Or for the tiny jolt that shot through her, taunting sensitive places, turning the low heat liquid.

He pulled back far enough to see her face.

She had no idea what he saw, what it was that betrayed her. But her heart had barely jerked again when something darkened the chips of silver and he kissed her once more.

There was no demand. No attempt to claim. Nothing but warmth, heat and the incredible feel of him as he drew her closer.

He feathered his mouth over hers. Once. Again. Her own lips parted, her breath shuddering at the exquisite sensations he caused to dart through her. Yet what she felt in those moments paled during the next. As naturally as breathing, his tongue touched hers and he drew her closer still.

The beat of the rain merged with the pounding of her pulse in her ears. She had never in her life been kissed the way Cord kissed her. With nothing more than the slow invasion of his tongue, he stroked and savored, teased and taunted. And all the while, he held her there with nothing more than the touch of his hand at the back of her neck.

The tiny sound she made was part sigh, part longing. Cord swallowed that kittenish moan even as he fought a more guttural one of his own. She wanted his kiss. He could hear it in that small whimper, feel it in the tempting and tentative touch of her tongue to his.

He hadn't been thinking when he'd first leaned toward her. If he had, he might have considered how she had always pulled away from him when he touched her before. But she wasn't pulling away from him now. That was all he cared about, too, because he didn't know what he would have done if she had. He hadn't expected the shaft of heat that had torn through him at the sweet taste of her. Or the sharp need that caught him in the gut when he'd taken the kiss deeper and she'd started kissing him back. He was a healthy, red-blooded male with healthy, red-blooded needs, but as he drew her as close as he could get her with a console jammed between them, he couldn't remember the last time he'd simply kissed a woman and forgotten about everything but her.

The thought had no sooner occurred to him than he felt her stiffen. He would bet his new sailing trophy that she'd just realized how visible they were from the street, even with fogging windows. He'd all but forgotten it himself.

Willing his heart to slow, he leaned back far enough to see her face. Her lush mouth gleamed damp from his kisses. Her eyes dark with awareness, she lowered her gaze an instant before she lowered her head.

Catching her cheek with his palm, he turned her face back to his. With the pad of his thumb, he slowly traced the enticing fullness of her bottom lip.

"I know my reputation isn't the best," he admitted, his voice husky and low. "But I meant it when I told you that you shouldn't believe everything you read about me. I may be seen with different women, but that doesn't mean I'm sleeping with any one of them. I've learned to be very careful about who I trust."

His thumb traced its way back, tugging slightly when it reached the center. He couldn't believe how soft her mouth felt. Or how badly he wanted to taste her again. But he could feel her hesitation. He could see it in her eyes.

The last thing on earth he wanted was to scare her away.

"I will never try to charm or seduce you, Madison. I promise you that." It surprised him to hear what he was saying. But he meant every word. "I just like being with you. Okay?"

He had no idea what went through her mind at she sat with her eyes wide on his. For all he knew she could be dredging up every derogatory headline she'd ever seen about him, or she could be wondering how to gracefully tell him to drop dead. All he knew for certain was that he felt an incredible sense of relief when her head finally moved in an almost imperceptible nod.

Reluctant to stop touching her, knowing he wouldn't trust himself much longer if he didn't, he edged back a little farther. "And by the way," he murmured, tucking a strand of her hair behind her ear. "I don't know Taylor, but I can't imagine that she would have handled the situation with your sister and your brothers any differently that you did."

Madison felt her breath leave her lungs when he finally drew away. She didn't know which felt more dangerous at the moment, the heat burning wherever he'd touched or the longing she felt for the understanding he offered.

He'd said he would never try to seduce her. But he didn't have to try. He seemed quite capable of doing it without any effort at all.

"Thank you," she murmured, torn between gratitude for the understanding and the incredible pull she felt toward him.

She touched the back of his broad hand, immediately pulled away. He had such capable hands. Big, strong. Just the touch of his fingers to her face had stolen her breath, stalled her heart. She could only imagine the sort of magic they could work roaming over her body.

She reached for her door.

"I think I'd better go."

"Madison…"

"No, I really should." With her thoughts now sabotaging her, she desperately needed perspective. "I didn't get my bookwork done last night and I need to be up early in the morning to bake."

"What about your business plan?"

"Can we talk about it tomorrow?"

"I'm in meetings in Boston tomorrow."

"Tuesday?"

He didn't know who it was she didn't trust just then. Him. Or herself. Either way, she wanted distance. That was as clear as the caution in her eyes.

"I'll call you"

"Thank you," she said again, and gave him a faltering smile just before she slipped out and ran for the stairs in the rain.

Cord watched her until she disappeared. Even then it was nearly a minute before he gave up the idea of going after her, started the engine and backed out of the alley.

He hadn't wanted her to go. He'd wanted to sit down with her and talk about how much she would need for equipment and advertising and convince her, somehow, that she would need to hire help. There was no way she could do what he had in mind for her all by herself.

He would be lying to himself if he didn't admit there was something else he wanted now, too. He wanted her in his arms. He wanted to hear her breath catch at his kiss. He wanted to know how she would feel against him. He wanted to know the shape of her breasts, how they would feel in his hands, taste against his tongue. He wanted to know every silky inch of her. But more important than any of that, he simply hadn't wanted her to go.

When he was with her, he wasn't so aware of the restlessness that made him feel as if he should be someplace else. It was only when they got to talking about his family that he tended to feel it with her—and even then, the need to find some other place to be didn't feel nearly as compelling as it once had.

Plowing his fingers through his hair, he blew a long, low breath. The only place he had to go now was to the house on the Chesapeake.

In no mood for solitude, he thought about heading for a favorite haunt near Gloucester Point. Mike's Pub appeared to be closed on Sunday, but the bar at the Gloucester Inn usually had a little action going, even on the slowest night of the week.

Having backed up to the street, he glanced at the blue door. The thought of sitting in a smoky bar held no appeal at all.

He backed up the rest of the way, too preoccupied to pay much attention to the dark sedan that had pulled up to the curb. He'd just decided to call Matt when he remembered that his friend had gone home to Richmond and his wife for the weekend. Since Matt's wife was Cord's sister, Ashley, and Cord didn't think Ashley would appreciate him asking Matt to come back tonight so they could grab dinner, he moved on to plans C and D.

Unfortunately, plan C was out. Even if it hadn't been raining, he couldn't take his boat for a short sail because he'd left it in Annapolis when he'd flown back that morning to see Madison. Friends and his crew were bringing it back. That left picking up takeout and putting in a DVD so he could spend the evening watching chase scenes and buildings explode.

Or, he thought, pretty sure he would just wind up pacing despite the carnage on the screen, he could go to Boston tonight instead of in the morning as he'd planned.

He opted for Boston.

He was still there when he called Madison two days later.

Cord hated meetings. As far as he was concerned, they were seldom more than a waste of everyone's time. Except when he was negotiating a land deal. Then, meetings became a game of strategy, wit and will and, as always, there wasn't much he enjoyed more than a challenge.

Except, possibly, celebrating the victory afterward.

He had reason to celebrate tonight. He'd just put the wheels in motion on a multiparcel land acquisition that would make Kendrick Investments another small fortune. Yet, as he stepped from the elevator into his suite on the top floor of the Ritz-Carlton Hotel, the adrenaline was already wearing off. That surprised him a little. Deciding to move forward on a new project usually kept him pumped up for days.

Tossing his key on the mahogany credenza inside the marble foyer, he crossed the expanse of lush gold-colored carpet that matched the elegant room's sofa and chairs and heavy damask drapes. An enormous bouquet of fresh flowers occupied the coffee table. The brass lamps had already been turned on by the staff.

Reaching the desk by the massive television armoire, he flipped open the room service menu. He needed to get himself pumped back up again before he joined his acquisition team for a little post-game libation. In the meantime, however, he needed food. He could have joined his team—two Harvard lawyers and a smart, sexy accountant from Yale—for dinner, but he wanted to call Madison before she went to bed. Since he also needed to make sure his boat got back and to change his shirt because a young and rather rattled secretary had spilled coffee on him, he'd told them he would join them in the bar later.

Picking up the phone from its base, he punched in the number for room service and ordered. After being assured that his order would be delivered in twenty minutes, he headed into the bedroom with its lavish drapes and king-size four-poster bed and picked up another phone from its base in there.

Having played phone tag with Madison a couple of weeks ago, he knew her number by heart. He just hoped she was home and not down at the pub. He knew the regular cook was back, so she wasn't working for Mike tonight. But he also knew she sometimes ate dinner down there. With any luck, tonight she was watching her taped TV shows.

She answered on the third ring.

"You're home," he said, peeling off his favorite Versace tie.

He hadn't spoken to her since she'd more or less bolted from his car. He didn't take it as a good sign now that she wasn't saying a thing.

Five hundred miles away, Madison sank down on the royal-blue sofa she'd bought from a consignment store, tugged the stretched-out neckband of her favorite sweatshirt up from her shoulder and tightened her grip on the phone. She couldn't believe how she'd run from Cord. Literally, flat-out run. Granted, it had been raining and she hadn't wanted to get soaked, but she knew she'd have run, anyway. She'd had no idea how to handle what seemed to be happening between them. Or what was happening inside her.

She didn't believe for a minute that a man like Cord could ever be serious about a woman like her. She couldn't believe, either, how badly she had wanted to hear from him. With her pulse beating a little too quickly, she finally murmured, "Hi."

"Am I calling at a bad time?"

"No. No," she repeated, forcing herself to sound totally nonchalant. Grabbing the remote control, she muted the television below her posters of Paris, Venice and Barcelona and grabbed another T-shirt from the pile of freshly dried laundry beside her. "Now's fine." Needing motion, she gave the shirt a snap. "Are you back?" she asked, folding it.

Cord reached into the closet for one of the pressed shirts the butler had brought that morning with his freshly polished shoes. "That's why I'm calling. I'm in Boston. I have to go to Richmond from here, so I won't be back for a couple of days. How does Friday evening look for you to go over the plan?"

As he laid the shirt on the bed, Cord heard her hesitate.

"I have a job Friday night," she said with a note of disappointment. "A friend of Amber Johnson's booked me." Disappointment faded to anticipation. "And I have dinner for eight at Amber's Saturday, and next Saturday for ten."

Tugging his shirt from his pants, relieved by what he heard in her voice, Cord felt himself smile. "Hey, that's great."

"Thanks. And thanks for having the dinner where I met Amber." It sounded as if she was now smiling, too. "Another friend of hers called me about doing hors d'oeuvres and a cake for her niece's bridal shower. It's not for a couple of months yet, but that's exactly the kind of thing I want to do. Oh," she added quickly, excited, "and she wants me to cater her art committee luncheon in June."

"Amber's friend?"

"No," she said, making two syllables out of the word. "Amber. She said she wants to book me as far ahead as she can before everyone else does."

The disbelief at how quickly she was coming into demand was evident in her voice. So was her excitement. He could practically feel her delight washing over him as he unbuttoned his shirt and shrugged out of it. That excitement made him feel good. What made him feel even better was knowing he'd helped put it there.

"Just wait until we start to market you." Telling himself he was just grateful that his initial step to expand her business had worked, he tossed the soiled shirt into the bottom of the closet and peeled the fresh one off the hanger. "The best caterers are booked a year in advance." Holding the phone between his ear and his shoulder, he stuffed an arm into a sleeve. "Are you really sure you want to tie yourself up like that?"

"You know I do."

She hadn't hesitated. But then, he really hadn't expected her to. What surprised him was that he wasn't so sure he wanted her that occupied. He didn't have time to question why that was, though. Over the hum of silence on the phone pressed to his ear, he heard the electronic chirp of the cell phone in his pocket.

Pulling the palm-size instrument from his slacks, he frowned at the name and number on the caller ID display.

"Cord?" he heard Madison ask. "Are you there?"

"Yeah. Sorry," he murmured. "Just checking another call."

"I should let you go."

"No." This time he was the one who didn't hesitate. The one thing he did not want was for her to hang up. "It's the AP. I have no idea how they got my cell number."

"AP?"

"Associated Press."

"What have you done now?"

Had anyone else asked him such a question, every muscle in his body would have tightened in an instant. The thick skin he wore in public was painfully thin when it came to how he truly felt about the press's invasion of his life. Or, its fondness for finding new dirt, digging up old, or developing some means to exploit whatever it was he did. But the unexpected teasing in her voice put an equally unexpected smile in his.

"Nothing that will rate more than a few paragraphs on the business page," he replied, reminding himself to get his cell number changed. It was annoying enough to have been caught by the flashes of a photographer lurking outside the hotel. Knowing a member of the press had obtained his direct line irritated him even more. "We just put together a deal to create a new industrial park. We just got the land. Now we have to build."

"Your meetings went well, then?"

He told her that they had as he walked to the window and looked down at the lights sparkling on the back bay. He liked hearing her voice. He especially liked hearing the interest in it when she started asking questions about the next steps in the project and how involved he would be with them.

"My job is just to acquire the property and turn it over to the trust for development," he told her, wondering if she'd noticed the dark sedan parked on her street the other night. He hadn't thought about it much himself at the time, except to note that it hadn't been there when he'd pulled in behind her van. The only reason the vehicle had stuck in his mind was because one similar to it had followed him to the airport later that night.

"But you're involved with the mall project, aren't you?"

"Only because Matt is my friend."

"Don't you want to see this one through, too?"

Her question gave him pause.

Once the bartering for all the pieces of land was over, the real work began. To him, the fun was in the chase.

"I like to stick with what I know best."

"I know what you mean," she murmured, but her simple question stuck with him as she moved on to ask about other projects he'd put together, other things he had in mind to do. Her mind was quick, sharp, and though he'd felt his enthusiasm for his latest deal flagging as he'd come into his suite, she had it building in him again in the minutes before a knock sounded on the main door of his rooms.

The sound had barely registered when the ring of her doorbell filtered through the connection.

As he had the night they'd stood in his driveway after she'd fed his guests, and again the last time he'd seen her, he felt a definite reluctance to let her go. So while she answered her door and he listened to her pay for her pizza and double-check to make sure it had extra cheese, he answered his door and signed for his braised sole and asparagus, double checking to make sure he had extra béarnaise.

He heard her close her door a moment after he closed his. "So, how's your family?" he asked before she could say again that she should let him go.

"They're fine. That reminds me," she hurried to add, apparently in no particular rush to hang up, either. "I've been thinking about those dance lessons for Jamie. I'm going to find someplace close where she can take them."

He'd had the young man from room service leave the

linen-draped cart in the middle of the living room. Removing the silver lid from the plate, he lifted a forkful of sole. "Are you planning to pay for them?"

"Of course I am."

He took a bite, swallowed. "Listen to your mom and save your money. I can teach her to dance for free."

She must have taken a bite herself. The choking sound she made was followed by a moment of silence where, presumably, she swallowed, too. "You're joking."

"I am?"

"Aren't you?"

He picked up his plate, carried it to the desk rather than sitting at the dining table.

He'd actually never been more serious in his life. "What time does your sister get home from school?"

Madison balanced a slice of pizza in her hand, frowning at it as she plopped the cardboard box containing the rest of it onto her tiny kitchen table and sat down in one of her two bistro chairs. She told him her sister got home a little after three—and would have asked again if he was serious had he not sidetracked her completely by asking if she'd noticed any paparazzi hanging around.

Chapter Eight

Madison had no idea what paparazzi looked like. Other than for a few photos in *People* magazine of men who swarmed like honeybees around celebrities and had a penchant for wearing large-lensed cameras around their necks, she'd never actually seen any.

Cord had told her they could look like anyone else, except they had an uncanny ability to lurch from behind columns, foliage and from around corners when a person least expected them. Those where the subtle ones. The more brazen type simply followed a person around, snapping away, practically begging for someone to challenge his First Amendment rights.

She'd told him she hadn't seen anyone like that.

He'd told her to keep her eyes open for them, anyway, then shifted the subject of their conversation again. He hadn't mentioned anything else about the dance lessons, though. Those she'd heard about from Jamie herself when her little sister called Thursday evening, waking her from a sound sleep within seconds of Cord leaving their grandma's house.

"Omigosh, Madison. You're never going to believe what just happened! Well, maybe you will," she hurriedly qualified, her words tumbling over themselves, "because Cord said he told you. But he was just here. He's giving me dance lessons! He's going to teach me so I can ask Steve to take me. He said men like it when women ask them out. He's going to help me figure out what to say to him, too. But I'll tell you all that later."

As excited as she'd been, and as apologetic because she knew she'd wakened her, she promised not to keep her on the phone and said she'd give Madison all the details when she came on Sunday. She'd just been dying to say something to someone and since she knew he didn't want them talking about him, Madison was the only person she could tell. What she hadn't mentioned in her elation was that Cord would be there on Sunday, too. She didn't learn that until two hours before she was due at her grandma's house to start dinner.

"He's coming about noon," her grandmother informed her. "That'll give him time to give Jamie her lesson and relax before dinner. You sure you're peeling enough potatoes? He seems to like potatoes."

"She has enough potatoes, Mom." Beth wore a suit today. Navy blue, of course, and pearls. Madison suspected that the reason she'd worn the outfit to church that morning was so it wouldn't appear that she was dressing up just because Cord was coming.

Grandma's jogging suit was lime green with appliquéd pineapples on the pockets. She didn't seem to care at all for what Madison was wearing.

Her eyebrows pinched above the silver rims of her bifocals as she looked from the purple tank top tucked into Madison's jeans to the sandals baring her pink toenails. The jeans were faded, worn soft and fraying slightly at the hem and back pockets. The designer version cost a fortune. Hers had cost less than thirty dollars on sale and simply been washed to death.

Grandma Nona poked at the bacon, onion and cubed beef Madison had braising on the stove top. "You have time to go home and change, if you'd like."

As hints went, hers were seldom subtle.

"I'm fine, Grandma. It's warm out today. I wanted to be comfortable." The showers of last week had passed. Today was gorgeous. Blue skies. Seventy-five degrees.

She was sure Cord would rather be sailing.

Her grandmother's mouth pinched. "Since it's so warm, why are you making stew? Stew is for cold weather. And it isn't company food."

"It's beef bourguignon. And it's what I was going to make before anyone told me he was coming."

Sounding as patient as Job, or maybe as beleaguered, Beth looked up from where she was polishing the good silver. "She looks fine, Mom. And I'm sure Cord will appreciate anything she prepares."

"I just think she could have fixed up a bit," the older woman defended. "It's not every day a girl has a man like him come calling."

From where she stood at the sink, Madison gave an inward sigh and kept peeling. Her grandmother, still in her marry-off-Madison mode, wouldn't hear a word she said. It therefore seemed pointless to mention that Cord wasn't "calling" on her. She wasn't exactly sure what he was doing beyond confusing the daylights out of her. She just knew that it seemed imperative to maintain the status quo. That was why she didn't want to do anything any differently than she would have done on any other Sunday.

She'd come to that conclusion after she'd spent a solid hour trying on one top after another. She'd pulled her hair up, let it down, pulled it up again. She'd put on full makeup, doing her eyes the way she'd learned from Tina Deluca's mom, who sold Mary Kay, to make them look larger, darker, more sultry. Then, she'd wiped it all off and settled on her usual mascara and trace of liner pencil.

If she did anything other that what she would have done normally, it would mean that she was getting her hopes up about Cord. It would mean that she wanted more from him than his help with her business and replacing her truck. It would mean that she wanted to believe that the two hours they'd spent having dinner on the phone and talking about whatever he could think of to keep her from hanging up actually meant something to him.

It would mean that she wanted him to touch her again, to hold her and make her feel the totally unfamiliar heat she'd felt when he'd kissed her.

She couldn't let herself admit any of that.

She was Madison Margaret O'Malley from the Ridge.

He was Cord Kendrick of the Kendricks of Camelot, and light years beyond being truly interested in someone as ordinary as her.

He was also ten minutes early.

"Oh, shoot," her mom muttered when the doorbell rang. "I wanted to have the table set."

Peeking past the yellow Priscilla curtains above the sink, her grandmother double-checked to make sure it was him.

Apparently, it was.

"Wonder what's in the bag?" she mused. "Why don't you get the door, Madison?"

"Got it!" Jamie called over a thump from the living room.

Madison reached for a bag of mushrooms.

Her grandmother took it from her hand. "Go say hello. I'll clean these."

"He's here to see Jamie, Grandma. Not me." Edgy, trying not to be, she took the bag back. "Besides, I need to get this put together and into the oven or it won't be ready by two o'clock."

Her uneasiness was showing. Madison felt certain of that as she dampened a paper towel and started wiping mushrooms. She just wasn't quite sure what to do about the odd and unfamiliar disquiet filling her, other than to keep herself occupied right where she was—and hope it would wear off before she said or did anything else to make her mom and grandma suddenly look at her with such concern. It wasn't like her to be touchy or impatient. And she truly didn't mean to be. But at least her grandma wasn't pushing her now. The possibility of not having dinner at its usual time had finally silenced her.

Voices drifted in with the sound of the front door closing; Cord's deep and rich, Jamie's sweet and light.

"Grandma and I will go say hi," her mom said to her, motioning her mother toward the kitchen door. "We need to move the coffee table, anyway. When he was here the other night, we pushed all the furniture almost to the walls."

"I'll move the furniture," Cord announced.

The sound of him so near pulled Madison's glance over her shoulder.

His big body practically filled the doorway. His presence seemed to fill the room.

"I know I'm early." His apologetic smile moved from the suddenly smiling gray-haired lady in tropical lime green to the more subdued one in navy and pearls. "But I didn't want this to melt."

He'd dressed casually. Tan chinos hugged his lean hips. A casual black T-shirt defined his broad shoulders. With a lazy, athletic grace he walked into the room, set the large sack he carried on the yellow Formica table and pulled out two pints of Ben and Jerry's. "Jamie said it's her favorite."

"You brought me ice cream?"

Jamie had moved into the space Cord had abandoned. Framed in the doorway in a long blue skirt and the snug print top she'd begged for for her last birthday, she leaned on her crutches, grinning.

"Think of it as a reward for suffering through my two left feet."

"I'll take care of that," Beth said as Jamie giggled.

"And there's these," he said after her. "I didn't know what we were having, so I brought a white and a red."

"By the way, whatever it is smells great." Paper rustled as he finally glanced toward Madison. "If you want to serve the white, it should probably go into the fridge."

He held out the two bottles he'd pulled from the sack. "Which one goes best?"

Wiping her hands on a towel as she turned, she looked from the labels of what she felt certain were insanely expensive wines and cautiously met his eyes. The stark black of his shirt turned them a sharp, crystalline blue.

Feeling his glance laser right through her, she murmured, "The red."

The overhead lights caught the shades of silver in his wheat-colored hair as he tipped his head, studying her closer. Something that looked like curiosity slipped over his compelling features, only to vanish with his smile when he turned and set both bottles on the counter.

"Mind if I push those two big chairs back again?" he asked Grandma Nona, who'd watched his every move.

"Of course I don't." Light bounced off her glasses as she gave Madison a significant glance. "We can all help."

To Madison's relief, Cord insisted that help wasn't necessary. He could handle the furniture while Jamie picked out her music. Once that was done, they'd be set for lesson number two.

Grandma followed him out anyway. So did Madison's mom so she could set the table. At least, that's what Madison thought her mom was doing as the scrape and thump of furniture being shoved around gave way to Jamie's request that Grandma not watch her and the easy syncopated beat of Hilary Duff singing that she was going to be okay.

Madison told herself the same thing. She would be fine. Cord wasn't acting any differently around her now than he had before he'd gotten a little up close and personal. She was simply overreacting. He'd kissed her. That was all.

It took Madison ten minutes of chopping and seasoning to get dinner into the oven. It took another ten to clean up the mess she'd made and admit that she probably wouldn't have gotten so worked up had she had more kisses to compare his to. It was entirely possible that she'd felt no more with him than she would have with anyone else. It was entirely possible that he wasn't even that good a kisser.

"Madison." Her mother whispered her name from the doorway, cutting off her attempt to be rational. "Come look."

Madison turned from where she'd nearly scrubbed the porcelain from the sink to see her mom and grandma lurking just outside the doorway. She had no idea how long they'd been standing there. At least, she didn't until she reached the doorway herself and noticed that the dining table hadn't yet been set.

Both women had been watching Cord and Jamie. Spying on them, actually. They were all but hidden by the foliage of the potted avocado tree her mom had grown from a pit.

Her mother's whisper sounded a bit worried. "I'm so afraid she's going to lose her balance. He's not supporting her the way he was the other night."

The coffee table and overstuffed chairs had been pushed to the middle of the living room and the oval rag rug flipped halfway back to reveal the shining and smooth hardwood floor. The room pulsed with the beat of something by Britney Spears that was a little too fast to be slow, but Cord had Jamie dancing to it, anyway.

Many of Jamie's surgeries had been to add length to her damaged leg so it could keep pace with the growth of the other. Her last surgery, last year, had brought her to what her doctors felt would be her full height. Now, a couple of inches shorter than Madison's five-five, and more coltish than curvy, she looked even more like a child, dwarfed as she was by Cord's tall, muscular body.

He held her with one hand firmly on her waist rather than her back to allow her room to move her shoulders and arms to the undulating rhythm. He moved with her, reminding her to loosen up and get her shoulders into the action while she grinned, put more shoulder into it, then grabbed his arm when she started to lose her balance.

He caught her before there was any chance she would fall, then eased her back to start over again.

She wasn't steady without at least one crutch. And without him to lean on or brace her, she would have been on the floor. But Jamie looked utterly determined to lean on him as little as possible so she could master some of the upper-body moves she'd seen on MTV. And Cord seemed just as determined that she would.

As Madison watched him through the foliage, she couldn't help being drawn by his patience and his completely unexpected generosity. He was giving Jamie a chance to do something she'd once only dreamed of, and she would forever be grateful to him for that.

He was also testing the strength of her mother's heart.

The CD moved to a slower track. Adjusting their positions to the easier beat, he moved closer, holding her as if they were in a ballroom. From the way he asked if she was ready, it sounded as if the step might be one they had practiced before.

Smiling, she nodded, looking as carefree as the swing of her hair, then let out a little shriek when he pivoted her on her stronger leg and dipped her backward.

Madison felt her mom stiffen and start to dart forward.

Grabbing her arm, Madison stopped her. "Wait," she insisted, loud enough that Jamie and Cord both looked to where they were all half-hidden by the plant.

Head upside down, eyes bright, Jamie grinned before Cord swung her back up.

"Do that again," she demanded, and grabbed his arm to repeat the move so she could learn to be dipped just like any other girl.

Her little sister was clearly having a ball.

Her mother was not.

"Maybe you'd better not watch," Madison murmured beneath the music.

"I'm just so afraid he's going to drop her."

"He won't." Madison's grandmother spoke with utter conviction. "The man lifted those chairs as if they didn't weigh a thing. He's not going to drop a hundred-pound girl."

"Hey, Madison," Cord called, moving sideways with her sister in his arms to get a better view of her behind her mom. It seemed he'd known all along that he'd had an audience. He'd also seemed to known that Jamie was self-conscious about being watched while she learned, so he'd kept her back to them. "Come here and help me show Jamie what this is supposed to look like."

The thought of being in his arms bumped her heart against her ribs. But it was the thought of being in his arms with the women in her family watching their every move that set her into motion.

Suddenly looking quite concerned about dinner, she hitched her thumb toward the kitchen. "I have to check the stew." Giving her mom a nudge, she took a step back. "Mom's a great dancer. She'll help."

"Oh, Madison, I can't..."

But she did. Which brought Grandma out from hiding and, eventually, proved to her mom that she had nothing to worry about when it came to Cord keeping a woman on her feet. Gasps and giggles filtered into the kitchen from the living room, along with the music that filled the usually quiet house.

Her little sister wasn't the only one enjoying herself.

Knowing that should have pleased Madison. And it did. In some ways. In others, it only fed the disquiet that accompanied her as she moved between the kitchen and dining room, setting the table herself because her mom and grandma were busy offering suggestions to Jamie before Madison announced dinner was almost ready.

At dinner, which Cord pronounced the best food he'd

had in a week, the conversation seemed more animated. A debate about when Jamie would feel ready to ask Steve Balducci to the prom led to the necessity of buying a dress, which Jamie said she wouldn't do before she knew for sure if Steve would take her. That led Grandma to ask Cord if he'd ever been to a prom, which brought the admission that he had not, even though he'd been forced to take dance lessons as a child. He'd had formal training in ballroom dance with his brother and sisters, he admitted, making it sound like one of the more painful experiences in his life, then deftly turned the conversation from stories from his childhood to Madison.

He wanted to know about the catering jobs she'd had last night and the night before. Aware of how neatly he'd avoided any betraying details about his troubled youth, just as aware of everyone watching him watch her, she simply told him that they had both gone well, then asked if everyone was ready for the dessert Jamie had helped make.

Cord couldn't help notice the teenager's suddenly shy smile at mention of her contribution to the meal. It hadn't escaped his attention, either, how Madison had avoided him most of the afternoon. As much as she could, anyway. He couldn't put his finger on the problem. He wasn't even sure there was one. There was just a reserve about her, an odd sort of reticence that he'd never noticed before.

That distance was there even as he said his goodbyes, told Jamie he'd see her again Thursday evening and asked Madison if she was ready to go. When she told him she wasn't, he asked her to walk him out to the porch.

They hadn't been alone since the moment he'd set foot

inside the house. Alone now, he watched her move away from the closed door and cross her arms.

The late-afternoon sun cast leafy shadows on the wide porch with its old-fashioned swing and planters of geraniums. A faint breeze, warm and scented with those flowers, rustled the rosebushes climbing the trellises behind him. From somewhere down the street came the bark of a dog, the laughter of children.

Wondering at how peaceful the ordinary sounds seemed, he quietly studied the wariness in her upturned face.

"What are you doing?" she asked.

The question threw him. "I'm not sure I know what you mean."

"Coming here like this. I know you were invited," she hurried to explain, her voice concerned and quiet, "but why do you want to help Jamie to begin with? I'm sure there are hundred more interesting places you could have been this afternoon."

"What I'm doing," he replied, his tone just as low, "is saving you money, getting a great meal and having a good time. In all honesty, I can't think of anywhere else I would have wanted to be today."

Disbelief replaced wariness. "Come on, Cord. The weather is beautiful. You could have been sailing. You could have had friends over and had a party." He could have flown to the Hamptons, Nantucket, Paris.

"I thought I was with friends."

His simply spoken words jerked hard at her heart. There were so few people he trusted. "I didn't mean it like that."

"Would you rather I hadn't come?"

"Of course not." He considered her family to be his friends. Knowing that only seemed to prove just how few close ones he actually had. "I'm just…" *confused,* she silently concluded.

"Come on," he murmured. The shuttered look in his eyes vanished as quickly as it had appeared. Reaching out, he gently skimmed his knuckles along her jaw. His touch felt light, intimate and instantly familiar. "Let me give you a ride home."

She was in trouble here. Big trouble. As her head moved as if seeking more of his touch, there wasn't a doubt in her mind that she was getting deeper into trouble by the second, too.

She absolutely did not trust the attraction she felt toward this man. Yet, denying that it existed wasn't working at all. She knew Cord would be the first to admit that he truly deserved much of his notoriety. Yet, in so many ways, he kept proving himself to be far different than the press portrayed him to be. He seemed far less self-focused. Far more sensitive. Infinitely more reliable.

When she had first met him, she never would have expected the total responsibility he had shown for his role in wrecking her truck. And no way on God's green earth would she have anticipated his thoughtful kindness toward a disabled teenage girl. But beyond even those remarkable and telling qualities, she had never suspected the deep-seated loneliness she sensed in him each time they parted.

That loneliness seemed to exist even now, masked though it was by his easy smile.

"I can't leave. I have to stay and help with the dishes." Pitiful as it sounded, it was the only excuse she had to keep from being alone with him and even more vulnerable. "But you don't have to go," she wanted him to know, not wanting him to feel alone, either. "You can help. While you're at it, you can tell me your plan."

"I forgot to bring it."

"You don't remember what you wrote?"

Indulgence swept his features. "I want you to see the charts. It'll be easier for you to see why you're going to have to do some of the things you don't want to do."

"Such as?"

"We can talk about it later."

"I told you, I don't want to—"

"Hire help. I know," he said, suspecting from her quick frown exactly what she would say. "But I think you'll change your mind once you see how practical it will be.

"I'll take a rain check on the dishes," he told her, far more interested just then in the way she'd moved into his touch than he was in business. Wanting to feel the softness of her skin once more, he crooked his index finger under her chin, brushed beneath her bottom lip with his thumb. "Is that okay with you?"

She said nothing. She just stood with her arms crossed tightly beneath her breasts while the unmistakable light of awareness flickered in her eyes. He felt her breath tremble against his thumb, felt the quick flutter of her pulse when he carried his touch to the delicate hollow at the base of her throat.

She didn't move. She did nothing to let him know what was going through her mind. Yet he knew, just by touching her, why she'd seemed so different that afternoon.

She was protecting herself. Between her betraying response to his caress and her tight body language, there wasn't a doubt in his mind.

He eased away. He hated that she felt the need to shield herself from him. He didn't want her guarding herself with him at all. Feeling the same need he had before to keep her from withdrawing any farther, he pushed both hands into his pockets.

"I'll call you when I get back."

The light in her eyes shifted with the tilt of her head. Interest eased her caution. "You're leaving again?"

"Only for a few days," he replied, suddenly conscious of a prickling sensation at the back of his neck. "We're signing the final contracts on the Boston property."

He was being watched. He could feel it. Thinking it might be the kids he'd heard earlier, he tossed a casual glance over his shoulder.

An instant later he swore.

The low, succinct sound pulled Madison's glance past his arm. An instant later she caught a flash, like sun reflecting off glass. "What's wrong?"

"That black car parked down there. The driver just ducked below the wheel."

The only black car other than Cord's relatively modest SUV parked out front, sat a block down on the opposite side of the street. Madison had barely caught the flash herself before the driver disappeared.

"Is that the guy you were talking about the other night?" she asked, even as the driver reappeared. Slouched in the seat with a dark ball cap pulled low, he gunned the engine and swung the car around the corner.

Four children were playing ball in the street.

Tires screeched as he hit the brakes. An instant later with kids darting between parked cars for the sidewalk, tires squealed again and he took off like a rock shot from a sling.

This time it was Madison who swore.

Cord bolted for the steps.

Alarmed as much by the dark anger clouding his face as the near disaster down the street, she started after him.

"What are you going to do?"

"I'm going to get his film."

"Like he's just going to give it to you?"

"I doubt it. But I want it, anyway."

"Cord, wait!" She stepped off the last stair a second after he did, catching him in the middle of the cracked sidewalk. Tension radiated from his body like sound waves, surrounding her, knotting her nerves, her stomach. As angry as he looked, he also looked frighteningly in control.

Suspecting he knew exactly what he was doing, suspecting he'd done it before, made her extremely nervous.

"Don't chase him. Please."

The hard line of his jaw looked chiseled of granite. The quiet fury in his eyes turned them diamond bright. "I'm not going to hit any of the kids," he assured her, his voice tripwire-tight. "But I am going to let him know what I think of him for nearly doing it himself."

The thought was noble. The results, she knew, would not be worth the effort.

"Let him go, Cord. Please?" she repeated. "You'll just wind up in the papers again."

The plea in Madison's voice pulled his glance to the quiet appeal in her eyes. She stood at his side, her fingers curled tightly around his arm, totally oblivious to the neighbors flying out their front doors to see what had just disturbed the peace in their neighborhood.

With everyone looking toward the corner where the kids pointed in animated gestures in the direction the car had gone, he edged her toward the house. A trellis of climbing roses by the porch protected them partly from view.

Protecting Madison had been his first thought. Her and her family.

Ever since paparazzi had take the photos of him learning to play craps in Luzandria as a teenager, he'd harbored a dislike of the breed that bordered on disdain. He'd had more than one run-in with their obtrusive ilk. He'd even once been charged with assault for relieving one particularly bothersome photographer of his equipment—a matter that family lawyers had handled with a hefty payment and the warning that next time he could wind up in jail. He had also received the admonishing reminder from his mother that, while she would dearly love to see all of that particular element removed from the planet herself, no Kendrick had ever been incarcerated. She would greatly prefer that he not be the first.

He had learned to live his life in a fishbowl. He hated it. But he did it. There were just times when the invasions into the few nooks and crannies he could find for escape pushed him harder than others. What had pushed him now was the fact that Madison's privacy had been invaded, too.

He didn't question why that mattered so much. He didn't even question why his first thought had been of her instead of getting the film to protect himself. With her looking as if she was truly worried about the consequences his actions would hold for him, he was aware only of her concern.

She seemed to be protecting him, too.

The front door opened with a sharp squeak. The quick arthritic groan of the screen door followed.

"Was that the Donnatelli boy racing around out here again?" Grandma Nona demanded. "If that was him, I'm calling the police right now and having him pulled off the street for good. If I've told him once, I've told him a dozen times that this is a decent—"

"It wasn't anyone we know," Madison hurried to assure her. "I didn't recognize the car at all." *But I will if I ever see it again,* she thought.

"Oh. Well," her grandmother muttered. Having had the plug pulled on her indignation, she finally looked to where they stood by her climbing roses.

"Oh," she repeated, watching Madison's hand slip from Cord's arm. "Don't let me interrupt," she admonished, and hurried back inside with another groan of the screen.

The inner door had just closed when, down the street, Madison saw nosey old Mary Schneider heading toward them. Next to Mavis Reilly, Mary was the biggest gossip in the Ridge.

"Unless you want to be recognized," she murmured to Cord. "You'd better go."

Catching sight of the barrel-shaped woman in floral print bearing down on them, he took a step back.

"Are you okay?" she asked.

"I won't go after him," he muttered, though he still looked as if he wanted to.

"Thank you."

"I'll call you later. In the meantime, you don't have to worry about whoever-that-was approaching you for an interview. That kind just wants pictures to sell. You might want to keep your curtains closed, though. They're notorious for trying to get money shots."

"Money shots?"

"The ones that catch a person in a way they'd rather the world didn't see. This guy isn't going to be a problem, though. I'm going to make a call and get someone out here to take care of him."

Take care of him? "What are you talking about?" she asked, worried all over again.

"I'll explain when I call."

Anxious to go, he slipped around to the driver's side of his SUV. Mary was moving in with the speed of a fast-moving hurricane, disaster waiting to happen.

"Hi, there, Madison!" she called, waving.

"Hi, Mary," she returned, waving back.

"Did you hear those tires?" she asked, eyeing the SUV, trying to see through the back window.

"I think we all did. How's Lester?"

"He's fine. Gout flared up again last week, but it's under control now. Who's your friend?"

Her carrot-red head was still doing a bob-and-weave as she tried to see through the tinted windows of Cord's vehicle. Between the shadows of leaves on the windows and the fact that he was pulling away, she couldn't see a thing.

"The man who's helping me get my new truck," she replied, because it was the truth, as far as it went.

Mary had apparently already heard that such a man did exist. Looking a little deflated that she had no new news to share with anyone, she moved on to declare how awful it was for someone to race around the neighborhood with children playing in the street. Mary thought it had been the Donnatelli boy, too.

Having a new appreciation for how unfounded rumors could eat at the person so wrongly accused, Madison made certain that Mary knew it absolutely was not that particular teenager before she excused herself to do dishes.

The fact that she did know who had been in the car—or at least what the person did for a living—felt decidedly unnerving. Almost as unnerving as knowing that someone had been watching her through a camera lens. She wasn't feeling terribly comfortable, either, not knowing what Cord planned to do about him.

She thought it highly unfair that he waited nearly a week to tell her.

Chapter Nine

The phone rang as Madison peeked out her window at six o'clock Friday evening. Clutching the cookbook she'd been going through, she hurried across the room, praying it would be Cord. He'd left a message while she was on her route Wednesday that he would call tonight. He'd also left her his new cell phone number to call if she saw the guy in the black car again.

She'd almost called him. Twice.

Edgy, anxious and feeling a tad out of her comfort zone, she snatched the receiver from its base. Taking a deep breath, she forced a casual "Hello?"

He chuckled. "You sound harried. Did you just get in?"

"No. Yes. A while ago," she amended, not bothering to deny how glad she was it was him. Clutching the book more tightly, she sank to the sofa. "I got back from the market a few minutes ago."

''Are you going to have time to go over the plan tonight?''

She closed her eyes, rubbing her forehead as she wrinkled it. ''I can't tonight. I have to figure what to serve for an appetizer for Amber's dinner party tomorrow night. She was very specific about the main course, but for the appetizer she just said to surprise her with 'something spectacular.'''

''No pressure there,'' he muttered.

''No kidding. I need to stay here and experiment.''

''Is that why you sound so stressed?''

That was part of the reason. The other part could well be all in her head. ''May I ask you something?''

Suddenly sounding as serious as she did, he said, ''Of course you can.''

''How can you tell if you're just being paranoid, or if you really are being followed?''

His pause lasted all of two seconds. ''You can't always. Why?''

''Because I think I am. Being followed I mean. Not all the time,'' she hurried to add, fearing she sounded paranoid, anyway. ''And not by the black car. I've only seen it once. I was leaving the construction site to head for the docks when I saw it behind me. I don't know where it had been parked. But I lost sight of it when another car pulled out in front of him and nearly ran him into the curb.''

''You haven't seen the black car since?''

''Not since Tuesday,'' she admitted, too new at being stalked by people with cameras to understand why she couldn't shake the feeling he was still around. Or that someone was. ''I think he's switched to a beige one. Either that, or there's someone else out there now. I've seen this beige car off and on all week. It stays too far away for me to see much, but the guy in it looks huge.''

''That's Bull.''

''Excuse me?''

''Bull,'' Cord repeated, suddenly sounding far less displeased. ''His name is actually Jeffrey, but no one calls him that. Except my sister,'' he qualified. ''He's a bodyguard.''

It took a moment for what he'd said to register. *Bodyguard* was not a word that popped up in her everyday conversation.

But, then, neither was *paparazzi*.

''A bodyguard?'' Was he serious? ''You have a bodyguard following me?''

''I use him a lot,'' he said as easily as most people would talk about a preferred plumber. ''I like to have him with me when I'm in Monaco or Vegas. He's ex-military from the security service my family uses.''

The family security service, he'd said, as if all families had one.

''I asked him to keep an eye out for anyone who might be following you. Or, hanging around your place, or your grandma's.''

He was having her watched by a bodyguard. The thought seemed as unbelievable as it did unnerving.

''Why didn't you tell me? I thought he was one of those paparazzi guys,'' she insisted, only marginally less uneasy with the thought of the Incredible Hulk watching her every move. ''The least you could have done was leave me a message,'' she insisted, unable to believe that he hadn't. It wasn't as if she'd ever felt endangered. What she'd felt was defenseless and exposed, but those sensations had been distressing enough. The only place she'd felt safe from a potentially prying lens had been in the pub's kitchen and her apartment. Even then, she'd wondered who might be lurking outside. "I've been looking over my shoulder all week."

The distress in her voice caught Cord off guard. It honestly hadn't occurred to him that he should tell her about Bull. He'd just taken care of what needed to be done. When he'd called the stocky ex-marine, his only concern had been with keeping press of any sort away from her. For her sake.

And his.

A few pictures of him simply talking to a woman would be of no value to a tabloid, much less a newspaper, unless there was some hint of a story or scandal that could be conjured up to go with it. He had learned to never underestimate the inventiveness of some journalists and all tabloid writers, but so far, except for the lone paparazzo Bull was making work harder for a close-up, he had attracted little attention where Madison was concerned. He wanted to keep it that way. As long as the legitimate press didn't start digging around trying to find out why he was interested in her, he could keep things as quiet and uncomplicated as they were—as far as unwanted publicity went, anyway. Things didn't seem quite so simple where Madison herself was concerned.

He'd never put a bodyguard on a woman before.

He also wasn't in the habit of explaining his actions to anyone.

"Bull is usually so discreet people don't notice him. I told him to stay inconspicuous."

"That's no excuse for not letting me know he was there! I won't even ask how someone that size can *not* be conspicuous," she countered, clearly not appeased, "but just because you didn't think I'd notice doesn't mean you shouldn't have told me. All you had to do was pick up a phone. How would you feel if someone did something like that to you?''

He would have hated it. But he hadn't been thinking in those terms when he'd done what he had, simply because thinking of how certain of his actions affected others didn't always occur to him. He just did what he felt compelled to do.

He could feel his mental defenses rise at her challenge like rockets in a missile silo. Yet they never locked into place. Not the way they would have if nearly anyone else had called him on something he'd done that they hadn't liked. What he had just acknowledged to himself, what she had just made him realize, stopped him cold.

Over the years he had been called thoughtless, self-indulgent and irresponsible. He'd seen himself described as everything from rebellious to defiant and let the world think the labels rolled off his back.

His self-protective armor just didn't seem so impermeable with the woman whose smile touched something sheltered inside him, the woman he'd thought about every day he'd been gone—even if he hadn't thought about how what he'd done had affected her. He had known that Bull had been watching out for her with the press, so he hadn't given that aspect another thought.

It was entirely possible, he supposed, that she regarded Bull's presence as nearly as much of an invasion of her privacy as being followed by a photographer. He'd never considered that, either.

"You're right," he admitted, though admitting he'd been wrong wasn't something that came easily. "I guess I never thought that what I accept as common might throw you a little."

For a moment she said nothing. When she did finally speak, the challenge had left her tone. "You have a gift for understatement,'' she muttered. She paused again. ''Is he out there now?''

''He left this morning. He had another job he'd committed to,'' he told her, needing her to know she could relax. For a while, anyway. ''When he checked in, he said he hadn't seen the guy we'd seen for three days. Apparently, the little talk he'd had with him after he'd cut him off made him think twice about hanging around.''

Madison took a deep breath, slowly blew it out. She now understood what Cord had meant when he'd said he would take care of the guy. She also realized that the car that had pulled in front of the darker one outside the construction site had been the bodyguard's. She just couldn't quite believe what she was hearing.

Cord had actually sent someone named Bull to talk to the photographer who had followed her. She thought people only did that on TV.

Feeling a certain sense of unreality about the entire situation, she reached for the rational. ''Won't sending this Bull-person after that man make him think that there's something you want to hide?''

She could practically hear the shrug in Cord's voice. ''They're used to being told to back off. Not always by men as respectable as Bull, either. Bull's actually kind of reserved. His size just says a lot.

''Look,'' he continued, sounding as if he pretty much knew she couldn't believe she was having this particular conversation, ''I haven't eaten and you have experimenting to do. Why don't I come over, bring the plan and you can use me as a guinea pig?'' He paused. ''Unless you're still upset with me.''

Madison hesitated before she said she wasn't, but in

the moments before he told her he'd see her soon, she had the distinct feeling Cord didn't quite believe her.

She really wasn't upset with him. Not in the sense that she felt anger or resentment for what he'd done. After all, he had been watching out for her. And he had admitted that what he considered a routine part of his world might tend to throw her just a tad. But having a bodyguard added to the sense of unreality about Cord's presence in her life, along with a healthy dose of respect for the privacy, and anonymity, he seldom ever knew.

It was no wonder he seemed to enjoy being at her grandma's house, she thought in the moments after she hung up and hurried in to start concocting appetizers and dinner. Life was normal there.

By the time Cord arrived half an hour later, her flare of annoyance had dissolved into a confusing combination of anticipation and uncertainty that accompanied nearly every thought of him. Even if it hadn't, irritation would have been hard for her to hang on to when she opened her door to see him carrying the file she truly did want to see—and a dozen bloodred roses.

"I caught the florist as she was locking up," he said when she just stood there, staring.

Glancing past her to see which way he should go, he walked into her little living room, seeming to take up most of the oxygen and all of the room as he stopped by her comfortable blue sofa with its bright poppy-print throw pillows. Looking around for a place to put the flowers, he decided to set the crystal vase holding the huge bouquet on the antique coffee table. It barely fit between the stacks of magazines and a bowl of cinnamon-apple potpourri. The file landed on the cookbook she'd abandoned.

"I told her I screwed up and she let me in." He straightened as he spoke, his shoulders looking a yard wide in the white Manhattan Athletic Club T-shirt tucked into his comfortably worn jeans. "She said she gets guys like me a lot. Ones who need to apologize, I mean."

Not totally certain of his welcome, Cord watched Madison close the door on the darkness that had fallen outside. She had said on the phone that she wasn't upset, but the self-protectiveness she'd shown around him last Sunday was still fresh in his mind. He also knew she was as good as he could be at masking feelings. For practical reasons, and a few that felt entirely too personal, he wanted to make sure he'd been forgiven.

From the expression on her lovely face, he suspected that he had.

She looked from the arrangement of ferns, roses and baby's breath, her eyes wide with disbelief as they met his. That same disbelief slipped into her voice. "You brought me flowers?"

"The florist said nothing begs forgiveness like red roses." Watching her walk over to touch the petal of one delicate bloom, he ducked his head to see her eyes. Those warm brown depths were bright with something even more compelling than her smile. "Am I forgiven?"

It was a moment before she looked up. When she did, the light from the lamps on the end tables caught the shades of gold and ruby in her rich dark hair. She wore her hair up, as always. And, as always, his fingers itched to take it down.

"Only if you promise not to do that again," she replied, sounding teasing, still looking touched.

"Which? Get you a bodyguard? Or not tell you?"

"Not tell me." Consternation crossed her delicate features. "Do you think another one will be necessary?"

"It's possible," he conceded. "I never know when press is going to get persistent. But I'll tell you if I think I need to call Bull again," he promised. Although, promising something—anything—to a woman was something he'd thought he'd never do. "Okay?"

She looked thoughtful. Or maybe it was resigned. "Okay, then."

"Okay, what?"

With her eyes smiling cautiously into his, her lush mouth curved in an expression as soft as it was accepting. "You're forgiven."

"Thank you," he murmured, relieved, and would have reached to touch her had the quick, electronic ring of a timer not snagged her attention.

"That's my bread."

Looking relieved herself, she turned on her heel and darted past the front door and the bistro table-for-two beneath the white-shuttered window. Aware that her guardedness with him was still there, not totally sure what to do about it, he watched her go—and promptly found his thoughts sidetracked by the glimpse of bare skin below the hem of her pink shirt and the low waist of her jeans. Wondering if the skin there was as soft as the skin of her face, his focus drifted to the heart-shaped curve of her backside and down her long legs.

She was barefoot.

She wasn't at all like the other women he knew. There was nothing overtly sexy about her. Yet she possessed a quiet sensuality that had begun to constantly taunt him, his thoughts and the nights that had become even more restless than they had once been. There had been a time when he could escape that restlessness with people, loud music, high stakes at a roulette table. A woman. For a while, anyway. Since he'd met Madison, the only escape he'd found was when he was with her. When he wasn't, nothing worked.

She disappeared behind a wall she'd painted a bold apple red. Pushing his fingers through his hair, he drew a breath that brought the delicious scent of something toasting, and glanced around the welcoming and cozy space.

The room looked smaller than his walk-in closet. The one in the house he currently occupied, anyway. On a tall bookshelf, photographs of family and friends filled the open spaces between books. The muted television was tuned to a travel channel. What caught his attention were the large, framed posters above it.

He didn't have to read the captions below the prints to recognize the scenes from Venice, Paris and Barcelona. Just as he didn't have to ask to know that she'd never been to any one of those distant cities.

She'd barely been out of the state.

''I'm trying to decide between smoked-salmon tarts and a goat cheese bruschetta,'' he heard her call. ''Which sounds better?''

Shoving his hands into his pockets, he walked around the corner.

She stood at the stove, frowning at the toasted rounds of bread on the cookie sheet she'd taken from the oven. Behind her, three ceramic ducks marched beside bright red canisters by the white porcelain sink. A wreath of dried herbs took up the top half of the narrow end wall. A stainless steel rack of pots and pans occupied the bottom half.

He'd been on boats with bigger galleys.

''Which tastes better?''

''I'm not sure.'' Tossing aside a pot holder, she turned

on the burner under a large pot of water. "We'll just have to make them both and see."

There seemed to be no question that he would help. It was simply what he did when he was alone with her. The fact that he enjoyed it would have given him pause had he allowed himself to consider it.

"What do you want me to do?"

As if there'd been no question in her mind, either, she pointed to the ripe tomatoes on the cutting board by the sink. Asking him to dice them, she opened a cupboard for olive oil and salt.

Thinking it best to concentrate on something other than the strip of bare skin on her stomach that grew wider with her reach, he turned his attention to his task and turned his thoughts to why he was there. But his focus had no sooner settled on the charts and lists in the file on her coffee table than he realized that he didn't want to mention them now.

He knew Madison couldn't really concentrate on the technical end of her businesses while preoccupied with the creative end, as she was just then. Yet that wasn't what held him back. What did were the innocent remarks her sister had made last evening after Beth had pulled Grandma Nona into the kitchen to keep her from critiquing Jamie's dancing.

The thought of Beth drew a considering frown. Beth O'Malley seemed to need to protect her girls. And what she seemed to protect them from most was criticism. He could see where she would want to shield a disabled daughter, but Madison seemed entirely capable of taking care of herself, along with everyone around her. Because she did seem so capable, he couldn't help but wonder if Beth wasn't somehow trying to make up for all the blame Madison's dad had dumped on her. Blame she hadn't been around to prevent because she'd needed to be with her injured child.

"I saw your family last night," he said, abandoning his armchair analysis of her family dynamics when Madison reached past him for basil and garlic. Though she pulled back the moment her arm brushed his, the smooth feel of her skin lingered. So did the distracting freshness of her scent. "Jamie's really coming along."

With the sink separating them, Madison diligently started chopping, too.

"I heard. She called when I got home this afternoon," she murmured. It had been so much easier working with him in his own kitchen and down in the pub's. Here there was no space, no room to maneuver without bumping into each other. She'd been aware of him the moment he'd walked in the door. The nearness of his big body only made her more so. "I hope you know how much what you're doing means to her." And to me, she thought, but didn't say. She was afraid to. Everything he did, everything he said, was coming to mean just a little too much.

He'd brought her flowers. Not just any flowers. Red roses. She'd never received flowers from anyone in her entire life. Yet, more significant to her than the gift itself was why he'd brought it. He didn't want her upset with him.

"I'm getting as much out of it as she is. She's a great kid." The pause in his chopping underscored the thoughtfulness in his deep voice. "She really worries about you, though."

Keeping her focus on her own task seemed safer that looking at him. With her brow pinched, she poured oil into a ceramic bowl and tossed in sea salt along with what she'd chopped. "Why would she worry about me?"

"Because you spend so much time worrying about her," he replied easily. "She said she really wishes you'd get a life of your own and stop wasting your time with her and your mom and grandma."

Madison's frown stayed on the bowl. "I have a life. And I don't consider the time I spend with them a waste."

"'Wasting' was her word, not mine. And I don't think she meant it the way it sounds," he defended. "She just thinks you need to use your free time for yourself instead of spending it making sure she has everything she needs.

"She really appreciates what you do," he stressed as she silently reached for the tomatoes he'd cut up and dumped them into the bowl, too. "But she's afraid you're going to wind up like Harriet O'Something-er-other."

"Harriet?" Her glance jerked up. "Harriet O'Bannon?"

"That's the name. Who is she?"

Harriet O'Bannon was an old spinster with cats. She was a perfectly pleasant lady, but she'd always seemed terribly lonely—which was why Madison always made a point of visiting with her when she dropped off left-over muffins at the seniors' center.

Jolted by the thought that her sister saw a future Harriet in her, she said only, "Just someone we know."

"Well, whoever she is, Jamie doesn't want you to be like her. But she's afraid you will be because you won't go out with any of the guys who ask you. She said you fix them all up with somebody named Tina."

Madison reached for a spoon, nearly knocked over the oil. It was unsettling enough that her little sister had grown to develop such concerns and opinions. It was even more so to have had them passed on to the man she could feel so carefully watching her now.

Feeling totally exposed, she turned around with the bowl and quickly started spooning the mixture onto toast rounds. Pride demanded that she assure him her sister's fears were totally unfounded.

"The men I introduced Tina to were more suited to her than me," she defended, thinking it might be best to just let the spinster part go.

"That may be, but Jamie isn't concerned about Tina. She's concerned about you."

"She doesn't need to be. I know what I'm doing."

His knife landed quietly on the counter. "So do I."

She spooned faster. "So why are you telling me this?"

For a moment she heard nothing but a thoughtful silence, and the sounds of him moving behind her. Reaching past her arm, he took the bowl and spoon, set them aside with a clink and a thud and turned her by her shoulders to face him.

"Because I'm not sure that burying yourself in work is the answer for you. Because I think I'll feel guilty if I help you do that to the degree you seem to want." As if he was only now realizing the truth in what he said, the conviction in his voice grew stronger. "You deserve more than you're allowing yourself, Madison. Even your little sister can see that."

Looking big, quietly powerful and utterly male, he tipped his head toward the living room. "Those posters in there. When do you plan to go to those places? And who are you going to go with if you don't give yourself a chance to get out?"

Madison opened her mouth, closed it again. She'd never said a word to anyone about why she'd hung those posters. No one had ever asked, either. Yet Cord had walked into her apartment, taken a look around and promptly zeroed in on the one dream she'd allowed herself that didn't have to do with work. At least, the only one she'd had before he'd opened the lock on so many more.

Feeling more exposed by the second, hating it, she murmured, "I get out."

Indulgence swept his beautifully masculine face. "I don't mean with girlfriends. Jamie said I'm the only guy who's come around that you haven't fixed up with someone else." His too-keen eyes shifted over her face. "Apparently, I'm also the only one you've ever taken home."

Her little sister had an incredibly big mouth.

Bravado had always served Madison well. Grappling for it now, she sought to ignore his references to the guilt she felt about her sister—along with the heat of his palms burning through the thin cotton of her shirt.

"I didn't take you. You showed up on your own. Besides," she pointed out, feeling bravado fail, "our relationship isn't like…that."

His eyes held hers as the heat of his hands continued to seep inside her, messing up her heart rate, making her ache to be closer. She looked away, afraid of what he might see, afraid of what he might already know simply because she couldn't seem to move from his touch.

Slipping one hand up the side of her neck, he grazed her jaw with his thumb and coaxed her eyes back to his. "It's not?"

She gave a slow shake of her head.

"Are you sure?" he asked, quietly searching her face.

Madison told herself she should nod. She should let him know that she was absolutely certain their relationship had nothing at all to do with emotion or desire or the awful need that had built inside her to be in his arms. She just couldn't seem to move. Not with him touching her. Not with his eyes turning smoky. Not with the unfamiliar heat he caused to curl through her as his glance fell to her mouth.

His voice went dark and faintly husky. "Maybe it's exactly 'like that,' Madison."

Her heart knocked against her ribs as he cupped her face in his hands. She felt as if it stopped beating completely when he lowered his head. His breath whispered over her mouth.

"Maybe you should just stop fighting it."

Cord heard her breath hitch, felt her lips part beneath his as it eased out in a ragged sigh. Taking the small movement as invitation, he angled her head to kiss her more deeply.

He nearly sighed himself when he felt the little tremor that raced through her and she rested her fingertips on his chest. Her touch felt uncertain, as if she didn't know if she should allow herself the contact. The fact that she was touching him at all was all he cared about.

Catching her wrist, he drew her arm up around his neck.

Madison didn't know if she leaned closer or he'd drawn her into his arms himself. She was aware of little beyond the gentle pressure of his hand at the small of her back, his tongue touching hers, retreating, then touching again to invade more deeply, and the incredible feel of his granite-hard body.

His chest crushed her breasts, the hot solid feel of it causing heat to race inward and down. His powerful thighs burned into hers as he pressed her stomach more intimately against the hard ridge behind his zipper.

The feel of him created a heavy ache deep inside her. Knowing he wanted her robbed the strength from her knees.

She sagged toward him, slowly fisting his shirt in her

fingers. She didn't need experience to know when a man was aroused, or to understand the mechanics of what went on between a man and a woman when it came to making love. She had girlfriends. She read *Cosmo*. She just hadn't realized how amazing a man's body could feel until she'd felt Cord's pressed against the length of her own. Or how badly she could want the man she was falling in love with.

The realization that she was falling in love with him caught her unprepared. It shouldn't have, she supposed, easing her grip, resting her forehead against the solid wall of his chest. She'd been struggling against it pretty much since the day they'd met.

Maybe you should just stop fighting it, he'd said, but she wasn't sure that was a good idea at all.

She felt Cord's hands slide to her shoulders. His lips touched the top of her hair.

"See?" he murmured, smoothing her cheek when she lifted her head. "It is like that."

Cord's heart felt as if it could pound right out of his chest as he eased her back, willing his breathing to slow. Having craved her before he'd even touched her, it took every ounce of restraint he possessed to keep from backing her down the short hallway he'd seen and finding the room with her bed. Since she looked as if she wasn't at all certain how she felt about what he'd just pointed out, he settled for tucking back the loose strand of her hair instead.

Steam rose from the pot behind her. Thinking that she nearly made his blood reach that state simply by kissing him back, he nodded toward it. "The water is boiling."

Insides quivering, Madison blinked at the hard line of his jaw. "Pasta," she said, amazed that she could recall what it was for. "I was going to make you pasta with what's left in there."

She nodded vaguely toward the bowl. Other than that, she didn't move. Neither did he.

Across the tiny room the faucet dripped in the sink. From somewhere outside came the honk of a horn. With his fingers slowly drifting down her cheek, the sounds barely registered.

His eyes searched hers, questions slipping into their smoky depths.

Feeling far too vulnerable, she turned toward the stove, causing his hand to fall away. Motion seemed mandatory. Since pacing wasn't possible with him behind her, she reached for the narrow box of pasta near the pot.

"Would you rather I didn't touch you, Madison?"

His quietly spoken words stilled her hand on the box.

Loving him was not smart. She even knew that loving him wasn't particularly wise, as restless as he was. But she knew a different man than the world knew. She knew the man who collected homes like some people did cars, but never felt as if he belonged in any one of them. Especially the one in which he'd grown up. She knew the man who understood that she often felt a lot like that, too. She knew the man who could see things in her no one else noticed or bothered to understand. One who was generous and thoughtful and who made her sister laugh.

She knew the man who made her feel things she'd never experienced before.

The thought of not being touched by him was almost more than she could bear.

"No," she murmured, her voice nearly a whisper.

She could feel him behind her, towering over her, his eyes on the back of her head, his body utterly still.

"'No' what?" Caution laced his tone. "You want me to touch you, or you don't?"

She swallowed past the pulse fluttering in her throat. "I...do."

His breath feathered against her hair almost as if he'd been holding it. "Then, relax," he commanded softly, resting his hands on her shoulders. "Nothing's going to happen that you don't want. Okay?"

His fingers curved over her collarbone. His thumbs made little circles at the base of her neck. Not sure how he could so easily relax the muscles there when others felt so tight, she murmured, "Okay."

"Good." His head dipped, his lips grazing the side of her neck. His breath feathered over her skin. "If that's not it, then what's wrong?"

Little shivers shimmered through her, taunting nerves, scrambling senses. "What makes you think something's wrong?"

"You had that look."

"What look?"

"The one you get when there's something you don't want to talk about."

His hand snaked around her waist, flattened over her stomach. Beneath his broad palm, nerves jumped.

Concentration became more difficult by the second.

"I thought you were hungry."

"I knew it." His lips vibrated against her skin as his fingers slipped under the hem of her shirt to caress bare skin. "There is something you don't want to talk about. You're trying to change the subject."

He was right. But worrying about loving him didn't seem nearly as necessary as absorbing the feel of his body when he eased her against him. Cord made her feel more, made her want more. Of everything. He refused to let her hide inside the shell she'd created around herself that was so transparent few people knew it was there. He made her want the closeness they had somehow come to share. He made her want to dream, to experience, to stop holding back.

That wanting felt frightening, simply because she'd never allowed it before. But she felt as if she were dying inside, withering like a leaf torn from its branch. And not allowing herself to want what only he had made her feel felt more perilous still.

His hand eased over the slick fabric of her bra, cupping one breast as his lips grazed the skin behind her ear. The jolt of sensation snagged her breath, pooled heat low in her stomach.

"Do you want me to stop?" he asked, his voice rough in her ear. "All you have to do is tell me and I will."

It might well kill him, but he would do it. He would make himself take his hands away from the incredible feel of her and find himself a shower or lake to jump into. Or maybe he'd just sit on her porch and howl at the moon for a while. But he would stop when she asked.

"Maybe you'd better tell me to stop, anyway," he decided, nearly groaning when he felt the hard bud of her nipple against his palm. "Because I really don't want to."

His other hand had traced the delicate line of her collarbone to the hollow of her throat. Beneath his fingers, he felt the quick jerk of her pulse.

"You don't?"

"No."

Her soft voice grew breathy, and so quiet he had to strain to hear.

"What do you want, then?" she asked.

Madison could practically feel the tension in his muscles as his entire body went still. A heartbeat later he lifted his head.

"Do you really want to know?"

With his body burning into her back, his hands seeming to burn everywhere else, she whispered, "Please."

His voice grew dark as he spoke in her ear. "What I want to do is turn you around, strip away your clothes and taste here."

Through the thin fabric of her bra, she felt his fingers skim her taut nipple. The intimate touch nearly buckled her knees.

"Then, I'd get rid of these," he murmured, letting his hand drift down her stomach to the snap of her jeans, "and taste the rest of you."

The smoldering heat in his voice robbed the strength from hers.

"Then what?"

"Use your imagination."

The images he created in her mind already had her imagination working overtime. Emboldened by them, by him, she slowly turned in his arms. Now that she knew what he wanted, she could give it to him. She just hadn't been quite sure where to start.

Her heart was pounding so hard she thought it might crack a rib. Without a word, she caught the hem of her shirt, pulled it over her head and let it fall to the floor.

Never in her life had she done anything so bold, but never had a man made her feel as desired as Cord did. He'd told her before that she was beautiful. When his slightly stunned glance moved from her face to the bit of ivory lace covering the gentle swells of her breasts, he nearly made her believe it.

The light in his eyes turned feral.

"Show me?" she asked.

His glittering glance swept her face, his features beautifully taut as he nodded toward the furiously boiling water.

''Should we turn that off?''

Her fingers trembling, she flipped a knob. She'd barely turned back before he caught her mouth with his.

There had been restraint in him before. She hadn't realized that until she felt some of it slip. The tenderness she'd felt before in his kiss became laced with hunger, a kind of raw need that he still held in check even as he pulled her up hard against his body. She didn't want him holding back. She wanted all of what he felt, wanted to know all of what he wanted from her. Needing him to know that, she curved her arms around his neck, stretching against him, drawing a moan from deep in his chest as his hands shaped her back, the curves of her hips.

Turning her from the stove, he edged her backward while his lips took thrilling little forays down her throat. His fingers deftly freed the clasp at the back of her bra. Easing the straps from her shoulders, he slipped away the lacy garment and tossed it toward the sofa while he edged her along the path between it and the wall and into the tiny hallway.

His hand slipped between them, cupping her bare breast, causing little darts of fire to shoot the length of her body. She tugged at his shirt, freeing the hem from his jeans, marveling at how bold he made her feel, aching to get as close to him as she could. He let her go only long enough to grip his shirt between his shoulder blades and jerk it over his head before catching her back to him.

His shirt hit the back of the sofa, missed and slid to the floor.

They barely noticed.

Guiding her through the door next to the tiny bathroom, he backed her into her bedroom with its narrow twin bed, piles of pillows and impossibly frilly comforter. In the pale light spilling through the door, he freed her hair, carefully sifting his fingers the length of it, letting it spill to her shoulders.

His eyes devoured her as he shaped her sides with his hands, then framed her waist to draw her against the naked wall of his chest. He carried that debilitating touch up, over her ribs, spanning his fingers around them, slipping up to cup the soft shape of her breasts. Lowering his golden head, his lips followed the line of her throat to where he'd touched, his tongue creating a trail of moist heat as he did exactly what he'd said he wanted to do, tasting her there, tasting her everywhere.

She did as he did, imitating him in a sensual game of follow the leader that had her helping him tug off his jeans after he'd stripped hers away. Blue boxers landed on ivory briefs. She gloried in the feel of his corded muscles tensing beneath her tentative touch, and the strength in his arms when he eased her back on the bed. He followed her down, encouraging her until those somewhat uncertain caresses became as sure as his own. Only when her hand ventured down the hard muscles of his stomach did he stop her.

Catching her wrist before she could go any lower, Cord slipped his fingers through hers and drew their joined hands over the top of her head. His control hung by a thread. If she touched him that intimately, he might not have any at all. With her, he wanted more than just to seek release.

He had wanted her from the first time he'd seen her, craved her from the first time they'd kissed. He had spent every day of the past week telling himself that she wasn't interested in sex with him and wanting to believe that was okay. That he really did just want to be with her. Then, he'd gone on to spend those very same nights restlessly pacing his room, flipping through television channels, working out in the gym until his muscles screamed from exhaustion, wanting her, anyway.

He had spent his entire life living fast because he wasn't sure he would like what he found if he ever slowed down. But when he was with her, the awful feeling of not quite being good enough, of not quite measuring up was no longer there. She accepted him as he was. Him. The man inside. Nothing else. Yet, as vital as her acceptance felt to him, with her curvy little body trembling beneath his, forgetting control and slipping inside her felt even more essential.

He reached over the side of the bed, fumbled his wallet from his pants. Rolling their protection over himself, he realized that he truly hated using it with her. With her, he didn't want anything between them. With her, he wanted only the feel of her surrounding him. But the foreign and dangerous thoughts gave way to more demanding needs as he leaned down to seek her mouth and she eagerly reached to meet him.

Covering her with his body, he slid his hand along the back of her thigh to draw her leg over his. Raw need sank its claws deep as he eased against her, drinking in the taste of her, swallowing her sharp little moan as he pressed forward.

That quiet sound of pain and the unexpected resistance he felt turned him as still as stone.

"Don't stop," she whimpered, arching up, catching a breath as she did.

Need vibrated through him as he held himself in check. "Madison." Her name came as a raw whisper. "Talk to me."

"Now?"

"Now." With his blood pounding in his ears, he murmured, "How long has it been?"

"I don't under—"

"How long since you've had sex?" he asked, unable to make it any more clear than that.

"I never have." Desire had its claws in her, too. She arched a little more, taking him a little deeper. "Cord, please?"

The plea in her voice jerked hard at that thread of control. The feel of her seeking him, begging him, snapped it completely.

He couldn't seem to think now about the implications in her admission. Possessiveness swept through him, as strong and as powerful as the protectiveness that forced him to take it slowly even as his body ached to fill her in a single thrust. What *he* needed just then didn't seem nearly as important as taking away the discomfort she felt in the moments before he was finally buried in her heat. And when she began to move with him, seeking him as he sought her, the only thought in his mind was that this wasn't just sex, this must be making love. Never had it felt so incredibly right.

Chapter Ten

Cord cradled Madison in his arms. Her breathing had slowly quieted along with his, but their bodies were still damp where they touched. From somewhere below came muffled laughter and conversation. Or maybe the sounds from the pub came in through the vents.

They hadn't bothered to crawl between the sheets. Twined together with her on her comforter, its pale color muted in the slice of light from the hallway, he realized they hadn't bothered with many civilities at all. Throw pillows from the bed had been knocked to the carpet.

Their clothes were scattered pretty much everywhere, too. The floor. The living room. The kitchen.

Nudging back the silk of her hair, he tipped her face to his, quietly searched her delicate features in the shadows.

"Why didn't you tell me?"

His chest seemed to fascinate her. It also seemed like

a convenient place to look to avoid his eyes. Beneath his hand, her slender shoulder lifted in a shrug. "It's not the sort of thing that just comes up in conversation."

"It could have in ours. We've talked about a lot of things, Madison."

He couldn't tell what filled her eyes when she glanced up. It might have been concern. It could have been awkwardness. Talking about sex wasn't always as comfortable as just doing it.

"Would it have mattered?"

It seemed that it should have. It seemed that, had he known, he would have done things differently, taken them more slowly, taken more care. Yet she hadn't acted at all like a woman who'd been nervous or uncertain. She had given herself so freely, so willingly.

He had known that she hadn't been out with a man in a long time. He had known that he was the only one in her life right now. Yet, despite what he had learned from her little sister about her, it had never occurred to him that she was a virgin. As he smoothed the soft strands of her baby-fine hair from her face, he realized it had also never occurred to him that he could feel so possessive about a woman.

"Probably not," he murmured, touching his lips to her forehead. He needed her to smile, to somehow let him know she didn't regret having trusted him so completely. That trust meant more to him than he wanted to admit. "But I might have let you feed me first."

Madison drew back. The smile he hoped for glittered in her eyes as she brushed the tips of her fingers over his chest. "If I feed you, will you still help me figure out what to serve for an appetizer tomorrow night?"

"I really wish you didn't have to do that job."

"Why?" she asked, looking surprised by his displeasure.

"Because if you didn't, we could go to dinner ourselves tomorrow night," he murmured, trailing his hand along the side of her neck. "Then we could take the boat out and watch the sunset from the bay."

"Sorry." She swallowed as his fingers slipped past the hollow at the base of her throat. "I'm booked."

"Then, book me for Sunday night. We can leave your grandma's house early."

Her face looked hauntingly lovely as her eyes closed to savor his touch. When his fingers drifted over the swell of one breast, her breath went thin. "I have to be up early the next morning."

"I know." His mouth hovered over hers, food forgotten as his body stirred and hers eased toward him. "I promise I'll have you home and in bed by eight."

If it hadn't been for Amber and Ben Johnson's dinner party, Madison would have been a wreck. She felt a wreck, anyway. Part of her was shaken to the core by the depths of her feelings and the sense of abandon she'd felt with Cord. Another part, the part that had kept her life confined to work and family, kept whispering that she would be a fool to believe she had any sort of a future with him.

Fortunately, she had too much to do to let the emotional tug-of-war dominate her day. In the same way that she'd learned to bury her guilt about her sister by keeping too busy to think, she threw herself into preparations for that evening's dinner party so thoughts of Cord became little more than a thread of anxiety that ran beneath her more conscious thoughts.

He had, at least, helped her decide what to serve. Indirectly, anyway. After they'd eventually made it back to the kitchen, he'd helped her put together the rest of her test batches before, sometime after midnight, he'd kissed her breathless and left her leaning weak-kneed by her front door.

He had suggested she serve both appetizers, but because she'd overslept, she only had time to make the quickest, which meant the salmon tarts since she already had an extra batch of the bite-size pastry shells down in Mike's freezer. Aside from having to pick up the beef tenderloins she'd ordered from the butcher and make the dessert she'd intended to start last night, she had her usual Saturday-catering-route shopping to do before she was due at Amber's at six-fifteen.

She'd made it with one minute to spare.

Now, three hours later, standing in the Johnsons' butler's pantry slicing her torte, she finally began to relax.

Once Amber's maid served dessert, she could go home.

Madison hadn't had to do any of the serving herself, either this week or last when she'd catered for Amber. Elena, Amber's uniformed and quietly efficient maid took care of everything. All Madison had to do was prepare and plate dinner for ten—which meant she had spent the entire evening in a huge kitchen any chef would envy. Everything was professional quality, from the appliances to the cookware Madison promised herself she would someday own, too, if her business grew enough.

Because she had spent the evening cooking, she hadn't seen any of the guests, but she could hear their friendly conversation coming from the formal dining room with its fabulous Italian frescoes on the walls and the chandelier Amber had told her last week had come from a villa in Tuscany. She'd said she had bought it there herself and had it shipped back, along with the crystal on the table which she'd purchased in Murano and the gold chargers she'd bought in Florence. While her husband liked to spend his free time sailing, she much preferred to shop.

Madison was neatly placing a slice of lemon mousse torte on a plate she had embellished with a lattice of chocolate sauce—and thinking that her own idea of shopping would be to hit a mall rather than a foreign country—when she overheard one of the guests comment again on the entree.

"Honestly, Amber," a cultured female voice quietly announced, "I have to have the name of your caterer. The sauce on that tenderloin was fabulous."

"It's Roquefort and port wine," Amber replied over the clink of crystal and silver. "Her own creation. She's really quite good, isn't she?"

"Incredible. Where did you find her?"

"She catered a party at Cord Kendrick's a few weeks ago and I snatched her up from there. She's just getting started."

"You know Cord Kendrick?"

"Ben and Ron crew with him," she explained, speaking of her balding, physician husband and another guest at the table. "He's entering America's Cup next year. Cord is, I mean. Ben's dying to sail it, and sailing Cord's entry is probably going to be his only chance. It costs a fortune to get a boat ready and into that race."

One of the men cut in. It wasn't Ben. Madison knew Amber's husband's gravelly voice.

"Was that the party where that redhead was running around in a white thong?"

"Oh, Ron, will you get over that?" came a woman's faintly annoyed appeal.

"What?" choked the first guest.

"I was a little shocked myself," Amber assured her obviously scandalized friend. "We were having a perfectly lovely evening with Ron and Cicely here and another crew member and his girlfriend when some of Cord's other friends showed up. I think the redhead was with a rock musician."

"You were at a party with a rock musician?"

Amber, whose interests Madison now knew ran more to ladies' teas and charity fund-raisers, laughed lightly. "Hard to believe isn't it?"

"The man has interesting friends," Ben defended.

Amber agreed. "His friendships do seem…diverse."

"And some of those friends definitely seem uninhibited. It's no wonder some of his parties get crashed." The suddenly garrulous Ron grew a little louder. "To Cord," he said, sounding as if he'd just raised his glass.

The ring of two goblets bumping each other was followed by low laughter from several guests. Madison didn't know with whom he'd toasted, but she'd be willing to bet it hadn't been his Cicely.

"I'm just glad the police didn't show up at that one," he continued. "It would have been bad for business to have my name plastered all over the local front page. I can see it now. State's Top Auto Dealership Exec Busted in Hot Tub Raid." Madison imagined him lowering his hand from having traced out an imaginary headline. "Cord's given me a lot of business, but not enough to go through that kind of hassle."

The obvious newcomer to the group didn't seem terribly comfortable with the direction of the conversation. "So, Amber, this caterer," she said, getting back to her original query, "you say she's just getting started?"

Ron was not to be dissuaded. "Cord's backing her,"

he pronounced flatly. "I'm not sure what all happened, but I got a call from him on a Monday morning saying he needed a van delivered to her as soon as I could get it there. I met him at that mall he's building with the contract for it a couple of hours later. He gave me a check for full sticker and added a hefty bonus for my trouble because he needed ice chests in it. Then, I'm on my way out when this other guy comes in and wants to know if everything's taken care of. I never could figure out what she had on either of them, but it must be something," he concluded flatly. "I overheard him tell the other guy that he's off the hook and that he'll do whatever it takes to keep her from suing him."

"Suing whom?" Ben asked. "Cord or the other guy?"

"Cord. What he said was 'keep her from suing me.'"

The man's decisive claim caught Madison with a slice of cake poised above a skillfully adorned plate. For a moment she couldn't seem to move. She wasn't even sure she breathed.

"...good, no matter what his reasons," she could hear Amber say over the pulse suddenly hammering in her ears. "Shall we have coffee and dessert in the living room?"

The scrape of heavy dining chairs on travertine tile underscored the stronger voices of the men as they agreed that Cord did, indeed, seem to attract legal attention, and the women murmured something Madison simply couldn't concentrate on enough to hear.

It seemed to take all her focus to get the last slice on the plate without messing either up. Not until it was done did she start shaking.

"I'll take those out after I serve coffee." Carrying poured cups of coffee on a silver tray, Elena moved behind her and around the corner to go through the dining room.

Moments later Amber walked in wearing a stylish dinner suit, her dark hair cut in a swingy bob and her French-manicured nails wrapped around a wine goblet. Poised, polished and pretty, the thirty-something hostess also looked faintly annoyed.

"Remind me never to serve martinis when we have Ron and Cicely over. That man gets so mouthy when he drinks gin.

"Oh, perfect," she murmured, catching sight of the row of beautifully prepared plates. "You outdid yourself again, Madison. Thank you so much."

"You're welcome," was all Madison could think to say.

"Before you go, would you give me a couple of your business cards? I never did get one, and I'd like one for Lillian Turley. You probably heard that she adored what you did tonight."

It seemed Amber knew quite well that conversation carried easily from the dining room. She also seemed tactful enough to keep any curiosity she might have had about Ron's comments to herself.

On the other hand, Madison thought, from the speculation in Amber's expression, she could simply be waiting to see what Madison might be willing to divulge.

"I'm sorry." Willing her hands not to tremble, she removed her apron and added it to one of the boxes she'd brought in with her. "I don't have my new cards yet."

"Will you have them by next week? If you'll mail me some, I can give one to Lillian when I see her at our committee meeting."

Madison couldn't think to next week. She could barely think to the next minute.

He'll do whatever it takes to keep her from suing him.
The thoughtlessly spoken claim echoed in her head.

She didn't want to believe that Cord had manipulated her.

She didn't want to consider that, as close as they had become—as close as she *thought* they'd become, that she had all but forgotten he was a man who pretty much always got whatever he wanted. And that what he'd wanted from her was to keep his name out of the papers. He'd told her that himself.

Whatever it takes.

The thought that Cord had used her feelings for him put a knot the size of a lemon in her stomach.

The thought that he had used her family, to make her believe he was different from how everyone else in the world knew him to be, grew it to the size of a grapefruit.

"Madison?"

"I'm sorry," she repeated, groping to end the evening on the same professional note it had started. "I'll have to check," she said, only now remembering that she hadn't yet ordered cards at all. She'd meant to talk to Cord about them when they went over the plan he'd designed for her. Only, they'd never found time to sit down and discuss it. "Is there anything else I can do before I go?"

It seemed as clear as the pea-size diamonds in Amber's ears that her curiosity was growing stronger by the second. But with guests to attend to, she only smiled.

"I can't think of a thing," she said, and thanked her again before leaving Madison to collect her things and slip numbly out the side door.

Madison couldn't remember the last time she'd stayed home on a Sunday. She actually couldn't recall that she ever had. Her routine had been the same since she'd moved above Mike's pub. She usually slept in until six, had coffee while she indulged in the Sunday paper and did laundry in the stacked washer and dryer in the bathroom, then showered and headed to her grandma's at eleven o'clock.

Her grandmother's house was now the last place she wanted to go. Cord would be there to give Jamie her last lesson and because he would, she did the second thing she couldn't remember ever doing. She called her mom and told her she didn't feel well, that she had a headache and that she wouldn't be able to go over today.

Instantly concerned, since Madison had always been as healthy as the proverbial horse, her mom wanted to know if she had a fever, if she had chills, if she ached anywhere.

Madison assured her that her temperature was fine and that the only place she ached was her head. The latter was an outright lie, which was probably the third thing she'd never done. She did ache somewhere else. In her heart. Deep inside where it hurt so much the pain felt almost physical. So when she got off the phone after her grandma got on and told her to drink lots of liquids, she went back to bed, pulled the pillow over her head and reminded herself for the hundredth time that he was Cord Kendrick, she was Madison O'Malley—and that millionaire playboys did not get serious about working-class girls like her.

She also reminded herself that Cord had been victimized before by what people had said about him.

She was too new at being in love to know how to cope with all the awful insecurities that came with it. The thought of betrayal stung fiercely. But betrayal worked both ways. She knew by now that just because someone said something incriminating, or something incriminating wound up in print, that it wasn't necessarily so. What she'd overhead last night had sounded horribly straightforward and indefensible, but the part of her that had grown to trust him didn't want to let go of that faith. If she did, she'd be betraying him, too.

She didn't doubt that he had said what she'd overheard. And though she had no idea how he could make it sound less harmful than it felt, she needed for the man who'd held her in that very bed to tell her that what they'd shared hadn't just been a way to keep her quiet.

She couldn't lie there any longer. It didn't matter that her head ached. She could take care of the dull ache behind her forehead with coffee and a couple of aspirin. Uncovering her face, she climbed out of bed for the second time, put on coffee and spent the rest of the morning cleaning her apartment, since she hadn't had time yesterday.

By noon her kitchen and bathroom sparkled. By mid-afternoon, there wasn't a trace of dust to be found anywhere else.

Because the day had turned beautiful, she had opened the window next to the front door to let in the spring sunshine and fresh air. It seemed to her as she knelt in her living room replacing books in the bookcase she'd just polished, that she should feel a sense of satisfaction about what she'd just accomplished. She'd even cleaned out her closet and drawers.

All she felt was numb.

She glanced at the digital clock on the VCR. They would have finished dinner at her grandma's by now, she thought, and was replacing another book when the phone rang.

The knot that had taken up residence in her stomach

tightened. Staring at the instrument as if it had just grown claws, she slowly rose and answered with what she hoped was a normal-sounding "Hello?"

It was her mother. But any relief she felt at not yet having to confront Cord was short-lived. Right after her mom said she hoped she hadn't wakened her and asked how she was now feeling, she mentioned the other reason for her call.

Cord was on his way over to bring her some of the chicken and dumplings that Grandma had made. Her mom wanted her to know that, in case Madison was in her robe and wanted to get dressed before he arrived.

The thought that Cord would be at her door in a matter of minutes resurrected every ounce of the anxiety Madison had worked so busily to suppress. Trying desperately to keep that anxiety from her voice, she thanked her mom and, after reassuring her that she really would be fine, hung up seconds before she heard the sharp report of a car door slam in the alley below.

Her heart seemed to pound a dozen times for every thud of heavy footfall on the stairs. Hiding behind a mask of numb calm, praying that calm wouldn't desert her, she opened the door the moment after he knocked.

She had forgotten what he had planned for them that afternoon. He had wanted them to leave her grandma's early so he could take her out on his sloop. He'd wanted her to see the sunset from the bay. What reminded her was the Annapolis Bay Yacht Club cap he wore with black sunglasses and a casual navy cotton shirt.

Thoughts of the plans that had once sounded so exciting vanished like steam. The glasses hid his eyes, giving him an edge over her that she wasn't comfortable with at all.

Not caring for the idea that he could probably read

her chaotic thoughts while his remained hidden, she glanced away.

"Hi," she said, and stepped back.

Holding a foil-covered plate in one hand, he removed his glasses with the other and hung them on the neck of his shirt. Beneath the slash of his eyebrows, his eyes narrowed on the listing ponytail atop her head and her favorite threadbare gray sweats. The neck of the baggy shirt had stretched out over the years and hung slightly off one shoulder. The drawstring pants had a hole at one knee.

His quietly assessing glance worked its way back up. Her face had been scrubbed free of makeup, leaving her totally exposed to his scrutiny. In her cautious eyes, she suspected he found little of the welcome he'd expected to see.

"You really don't feel good, do you?"

"I've felt better," she admitted.

"Let me get rid of this."

He lifted the foil-covered plate and headed into the kitchen, dropping his cap on the bistro table on the way. Madison stayed where she was by the door, her arms crossed over the knot in her stomach, and her hurting heart holding the faint hope that she somehow had his intentions all wrong.

"Your mom said you have a headache," he told her when he reappeared around the wall. "Did you take anything for it?"

"It hasn't started working yet."

"Think it's stress?" Towering over her, he curved his hand over her shoulder, gently kneaded the muscles at the base of her neck. "It could be, you know? You push yourself all week, then you worry too much about getting things perfect for these new jobs. You need time to wind down.''

The warmth of his touch felt achingly familiar. Not knowing if she could trust the concern in his voice, hating that doubt, she turned her head and moved to the small pile of books still on the floor.

It frightened her how attuned to him she'd become. She could practically feel the shift in his concern.

''Hey,'' he murmured, watching her go. ''What's wrong?''

''I need to ask you something. I need you to know something, too,'' she continued, seeing no point in hedging. She could already feel her disquiet leaking out, filling the room. Or maybe that sudden unease was his. ''I need you to know that all I wanted from you was another truck and a way to keep my business going until it got here. You didn't have to do anything else just to keep me from suing you.'' Her arms tightened as she watched his brow pleat. ''I wouldn't have done that.''

For a moment he said nothing. He just stood as still and unyielding as a giant oak while the scope of her words sank in. The instant they did, she could practically see his defenses lock into place. They slashed his carved features, colored his tone with suspicion.

His glance swept her pale face. ''Who have you been talking to?''

There was no denial. No quick defense. He didn't even question what she was talking about.

The hope that he could make her believe what she'd heard wasn't as bad as it sounded vanished like smoke in a strong wind.

''Does it matter?''

''Who?'' he insisted, clearly wanting to know who he could no longer trust.

"I haven't been talking with anyone. It was something I overheard at the Johnsons' last night. The man you got the van from," she said before he could again demand to know who'd betrayed him. "He said he didn't know what I 'had' on you and some other guy at the mall site, but that he'd overheard you tell that man he was off the hook…and that you'd do whatever it took to keep me from suing you."

She could practically see the spinning of Cord's mental wheels as he assimilated what would have sounded confusing to anyone else, but obviously made total sense to him. He didn't ask a single question. He didn't seek to clarify. More telling to her, he didn't deny a thing she'd said about the overheard statement. All he did was jam his hands on his hips and stare at her as if trying to figure out how much she'd read into what she'd heard.

He also didn't sound terribly pleased with the man who'd blown his objective.

"Ron Brockton," he muttered, as if he might be wondering who else the man had mouthed off to. "He must have overheard me talking to Matt."

A muscle in his jaw worked as he carefully watched her. She'd pulled from his touch once. Since he did nothing to close the ten feet of tension separating them, it seemed he didn't want to risk having her do it again.

"The actual liability for your truck belongs to Callaway Construction and the owner of the crane," he explained, his male mind obviously thinking that mattered somehow. "If any insurance claim or suit had been filed, the claim representative or your attorney would have gone after Matt's company first, then the crane company they'd subcontracted, the crane operator, his foreman and anyone else they could find. And me," he added, "because I'm who you were upset with and you would have mentioned my name.

"You already know my name draws reporters like blood draws sharks, so it just seemed easier all around to keep things as simple as possible. I didn't want Matt or his company involved. I was the one who told you to ignore the warning sign, and he didn't need his insurance premiums going up because of me. That's what I meant when I told him that he was off the hook and that I'd take care of everything."

As decent of him as that sounded, his explanation of the legal food chain did nothing to address what mattered to her the most.

"And the part about doing whatever it takes to keep me away from those lawyers and claims people?"

He hesitated, studying her as if he needed to know how specific he had to get.

"What about it?" he asked, caution in his voice, unconscious defense in his stance.

"Is that why you wanted to help me expand my business?"

He didn't seem to want to answer that one at all. But his response wasn't necessary. To her his motives seemed painfully clear.

"You weren't interested in helping me because you thought I was all that good," she accused, strain in her quiet voice. "You just wanted to stick around to keep an eye on me. As long as you stayed close and kept me talking, you knew everything I was doing."

Her conclusion caught his conscience by the back of its neck, pulling him up short, stopping him cold. He hadn't thought of what he was doing in exactly those terms. He'd thought more along the lines of keeping her busy, keeping her happy. At least, he had at first.

"Madison…"

"Am I wrong?" she demanded, hurt breaking free.

"I did think you were good," he defended, wondering where along the line his purpose had blurred. "I still do. But, yes." He wouldn't look her in the eye and lie. "Damage control was my only intention at first. But it didn't stay that way," he insisted, needing her to know that, too. "It's not just that now."

It really wasn't, he realized. He hadn't been aware of it happening, but somehow his original intention had become all tangled up with feelings he'd never experienced before. Feelings he didn't even recognize, and wasn't at all prepared to do anything about.

He did, however, recognize the expression shadowing Madison's face. She looked as if she had expected him to say exactly what he'd just said, because what he just claimed was what any man in his circumstance would have said to defend himself.

"Was my sister 'damage control,' too?"

"Your sister? Oh, come on, Madison, you don't think—"

"I don't know what to think," she returned, more hurt than angry. "All I know for sure is that you'll do just about anything to keep from getting more bad press. Especially when it comes to me," she concluded, thinking of how he'd asked her and all of her family to say nothing about knowing him. "You even put a bodyguard on me to keep the press away."

"That's not…"

"Not what?" she pressed when he clamped his mouth shut.

The muscle in Cord's jaw jerked again. He had no explanation that wouldn't just dig him into a deeper hole. He couldn't deny that he'd wanted anyone with a camera away from her. Partly because he didn't want the press hounding her. Partly because he didn't want them finding out who she was and asking questions that would lead back to the very sort of publicity he'd wanted to avoid.

"I should have gone with my first instincts about you." She shook her head, the motion weary. "But I forgot who you are. I fell for your line and completely overlooked that you're accustomed to getting whatever it is you want. I just didn't realize how ruthless you could get, Cord. I was already cooperating," she insisted, as upset with herself for her lapse as she was with him for causing it. "You didn't have to make me think you actually cared about me to keep me quiet. You especially didn't have to involve my family."

Her voice dropped.

"You said you'd be around until you got your plan for my business into place," she reminded him, her accusations quietly slashing at his conscience "but that won't be necessary. My truck will be here next week. Since it wouldn't be long before you'd be gone, anyway, I'll let you off the hook now. I promise I won't say anything about you to anyone. Just do me a favor and stay away from me. Stay away from all of us."

The chirps of a bird drifted through the open window, the sounds oddly cheerful in the sudden silence. A patch of beige carpet separated them. It might as well have been an ocean. Cord couldn't think of a thing to say that she would truly hear, much less anything she would believe. She'd said she'd fallen for his line, making it sound as if everything he'd said or done had been calculated to deceive her. She'd said she'd forgotten who he was, as if her better judgment would never have allowed her to care about him had she remembered his less-than-illustrious reputation.

With her arms still protectively crossed, she turned her head to hide the hurt in her eyes.

She also thought he'd used her family. She thought he'd manipulated her and ultimately used her feelings for him. Considering what had happened between them the night before last, she undoubtedly figured he'd used her there, too.

"Please," she whispered. "Just go."

Cord had done a lot of things in his life that had left him feeling less than proud of himself. He had been accused of other things he hadn't done and felt used and angry. But never had the disquieting combination of guilt and injustice hit all at once.

Prompted as much by his own sense of self-preservation as the pain he'd heard in her plea, he turned away, slapped on his cap and walked out the door. He wasn't sure how things had gone as far as they had, how he had become so totally involved with her, but the defenses that had served him most of his life were telling him to cut his losses and move on. It was time, anyway. He'd never had a relationship with a woman that had lasted more than a month, and he was a day past that now. Madison was right. He'd planned to move on once her truck had been delivered and his plan for her business was in place. He'd never given a single thought to the two of them beyond that.

Refusing to regard that as merely an oversight, he pounded down the stairs. Irritation and escape were more familiar to him than the less definable feelings clawing at the void suddenly filling his gut. It had never been his intention to hurt her. It had never been his intention to care.

He'd closed himself inside his SUV, backed out of the alleyway and made it as far as the stop sign by the pub when he felt his hold on his protective irritation slip. He did care about her. Far more than he'd ever let himself care about anyone. He knew she cared about him, too. At least, she had. Knowing her as he did now, he was dead certain she never would have made love with him if she hadn't.

It killed him to know she thought he'd used her little sister.

He made the turn, headed for the highway.

He cared about Jamie, too. He felt about her the way he imagined he might have felt about his own sisters had they ever needed him to help them out with anything. Or, he conceded, had he paid enough attention to know whether or not they did. He knew Jamie needed his help now, though.

There had been no dance lesson today. Jamie had finally done what he had pretty much insisted she do and called the boy she had the crush on. She had worked up her nerve and asked him to take her to the prom. The kid had told her he'd already asked someone else.

Cord swore he'd felt as disappointed as Jamie had. But he'd said nothing about the idea that had occurred to him during the dinner they'd all insisted he stay and eat, lesson or not. Just because Madison wasn't there didn't mean he wasn't welcome, her mom had said. So, while he would rather have taken a rain check and gone to see how Madison was doing, he'd answered Grandma's questions about a movie premier he'd attended in Hollywood months ago, which she apparently knew about from an old *People* magazine, and thought about taking Jamie to the prom himself.

His problem now, however, was that he'd intended to ask Madison to pick out a dress for her and take care of the girl details he knew nothing about. But Madison wasn't talking to him.

She'd also asked him to stay away from her family.

It took Cord three days to decide that he couldn't let Madison go without making her understand that what had happened between the two of them had nothing to do with sparing his public hide. He also felt an obligation to Jamie. He was the one who'd gotten her hopes up about the prom. She had worked hard to learn to dance and she deserved to go. It wasn't right that she should miss the chance because of a problem between him and her older sister.

Having reached those conclusions, he also realized there was someone other than Madison he could trust to help get a dress.

He had never turned to his family for help with anything personal. For years he had felt the same way he'd acted, as if he had been entirely on his own, responsible only for himself or interests of his own choosing. He thought it vaguely ironic that Madison seemed to feel responsible for everyone *but* herself. Yet, because of her, he was beginning to understand how the inability to see things differently, or the refusal to change or even be willing to try, imprisoned a person.

It seemed apparent to him now that the emotional exile Madison felt was pretty much self-imposed. He didn't know about her other siblings, but neither her mom, her grandma nor her little sister blamed her for what happened so long ago. They loved and accepted her as she was. She was the one who couldn't put her past behind her.

Considering the number of invitations he'd turned down from his sister Ashley to join her and Matt for dinner, he conceded that maybe he'd imposed his own exile, too. There were certain areas where he and his family would never agree. He and his father, especially. But he knew a sixteen-year-old girl who needed a dress to wear to a dance. And because of her older sister, he realized that the time had come to stop letting his past hold such influence...where his family was concerned, anyway. Escaping his past with the press would be next to impossible.

Chapter Eleven

"**Y**ou're expected, Mr. Kendrick. Please, come in." The salt-and-pepper-haired woman in a gray house-keeper's uniform stepped back for Cord to enter. "I'll show you to the living room."

"I'll do it, Martha." Ashley Kendrick Callaway walked into the small marble foyer, her perfectly cut blond hair gleaming in the light of the overhead chandelier. Eyes as blue as Cord's own lit with an automatic smile.

"Matt just got home," she said to him. "He's in with the baby," she continued to her domestic help. "Would you please tell him Cord is here?"

"Of course," the woman murmured and slipped from the room.

The baby. Cord had all but forgotten about his three-month-old niece. Matt had shown him pictures, but he hadn't seen little Amelia Briana Regina Callaway himself yet. Other than to wonder why his family insisted on hanging so many names on its members and thinking how tiny the child looked, Cord had been more interested in how easily his oldest friend had adapted to doting fatherhood than the bundle of pink in the photos.

"I'm not here to see Matt, sis. I need to see you."

A thick gold necklace peeked between the lapels of Ashley's peach silk blouse. The necklace disappeared as she placed her perfectly manicured hand at the base of her throat. "Me?"

"You don't have to look so surprised."

A smile fought confusion. "You never come to see me. When you called and asked if we were going to be home, I thought you were coming to talk to Matt." The smile died. "Is everything okay? There's nothing wrong with Mom or Dad, is there?"

"I'm sure you'd know anything like that before I would." Trouble or bad news. It wasn't going to be easy getting past what his family thought at the sight of him. "I just need your help with something," he explained, trying to sound nonchalant about why he'd just made a two-hour drive in the rain.

He wasn't feeling anywhere near as laid-back as he usually did, though. His sister seemed to realize that, too. She also seemed aware that he'd given considerable thought to approaching her.

"Help with what?" she asked, curious.

"I need you to buy a dress for a prom."

Her expression didn't change. She just stared at him and blinked. "A prom," she repeated, as if wanting to make sure she'd heard correctly.

"You know, that dance the kids go to in high school. I need it for a...friend," he decided, not knowing what else to call Jamie.

"A prom," she said again. "This friend," she added, caution lacing her tone, "how old is she?"

"Sixteen."

For a moment Cord's perfectly poised sister didn't say a word. She didn't need to for him to know what she was thinking. Within seconds it became as clear as the sizable rocks in her wedding ring that she thought he was once again headed for trouble of the headline kind.

"You want me to buy a gown for a sixteen-year-old? Cord," she said, as if trying to appeal to his sense of reason, "what are you doing with a girl that young? Sixteen is—"

"Jailbait?" Matt suggested as he appeared behind his wife. The big, blond contractor held the equally blond baby against his muscular shoulder. His broad hand hid the back of the pink terry cloth thing that covered her from the toes tucked under her round bottom to the damp fist in her little rosebud mouth. Cord couldn't see the child's eyes. They were closed. But Matt had said they were as blue as her mom's.

Pulling his attention from the perfect and pale lashes curled against little Amelia's rosy cheek, Cord sent his friend a beleaguered glance. "You're not helping."

Matt lifted one T-shirt-covered shoulder in a good-natured shrug. "I'm curious, too. What *are* you doing with a sixteen-year-old?"

"I'm not doing anything with her. She's Madison's little sister."

Matt clearly recognized the name.

His wife did not.

"Who's Madison?"

"A woman Cord has been trying to keep from suing him."

The defense in Cord's tone slid in before he could stop it. "Madison's more than just a potential lawsuit."

Matt's sun bleached eyebrows arched. "She is?"

"Why does she want to sue you?" Ashley demanded.

"Can we just talk about Jamie, please?"

"Who's Jamie?" they both wanted to know.

"Madison's sister," Cord replied, striving for patience, growing exasperated. "I just need someone who knows something about clothes to buy a dress and shoes and whatever else she'll need so I can take her to her prom."

Poise faltered. "You're taking her?"

"You're kidding," Matt muttered.

"Forget it," Cord muttered himself and started to turn.

Ashley stopped him. Slipping one arm under his, her other beneath her husband's, she turned them both toward the living room. "I think we should all sit down. Then, Cord, you can start from the beginning and tell us that this isn't anywhere near as strange as it sounds."

Cord didn't want to sit. He didn't want to go into detail, either, but he could see where avoiding it was going to be impossible as he crossed the thick carpet in his sister's Richmond condo. Matt and Ashley were in the process of building a house on a two-hundred-acre parcel of land Matt had purchased shortly after their impromptu wedding in Luzandria last year. According to Matt, until it was complete, the condo was home.

Cord hadn't been there before, yet the place still felt familiar. The high-ceilinged room with its wall of arched windows, shades of taupe and ivory, original art and lush greenery reminded him in many ways of the rooms at the family estate. There was none of the European formality here, but quality and class fairly leaked from the carved mahogany woodwork.

A quiet elegance, so like that possessed by their

mother, fairly seeped from his sister, too. As she gracefully sat on the arm of an overstuffed chair and touched
her baby's peach-fuzz-covered head when her husband
sank to its cushion, Ashley seemed the epitome of a lady.

Cord still found it nearly impossible to believe that his
reserved, polished and pampered younger sister had tem-
porarily abandoned her administrative duties for the Kendrick Foundation's charitable trusts to spend weeks in the
humidity and heat of a Florida summer helping build a
house for a family of working poor.

He also had a hard time believing that his best friend
had possessed the audacity to put her up for bid at a
charity auction to get her to do it. Stranger things had
happened, though, he supposed. There had been a time
when Matt and Ashley had barely spoken to each other.
Actually, none of his family had cared much for Matt all
those years ago. Matthew Callaway had been his cohort
in crime in high school, the only guy he knew who
matched his disdain for other people's rules and, to
Cord's knowledge, the only person ever declared persona
non grata at Camelot.

That was before Matt had cleaned up his act, made his
own millions and helped provide their parents with their
first grandchild.

That child was actually kind of intriguing, Cord realized, finding himself drawn by Amelia's perfect little
nose and tiny fingers as he planted himself by the chair
a few feet away. Her whole hand gripped the top of
Matt's index finger. A miniature, incredibly perfect nail
topped her thumb. He'd never seen a baby that small so
close up before. Whenever he'd been around his little
second cousins at family functions, he'd pretty much
avoided any under the tumble-and-tackle or piggyback
stage.

He'd never seen his friend as content as he looked now, either. From what Ashley had said, it sounded as if Matt hadn't been home long. Since the child was sleeping, it seemed that he'd come in, changed clothes and picked up the baby just so he could hold her.

Watching Matt with his wife and daughter, and seeing Ashley smiling softly at them both, he thought it no wonder Matt so often made the long drive from the mall site. He wanted to be with them.

Like Cord wanted to be with Madison.

"Okay, buddy," Matt said, one big foot resting on his knee, his baby on his chest. "Do you want to tell us what's going on?"

Pushing his hands into his pockets, Cord turned toward the marble fireplace. He needed to focus on one challenge at time. He had no idea how to get Madison to listen to him. But he did know what to do for her sister.

"I want Jamie to go to her prom," he said, because that was the bottom line. "She's this great kid who's overcome some tough odds to even be on her feet. Going to this dance will mean a lot to her."

"Is she ill?" his sister asked.

"She's disabled. She has been since she was a kid," he explained, seeing no need to offer more than that. He saw no need, either, to mention that he had helped her learn to dance. This wasn't about him. "This thing is important to her, and she deserves to go. But I know she doesn't have anything to wear. That's why I need your help.

"You know what it's like out there," he said to Ashley. Like the rest of their siblings, she had lived her life in the same family fishbowl, suffered the same intrusions. "If I walk into a men's store and buy something, it's no big deal. I walk into a boutique and buy a dress to have delivered to a female, there's a good chance that will be noticed. There are no guarantees that the salesperson won't be on the phone to heaven-knows-who the minute I leave. They'd have Jamie's address, too, and I don't want some reporter or photographer showing up at her door. Since you buy clothes all the time, I figure you know someone you can trust to be discreet.''

Ashley definitely seemed to understand his problem. Being intimately familiar with the meddling of the press, concerns of her own shifted into place.

''What about the night of the prom itself? Can you trust Jamie to not say anything to her friends ahead of time? The media will be on this in a heartbeat, Cord. Especially if they know she's disabled.''

His brow slammed low. ''What does her disability have to do with anything?''

''We never know what slant those people are going to put on something,'' she reminded him. ''But you know as well as I do that if you show up at a high school prom, it will be news. If anyone knows about it ahead of time, it could turn into a media circus.''

She considered him, seeming to choose her words carefully.

''From what I've heard, the only publicity about you lately has been good. And low-key,'' she emphasized, because understated was good, too. ''Mom's mentioned a couple of financial pieces. And I saw a couple of articles about your win at the yacht races.

''Congratulations, by the way'' she offered, generously refraining from saying how relieved the members of the family grapevine were by his less-than-sensational publicity of late. ''No offense,'' she continued, getting back to her point, ''and I don't mean to offend your little friend, but with your reputation, some reporter could decide that the slant he wants on a story about a prom is that you're trying to clean up your act by taking on charity cases.''

''Or that you're playing with jailbait,'' Matt added, because that seemed most obvious.

At the blunt, and regrettably possible, suppositions, the muscles in Cord's jaw tighten. He had been so focused on losing Madison and getting Jamie to the prom that he'd again forgotten that their quiet little world was not his.

The thought of anyone thinking Madison's little sister a charity case galled him.

''Then I'll just have to make sure no one knows. We won't stay that long. She just wants to dance at her prom,'' he muttered, hating that everything he did was somehow suspect. It was no wonder Madison wanted nothing to do with him. ''An hour and we're out of there.''

A muscle in his jaw jerked as his sister quietly watched him. Her expression was thoughtful, almost... speculative.

''What kind of gown do you have in mind?'' she finally asked.

He hadn't considered that, either. Considering it now, he tried to recall the magazine pictures Jamie had shown him of gowns her friends were wearing. She'd seemed to like all of them. Except one.

''One without ruffles,'' he said because that was the one she'd wrinkled her nose at. ''All her friends are wearing ones with thin straps. It should probably have a full skirt, too. She wears a brace, so anything tight would make it hard for her to move.''

''Does she have a favorite color?''

His shrug told her he hadn't a clue.

"What about her coloring?"

"It's like Madison's. Only her eyes aren't as dark. Her hair is, though."

"What size is she?"

He had no idea there, either.

"Can you ask her sister?" Ashley suggested when he just looked at her.

The muscle twitched again. "Madison isn't exactly speaking to me right now." The fact that she'd told him to stay away from her family wouldn't bode well for such a conversation, either.

Matt shifted the baby higher on his chest. "Why not?"

The child squeaked in protest.

"It's complicated," Cord muttered.

Matt's eyes narrowed. "Complicated?"

Ashley rose, gave her husband a look of forbearance and reached for the baby. Matt reached up as she did, transferring a white cloth from his shoulder to hers. "Who is this woman?" she asked. "Other than someone who wanted to sue you."

Until a little over a year ago, Cord would have thought his sister wanted to know what Madison did for a living, who her family was, where they were from, what they owned. But he'd learned that, unlike many in their parents' elite social circles, she wasn't impressed by status or lineage. Though she moved within those pedigreed spheres with ease, she had been among the first to defend their brother, Gabe's, choice of a bride when he'd married the family's pretty young groundskeeper. Her own husband had the bloodlines of a mongrel.

She just wanted some idea of who they were talking about.

"She's this woman with a great smile who's honest and generous and works way too hard. Everyone she knows is a friend. A real friend," he emphasized, because true friendship always impressed him. "You can tell they'd be there for her no matter what she needed. And she cares about them the same way." She'd cared about him, too. Truly cared, he thought as he paced past the fresh flowers on the coffee table.

He stopped when he reached the end of it, his jaw working as the truth of the feelings he'd tried to sort through the last three days finally caught up with him.

"She makes me want to just be with her," he said, his voice quiet, his focus inward.

Aware that he was being watched, he glanced to where Ashley stood next to Matt rocking her baby. "She makes me want what you two have," he finally admitted.

With the baby settled on her shoulder, Ashley's motion suddenly slowed. Her glance darted to her husband, then back to Cord.

Looking surprised himself, and more than a little concerned, Matt rose to study him more closely. "You're that serious about her?"

Cord pushed his fingers through his hair. "Yeah. I am."

"You know," he said, shaking his head, "I never thought you'd get serious about any woman." Looking as if he didn't know if he should clap him on the shoulder in compassion or shake his hand in congratulations, he simply planted his hands on his hips. "Madison seems like a nice gal."

"She is."

"So how bad did you screw up?"

An amused smile lurked in Matt's eyes. Cord was pretty sure he would have found that smile annoying, too, had he not suspected why that amusement was there.

It hadn't been that long ago that Matt had been in the

same position himself. That had also been when Cord had pointed out to him that he never had those sorts of problems with a woman because he never let himself get serious about one.

It seemed that bragging inevitably came back to bite.

"Why does it have to be something I did?" he challenged, practically daring his friend to grin. "Why couldn't it be something she misunderstood?"

"Because even if a woman misunderstands, it's still our fault. Get used to it," he said, the smile fading to sympathy. "Is it just a misunderstanding?"

It was, and it wasn't. "Like I said before, it's complicated." Though Matt was his best friend, he didn't care to air this particular situation in front of his sister. Unlike in Madison's family, with her grandmother in particular, not every subject was open to dissection and discussion. There were boundaries in their personal lives, and certain things the others simply didn't need to know. "Mostly I think my reputation got in the way."

Matt whistled in a breath, gave him an understanding nod. "I can see where that could be a problem."

"Yeah," he muttered, not caring to think about that with his sister there, either.

Ashley moved to join them. Seeming to sense that her presence was responsible for her brother's reticence, she turned the baby so Cord could see her sweet little face. Eyes as blue as a summer sky blinked up at him.

"Why don't we finish up with Jamie, then you two can talk about her sister while I feed Amelia. We still need to figure out what size gown she needs."

Relieved by the change of subject, Cord reached over and stroked the baby's smooth little cheek. Her pink little mouth immediately moved toward his touch.

Surprised by her reaction, he pulled back.

"What size are you?" he asked his sister, tucking his hand into his pocket.

"Six."

"You're about the same as Madison. Jamie's a little smaller that she is."

"That would make her about a five in juniors. Or a two in haute couture. What about shoes? She probably wouldn't want anything with a heel."

"No heels. She's on crutches. And I have no idea how to judge what size shoe she wears."

"Don't worry about that," his sister replied with an airy wave of her hand. "I'll just pick out something to go with the gown and have one of each size sent over. She can send back what doesn't fit."

"You'll do it, then?"

"Of course I will," she said, looking as if she couldn't believe he'd just asked. "I'll feel like I'm playing fairy godmother. It'll be fun. Just leave me her address and I'll take care of everything. When is the dance?"

"Friday."

"*This* Friday. As in the day after tomorrow?"

Cord touched the baby's cheek again. He couldn't seem to resist.

"I would have given you more notice if I'd had it myself." He gave her an apologetic smile. "I just realized it was you I needed to talk to about this a couple of hours ago."

Ashley tipped her head, watching him with his niece. "Mind if I ask what happened a couple of hours ago?"

Considering that he'd never approached her for anything before, he supposed he owed her that much. "I was just thinking about what I've learned from Madison."

His sister smiled, touched her hand to his arm.

"I'd like to meet this woman." With a pat to his

sleeve, she added, "I'll leave you two to talk. I'll call you as soon I've found the dress."

"Thanks, sis."

"Anytime," she assured him, and turned so Matt could kiss the top of Amelia's fuzzy head.

On her way out, she told them both to take their time. But Matt's only advice when his wife disappeared took no time at all to deliver.

"Go with your gut."

Cord turned to the man whose advice he valued as much as anyone's. "Is that what you did with my sister?"

"Pretty much," Matt admitted. "The only thing I knew for sure was that I wanted to be with her. When I finally found her after she'd left, I just hoped I'd know how to convince her to give me another chance.

"There is one thing, though," he warned, male sympathy back again. "In situations like this, groveling is usually involved."

Cord had never groveled in his life. "I was afraid of that."

"So when are you going to talk to her?"

Cord told him he wasn't sure. If he was going to go with his gut, then there were a couple of things he needed to do before he approached her.

First, though, he needed to take Jamie to the prom.

Chapter Twelve

Madison spent Friday night in the pub and its kitchen and returned to her apartment a little after one in the morning. She had an order for cocktail hors d'oeuvres for forty to deliver to Amber's friend Lillian Turley Saturday evening and she had needed to get her puff pastry started and into the fridge. She'd planned to cook and chill shrimp, too, but that part of the project had to wait until later in the morning. Working in Mike's kitchen early in the morning or on weeknight afternoons or evenings had never been a problem. But on Friday night the pub was packed, which meant that Jackson, the weekend cook, had required the space.

She'd needed to work tonight. She'd needed something to occupy her mind, to block the emptiness she'd lived with ever since Cord had walked out the door. So instead of making trays of artfully designed canapés, she'd helped Jackson serve up burger and shrimp baskets and refilled the peanut bowls for Mike. Then she'd visited with her friends in the noisy crowd, smiled and laughed and tried to pretend she felt just fine. But the only thing she'd felt all night was...lost.

The light on her answering machine blinked as she closed and locked her door. Walking over to where it sat on the end table, she punched the message button below the window that indicated she had two calls and listened to the whir of the tape rewinding.

She knew there would be no message from Cord. She hadn't heard from him in five days and she didn't expect to hear from him now. He hadn't even called after she'd picked up her new truck on Tuesday to make sure it was what she'd ordered. She'd honestly thought he might call then, too, to make sure she was satisfied enough with the truck to keep her from complaining. But she hadn't heard a word. It seemed he felt he had accomplished his purpose and gone back to his rarefied world. His silence only confirmed that she really hadn't meant anything to him at all.

The first message was from Lillian. She'd added four guests and needed to increase her order. She hoped it wouldn't be a problem.

The second was from her grandma.

"You should have told us!" she scolded. "We didn't even have film in the camera. I would have borrowed one from a neighbor, but Cord said they had to go because he didn't want the limo parked out there attracting attention. Not that it didn't attract attention the minute it pulled up," her recorded voice informed her over the scratchy sound of the tape and the muffled voice of her mother asking her to just leave a message to have Madison call. "That's the longest one I've seen that wasn't in a funeral procession. Half the neighbors were out here watching them go. And that gown,'' she continued, ''she looked like a princess in it, but it sure showed a lot of shoulder…''

There was a pause. ''Madison, it's Mom. It was a wonderful surprise, dear. But you really should have told us sooner so she could have had more time to primp. Call us when you get in will you? Cord said they'll be back by eleven. You really need to see her.''

Madison blinked at the recorder as it clicked off. The ''her'' could only be her sister. But she was lost about the gown and limo part—until she remembered the prom her sister had given up hope of attending.

She picked up the phone, glanced at her watch, put the phone down again. It was one-twenty in the morning. If Cord had returned Jamie by eleven, no doubt by now everyone would be wound down and asleep.

Cord had escorted Jamie to the dance. He'd bought her a gown. He'd taken her in a limo.

The knowledge tugged hard at her heart. She could only imagine how wonderful the evening must have been for her sister, how much it had meant to her to show up at her school in a limousine, looking like a princess, escorted by a gorgeous man whose bad-boy reputation and wealth were legend. He'd given her a fantasy. Instead of being the girl others felt sorry for, or avoided, or ignored, she would have been Cinderella at the ball, and the envy of every girl there.

She imagined Steve Balducci's date had wanted to trade places with her, too.

What she couldn't imagine at all was Cord's motive.

She turned from the phone, hating the thought, hating that she questioned an act of generosity that had made her sister's entire year. She didn't want to question Cord's motives. She didn't want to think about how kind he could be. Despite what she'd said to him about having forgotten who he was, there truly was a side to him she didn't think others saw.

Since thinking about those qualities hurt so much, it seemed better not to think of him at all.

She headed for the bathroom to shower off the smell of French fries and smoke. She hadn't told her family what had happened between her and Cord. She hadn't talked to them at all since Monday night when her mom called to see how she was feeling. She had no idea what he might have told them, either. All she knew for certain was that they thought she had known about his plans. Unless she wanted to explain why she didn't want him around anymore—and face questions from her grandmother she truly did not want to answer—she needed to go along with that assumption. Then, first thing Sunday morning, because she wouldn't have time until then, she would call him and ask again that he leave them all alone. She needed him to understand that it would require a whole lot less explanation on her part and be easiest on all of them if he would just quietly disappear from their lives.

Quietly was not an option.

News of Jamie's date had not only spread like spilled water through the neighborhood, it had reached the media. Reporters started showing up at Madison's grandma's house a little after eight the next morning. That was when Madison's mom called to see if Madison had tried to call them. The phone had apparently started ringing at 7:00 a.m. with a call from a reporter in New York, which was followed by a call from a television station. Those were immediately followed by another from a woman who didn't identify herself but demanded to know how her mother justified allowing an impressionable young girl to spend time in such a notorious older man's company, unless it was just for his money. They'd taken the phone off the hook and stopped answering it after that.

"A couple of reporters even showed up at the door a while ago," her mom said, sounding a little shell-shocked.

"What did they want?"

"The same thing as the ones who called. They all want to talk to Jamie. When I wouldn't let them, they wanted to know who I was and how Jamie knows Cord, what their relationship is, and how long she's known him. They know she's on crutches and want to know how she broke her leg. One asked me if she and Cord had been together when it happened. I told them it happened when she was a child and the woman immediately wanted to know if he was paying for operations."

Madison closed her eyes, rubbed the spot between her eyes. There were no more operations that could help Jamie. But speculation like that was how rumors got started. "What else have you said to them?"

"Except to confirm that he took her to the prom and say he's a friend of the family, I haven't said anything. I don't know what to say to some of their questions."

"I don't know what to say to those people, either." Grandma Nona's voice cut in from an extension phone. "I answered the front door and those reporters shoved their microphones straight at me. There was even a TV camera on the porch and I still had curlers in my hair. They were talking over each other, asking the same things your mom just said, and wanted to interview Jamie. I told them she was still sleeping and shut the door."

"Is she still asleep?" Madison asked.

Her mother's voice lost its uneasiness. "She'll probably sleep until noon. Cord dropped her off a little after eleven and left then himself, but it was one o'clock before we could get her out of that dress and into bed. I imagine she lay there for another hour just thinking about how much fun she had. She told us all about it. She had a wonderful time."

Despite Madison's growing trepidation, she couldn't help but smile.

"What does the dress look like?"

The question seemed to give both women pause.

"You don't know?" her mom asked, sounding genuinely surprised. "I thought you might have picked it out for her. That pale blue was perfect for her. And the full skirt was the only style she could wear with her brace."

Madison hesitated herself. The less said, the better. "Cord did this on his own, Mom."

"I didn't think she'd pick out something with no back," Grandma defended. "And that explains why there are so many shoes."

"Well, when you talk to him," her mom continued, "tell him again for us how sweet he was for doing this for her. And, please, Madison, ask him what we can do about these reporters. I'm looking through the front drapes now and the ones grandma closed the door on are across the street talking to the neighbors."

Madison promised that she would, then told her to call her on her cell phone if she needed anything else because she'd be in the pub kitchen working on the hors d'oeuvres she had to deliver that evening. Moments later she headed for the kitchen to dig the card with Cord's phone numbers on it from the trash. She'd torn it up yesterday after she'd pulled it from her purse while searching for her keys.

Five minutes later, with enough pieces rescued and taped back together to reconstruct two of the three numbers he'd given her, she called his house first, then his cell. She got voice mail on both phones. Afraid he might not check his messages, or want to return her call, she didn't leave a message on either one. Taking the card and her cell phone with her, she decided she'd keep trying until he answered one or the other.

By one o'clock she had finished 264 canapés, all of which looked like little oriental works of art to complement Lillian's Asian theme, arranged them on disposable black faux marble catering trays and stored them in the refrigerator. Next on her to-do list was her weekly shopping. She needed ingredients for next week's muffins and sandwiches, since she could now return to her full route. After that, she had to stop by the florist to pick up a stem of dendrobium orchids so she could place a single flower on each of Lillian's trays. She also needed to run by the printer and pick up the new business cards she'd ordered. Since Lillian wanted her order delivered at six o'clock, that gave her five hours with no time to spare.

The thought that maybe she would need to hire some help reminded her that she needed to try calling Cord again.

Again there was no answer.

She called her grandma's, let the phone ring twice as she'd told her mom she would do, hung up and called again so she'd know it was her.

Her mom told her that their phone had continued to ring and that, had she not known Madison would be calling, she would have left it off the hook. Another reporter had shown up, too. But she had gone away when they hadn't answered the door. A couple of Jamie's friends were there, though. They were with Jamie in her room, giggling over last night. Apparently, both girls had danced with Cord and labeled the experience amazing. From what her mom understood, they still hadn't washed their hands.

"I had no idea how much commotion this would cause," her mom confided. "We've had more neighbors drop by for coffee today than we've had in the past month. Have you reached Cord yet?"

Madison told her she hadn't, but that she would keep trying. Had she had any idea what she could do to ease the chaos at her grandma's house, she would have done it. Unable to come up with anything, and with the demands of the day ahead of her, she hung up to get started on her shopping.

She had barely set foot out the back door of the pub when a click and whir caught her attention. The faint sound seemed to have come from the direction of the street, but she couldn't see anyone except Tina Deluca. Tina, her dark curly hair flying, had just climbed from her car at the curb and rushed toward her to announce that she'd just heard from Suzie Donnatelli whose little sister had been at the prom, that Cord Kendrick—*the* Cord Kendrick—had taken Jamie to the dance and that Cord was actually a friend of Madison's.

"Where on earth did you ever meet him and why didn't you tell me?' Tina demanded as Mavis Reilly drove by and slammed on her brakes.

Seeing the neighborhood's biggest gossip zeroing in on her, Madison told Tina it was a very long story, that she was really pressed for time and promised she would talk to her later. Tina saw Mavis, understood completely and let her go. Dealing with nosy Mavis, however, would have been infinitely easier than dealing with the unsettling feeling that she was being followed again as she ran her errands—or with the headline that screamed at her from a newspaper at Reilly Brothers' Produce.

The *Newport News Daily Monitor* printed an edition of the Sunday paper that was available after five o'clock on Saturday.

Madison was standing at the checkout at five-twenty-five, running late and hoping the orchids in her truck wouldn't wilt, when seventeen-year-old Kevin Reilly, one of the family stock boys, cut open the bundle of papers by the front door. Picking up a copy, he turned around with a look of total disbelief on his face.

"Hey, Madison!" Light reflected off his glasses as he called across the two lanes of customers. He turned the paper around, held it up. "Is this you and Jamie?"

"Bring that over here," her checker, his mother, called. Beneath her short cap of strawberry blond curls, Rita Reilly's eyes narrowed. "And don't holler like that."

"Yes, ma'am," the boy respectfully replied, but his attention was on the way the color slowly drained from Madison's face.

The pictures were small, nothing more than little teasers that ran across the top of the front page with teasing tags to get people to look inside. But there was no mistaking the people in those photos. Not to anyone who knew them. One photo caught Cord with his hand on the side of Madison's neck, his lips inches from hers. The photo next to it caught him helping Jamie, beaming in her gown, from a limo. The tag running beneath the photographs read: Cord Kendrick Romances Locals, See Local Section.

The local section had the same photos, only six inches larger right below the two-inch headline suggesting A Family Affair?

"I'll take this, too," she said quietly, and hands shaking, offered cash since she'd just written a check for everything else.

Stuffing the paper into the bagged groceries in her cart, she thanked the dumbfounded Rita, declined help with her bags and headed for her truck with a dozen people scrambling behind her to claim a copy of the paper.

Within the hour she learned that the photos had also made the Saturday edition of *Entertainment Tonight.*

Jamie called to squeal that news to her as Madison left Lillian Turley's beautiful Tudor-style home by a road Lillian told her bypassed the development's main guard gate. Her little sister wasn't concerned at all with the publicity. Too young and innocent to grasp the repercussions, she was getting too much of a kick out of having been on television to realize how uncomfortable the situation could get for everyone else. She also quite proudly informed Madison that she'd known all along that Cord had a thing for her and she was glad he was Madison's boyfriend.

When her mother got on the phone, she didn't sound quite so thrilled. There were two news vans camped on the street. Reporters were stopping friends who came to the door. After pulling away from the phone to tell her mother that she could talk to Madison later about her affair with Cord, she got back on the line to ask how she was supposed to go to church in the morning with people blocking the driveway. Unless they wanted to get accosted with a microphone, they couldn't leave the house.

Hearing her mother's desperation, feeling her own, Madison told her to call the police and tried again to call the man who started this whole mess.

She was wondering if she might be able to track him down through Matt Callaway, though she had no idea how to reach the construction company owner on a Saturday night, when Cord answered his cell phone on the third ring.

"I need to talk to you," she said, not bothering to identify herself. "A guy on a motorcycle has followed me all afternoon, reporters are making prisoners out of my family and I'm afraid to go home because now that my name was in the paper and on television, they'll be at my apartment, too. What's my family supposed to do? What am *I* supposed to do?"

She thought she heard him swear, but the music in the background was too loud for her to be certain of so faint a sound.

The music suddenly died.

"Where are you?" she heard him ask.

"I'm just leaving Gloucester Point."

"You're being followed now?"

She glanced in her rearview mirror. The paparazzo on the black motorcycle that had followed her all afternoon hadn't been particularly discreet. She'd noticed him across the parking lot, taking pictures of her as she came out from the bulk food warehouse. He'd snapped away from across the street as she'd hurried from the florist and the market. He'd kept his distance, never getting close enough for her to see his features, but his brazenness and total disregard for her discomfort had made it feel as if he'd pushed his camera right into her face.

The last she'd seen him, he'd been hanging back from the main guard gate of the Turleys' exclusive neighborhood, presumably waiting for her to reappear so he could continue his pursuit. That was why she'd asked Lillian for another way out.

She fervently hoped that she'd lost him. "I can't see anyone right now."

"Then come here."

She'd reached him on his cell. She had no idea what she'd caught him doing. She didn't even know where he was. "Where's 'here'?"

"My house. You're only twenty minutes away."

Within twenty minutes Cord had called Beth to find out what was going on, asked if they all wanted to come to his house until he could somehow call off the press— an offer she graciously declined because the police had just told the news vans to stop blocking the street—and showered off the sweat he'd worked up after nine hours of polishing brass and oiling the teak deck of his boat. He'd needed something physical to do, something to work the edge off the restiveness plaguing him until he could talk to Madison. Because he knew her Sunday mornings were free, he'd planned to show up at her door first thing in the morning. He'd hoped that, by then, he would have figured out what he was going to say.

It had never occurred to him that she would show up before then looking as distressed as she'd sounded on the phone. After she'd asked him to stay away from her and her family, he'd been afraid she might not want to talk to him at all.

The crisp white blouse and black slacks she wore explained why she'd been in Gloucester Point. The way she had her arms snugged tightly beneath her breasts explained that she wasn't at his place because she wanted to be.

"I won't keep you," she said, stopping just inside the door when he closed it. As if she thought he might have company, she darted a glance past the arm of his navy-blue polo shirt and backed closer to the long stained-glass window by the door. "I just need to know how to make these people go away. There are pictures of you and me and my sister in the paper and on television and what they're implying is so totally—''

''I talked to your mother,'' he said, sparing her the details. ''She explained the pictures and told me about the headline.'' He tipped his head toward the living room, his carved features as guarded as her own. ''Come inside. We need to talk.''

Madison hesitated.

''There's no one here,'' he assured her. ''I've been out working on the boat all day. I'd just come in when you called.''

That explained his freshly shaved face, she thought, remembering the only other time she'd been to his house. She'd caught him fresh from the shower, then, too.

At least this time, mercifully, he was fully clothed.

Relieved to have found him alone, she followed him through the spacious entry with its view of the bay, past the dining table strewn with travel brochures and a map of Europe and stopped near the back of the long leather sofa dividing the airy space. From the looks of his reading material, it seemed he was looking for someplace to go.

The thought that there would soon be an ocean separating them shouldn't have mattered to her as much as it did.

''I don't know what to do about any of this,'' she said, wanting badly to keep him from knowing how much it hurt to see him. ''I really appreciate what you did for Jamie. We all do. But it's going to be all over the neighborhood by morning that you and I are having an affair, and I'm going to have to explain to everyone that we're not. No one who knows my family is going to believe what they're saying about you and Jamie dating, but they'll have seen that picture of us. They'll figure out that it was your car coming and going from grandma's house and my apartment. There's no way anyone is going to believe there isn't…wasn't…something going on.''

''It's going to go a lot farther then your neighborhood.'' Absolute certainty marked his tone. ''If it was on television tonight, it's already all over the country. The tabloids in Paris and London will pick it up, too.''

She couldn't believe how matter-of-fact he sounded. ''You think that helps? Do you have any idea how embarrassing it is to have to explain my personal life to my grandmother and her friends? How am I supposed to handle this?''

''I know exactly how embarrassing it can get,'' he reminded her, looking no crazier about the situation than she was. This was just the sort of publicity he tried to avoid. ''I'm sure I'll be hearing from my family soon, too.

''As for the best way to handle reporters or your neighbors,'' he told her, focused more on her problem than his just then, ''just answer the questions you're comfortable with and ignore the rest. I don't always do so well with the press, but my sister is a pro. She said to feel free to call on her until you get used to it.''

Madison opened her mouth, promptly shut it again. ''Until I get used to it?'' She shook her head. He'd talked about her to his sister? ''How long do you think this will last?''

Cord watched the consternation flicker through her eyes, felt a certain disquiet of his own. *Forever,* had just popped into his head, but she didn't look too receptive to the concept at the moment.

He drew a deep breath, rubbed his jaw as he blew it out.

Go with your gut, his friend had advised. That was exactly what he planned to do, too. He'd just hoped to be a little more prepared when he did it.

"There's something I need to explain before I answer that."

The distress that had masked Madison's caution shifted to confusion. "About reporters?"

"About me. Us," he amended, far more concerned about the woman quietly watching him than he had ever been with the media. "I don't blame you for backing away from me, Madison. I know my reputation isn't the best. And I know that when I met you I was only trying to save my hide. But I meant it when I said that the way I thought about you had changed."

Mention of their last encounter caused her glance to falter, then fall.

"I know you didn't believe me." He stepped closer, cautiously reached to tip up her chin. "I don't blame you there, either," he confessed, praying she wouldn't pull away. "I wasn't expecting what happened between us any more than you were, and I couldn't have explained what I felt for you if I'd tried."

With his eyes searching the wariness in hers, his thumb grazed her jaw.

"I know now what it is that I felt," he confided, his tone quiet and certain. "I want to be with you. I don't want to lose you, Madison. Ever. I love you," he said simply, laying himself, and his heart, on the line. "For what it's worth, I've never said that to any woman in my entire life."

He had no idea what thoughts crowded behind her lovely brown eyes as she stared up at him. She just stood there, immobile, while her breath shuddered in, and wariness shifted to what looked an awful lot like incomprehension. Taking it as a good sign that she hadn't backed away, needing her to know just how serious he was, he scrambled ahead before his nerve failed.

"I have to be honest with you," he said, thinking he'd be okay as long as he could keep touching her. "The idea of marriage has me a little nervous. A lot nervous, actually. But the thought of not being married to you frightens me even more. I'm sure the idea of being married to me would make any sane woman think twice," he hurried to admit as her eyes widened, "so please don't say anything now. Just consider it. Marrying me, I mean.

"And while you're at it," he added because he was afraid his reputation might not be their only obstacle, "consider what your sister said about getting on with your life. You've punished yourself enough for something that was never your fault. If you truly don't care about me, then I'll leave you alone. But if you do care, don't use your guilt about Jamie to push me away like you have every other guy."

He brushed her cheek with his fingers. "You don't have to deny yourself happiness because you think she's not happy, Madison. Jamie's doing just fine."

He'd said the wrong thing. He felt dead certain of that when she suddenly backed up, still staring in uncertainty, and turned away.

Madison blinked at the view of the bay, but she saw nothing. She breathed in slowly, telling herself to be calm, but her pulse continued to pound in her ears and her heart to batter the wall of her chest.

She didn't know which stunned her more, that Cord had just said he loved her, that he wanted to marry her, or that he could so clearly see how her guilt had overtaken her life.

She pressed her fingers to her mouth, her hand trembling. She'd never realized how much her guilt had caused her to deny herself until he had come into her life. She'd been content with what she had. At least, she had as long as she'd kept herself too busy to consider all she was missing. Yet even trying to working herself into exhaustion hadn't allowed her to stop loving him.

She'd never realized, either, that he could have been caught as unprepared as she had been by their relationship. She never would have imagined that he could be caught off guard by anything at all.

He loved her.

The thought echoed through her head, still unbelievable, still astonishing. He never would have said it if he hadn't meant it. She believed that with all her heart. He wasn't a man who promised a woman anything. Yet he was promising her a future with him.

Her hand slowly fell.

He was right, though. No sane woman would want to marry a man with his reputation. But the talk was far different from many of his actions. She knew the man who trusted her as a friend. She knew the man with a huge heart and kind soul who honestly seemed more content in her world than in his own. And she wanted that future as badly as she wanted her next breath. They would never be able to escape his name or notoriety, and in many ways his life was larger than she could imagine, but she could help build that oasis for him.

"Talk to me, Madison."

"I can't right now," she said, as the enormity of their situation sank in. "I'm—" *Hyperventilating,* she thought. "Thinking," she said.

"About what?"

"About what you said. About marrying you," she clarified. She'd walked in the door with her heart aching and bruised. As she turned around again, shoving back a lock of hair as she looked up at the caution etched in his face, it felt about to burst.

"I figure being together, we could help each other out," he said, strengthening his argument. "I know I need more structure in my life. And you could sure use a lot less in yours."

She gave a sage little nod. "You have a point."

Seeing a smile fighting to break free, Cord felt the tension leak from his muscles. Light danced in her eyes, warming their dark depths with shimmers of gold. He edged closer, nudged back the strand of hair she'd missed.

"So, about what you were thinking. Are you leaning in any particular direction?"

She moved into his touch. "Toward insanity. I love you, too," she murmured, and rested her hand on his hard chest.

"Yeah?"

"Yeah," she echoed.

The smile in his eyes met the smile in hers as he cupped her face in his hands. "Say it again."

She knew exactly what he wanted to hear. So she told him she loved him, and he told her he loved her back before he lowered his head and his mouth claimed hers. His kiss felt achingly tender, as full of relief and gratitude as it did the quiet hunger that had him kissing her more deeply, altering her breathing, weakening her knees.

Her hand had fisted in his shirt when he finally lifted his head.

He brushed her bottom lip with his thumb, the motion deliciously familiar. "You know," he began, glancing up as if he might be able to concentrate better with his focus on her eyes, "we never did get around to discussing your business plan. I made some changes to it."

She slipped her arms around his neck, loving how good it felt to be free to touch him again. "You did?"

"Mmm," he murmured, distracted by her mouth anyway. He brushed another kiss over her lips, lifted his head again. "I figured it might be good for business if you checked out some of the restaurants in Paris and Venice and Barcelona. We should check out some provincial towns, too. All the great chefs travel to expand their cuisine," he said, distracted by her earlobe this time. "I was going to talk to you about it tomorrow, but as long as you're here now…"

"You want to take me to Paris?"

"And Venice and Barcelona. I have brochures over there on the table." He touched a kiss behind her ear. "You're really going to have to give in on not wanting to hire help, though," he quietly insisted. "I figure you'll want to keep up with the catering, but we need to find you a space of your own and hire people you can train to do things the way you want. I need you to have time for us, too. Okay?"

He lifted his head.

She felt dazed. "Okay."

"There's one more thing."

Madison swallowed, hung on a little tighter. "What's that?" she asked gamely.

"We have a more complicated project to work on."

"The publicity," she said, only now remembering what had brought her there.

"Actually, we'll kill all that talk in the morning. We'll just tell everyone we're engaged and that'll stop all the rumors about your sister and speculation about what's going on.

"I'm talking about our wedding," he explained, pulling her a little tighter himself. "My family would think it just like me if they read I'd eloped to Las Vegas. But you probably want more than that, and, if you don't mind, I'd kind of like to do this right myself."

Epilogue

According to the etiquette books Madison nearly memorized, a proper wedding took a year's worth of planning. With the help of Cord's sister Ashley and his amazingly down-to-earth and welcoming mother, both working from Richmond, and her mom and Grandma Nona coordinating from the Ridge, Madison pulled it off in three months. It also helped that Cord's father, whom she discovered to be a rather formidable gentleman, had been so pleased to know Cord was settling down that he sprung for the whole affair.

The eight-tiered wedding cake, a creation that looked more like a work of art than dessert, had been flown in from New York.

The six-course dinner, including lobster and beef tenderloin with truffles, awaited the five hundred invited guests at the Gloucester Point Country Club.

Bayridge Floral had created the banks of white flowers

and greenery on the altar of St. Mary's Church by Jamie's school, along with the boutonnieres for Cord's father and Gabe, his brother and best man. That florist had also supplied corsages for his very regal-looking mom and sisters, Madison's mom, who looked stunning in royal blue rather than her usual navy, and Grandma Nona, who reminded Madison a bit of the queen mother in her pink evening suit and matching hat.

Jamie, her maid of honor, carried a nosegay of white roses, and wore the pale-blue gown Cord had bought her for the prom. Ashley, Cord's other sister, Tess, and his sister-in-law, Addie, wore similar gowns in sapphire. Madison's white gown wasn't so different from theirs. It had the same snug spaghetti-strapped bodice, only edged with pearls and a few more yards of skirt. She carried roses, too, because that was the flower Cord had first given her.

Cord, she thought, his name echoing in her heart, in her head as they stood at the altar, his lips touching hers. My husband.

"Congratulations," she heard the priest say as they drew back from their first kiss as man and wife.

"Thanks," she heard Cord murmur as he let go of one of her hands to accept the priest's.

He turned back to her, stunningly handsome in his black tuxedo, and smiled into her eyes. She smiled back, unable to imagine how she could ever be happier as church bells began to peal over the applause of the guests.

The organ struck the first chords of "Ode to Joy" and they turned, hands tightly clasped, to face the sea of smiling faces that stretched from the front pew all the way to the back door. On one side of the church, the cream of society rose to applaud them in stylish designer tuxedos and gowns. On the other, steamfitters, construction workers, patrons of Mike's pub and all her neighbors wore their Sunday best.

The doors at the back of the church opened as they moved together down the aisle. Her long veil and train flowed and rustled behind her. She knew she was still smiling. She couldn't seem to stop. It seemed Cord couldn't, either, as he turned her in his arms the moment they stepped into the early-evening air.

Cameras flashed. Beyond them, video cameras rolled. The mob of media was held back by red velvet cordons, and police lined the way to the white limousine parked at the curb, but Cord made no attempt at all to hurry them away from the eyes of the press. Instead he nudged back the veil the breeze pulled toward her face and kissed her. Hard.

When he pulled back, he was grinning.

"What was that for?" she asked, eyes shining. The past three months had been pure chaos, but they'd survived. They'd decided they could survive anything, as long as they were together.

"It was for them." He nodded toward the press, possession and protectiveness in the deep tones of his voice as he touched his hand to her cheek. "Because I love you. And because this time I've done something I want the whole world to see."

* * * * *

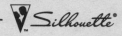

SPECIAL EDITION™

From award-winning author

MARIE FERRARELLA

Diamonds and Deceptions

(Silhouette Special Edition #1627)

When embittered private investigator
Mark Banning came to San Francisco in
search of a crucial witness, he didn't expect
to fall in love with beautiful bookworm
Brooke Moss—daughter of the very man he
was searching for. Mark did everything in his
power to keep Brooke out of his investigation,
but ultimately had to face the truth—he couldn't
do his job without breaking her heart....

THE PARKS EMPIRE

DARK SECRETS.
OLD LIES.
NEW LOVES.

Available at your favorite retail outlet.

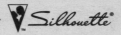

SPECIAL EDITION™

From bestselling author

VICTORIA PADE

Northbridge Nuptials

*Where a walk down the aisle
is never far behind.*

Wedding Willies

(Silhouette Special Edition #1628)

Although she's famous for bailing on two of her own trips to the altar, Kit McIntyre has no problem being part of her best friend's happy day. But when she's forced to spend lots of one-on-one time with the sexy best man, Ad Walker, Kit's eyes are finally opened to the very real possibility of happily-ever-after.

*Available August 2004
at your favorite retail outlet.*

And coming in January 2005,
don't miss Book Three, ***Having the Bachelor's Baby.***

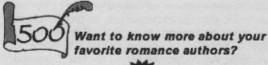

If you enjoyed what you just read,
then we've got an offer you can't resist!

Take 2 bestselling love stories FREE!

Plus get a FREE surprise gift!

Clip this page and mail it to Silhouette Reader Service™

IN U.S.A.	IN CANADA
3010 Walden Ave.	P.O. Box 609
P.O. Box 1867	Fort Erie, Ontario
Buffalo, N.Y. 14240-1867	L2A 5X3

YES! Please send me 2 free Silhouette Special Edition® novels and my free surprise gift. After receiving them, if I don't wish to receive anymore, I can return the shipping statement marked cancel. If I don't cancel, I will receive 6 brand-new novels every month, before they're available in stores! In the U.S.A., bill me at the bargain price of $4.24 plus 25¢ shipping and handling per book and applicable sales tax, if any*. In Canada, bill me at the bargain price of $4.99 plus 25¢ shipping and handling per book and applicable taxes**. That's the complete price and a savings of at least 10% off the cover prices—what a great deal! I understand that accepting the 2 free books and gift places me under no obligation ever to buy any books. I can always return a shipment and cancel at any time. Even if I never buy another book from Silhouette, the 2 free books and gift are mine to keep forever.

235 SDN DZ9D
335 SDN DZ9E

Name	(PLEASE PRINT)	
Address	Apt.#	
City	State/Prov.	Zip/Postal Code

* Terms and prices subject to change without notice. Sales tax applicable in N.Y.
** Canadian residents will be charged applicable provincial taxes and GST.
   All orders subject to approval. Offer limited to one per household and not valid to
   current Silhouette Special Edition® subscribers.
® are registered trademarks owned and used by the trademark owner and or its licensee.

SPED04   ©2004 Harlequin Enterprises Limited

SPECIAL EDITION™

Two's company...
but three's a family.

Don't miss the latest from

TERESA
SOUTHWICK!

After her husband's death, mom-to-be
Thea Bell had given up on passion.
Until she met Scott Matthews. But her
craving for the hunky contractor was
one she had to resist, for her baby's sake.
Because she wouldn't let a carefree
bachelor disrupt her dreams of a happy
home—even if he was the family man
she'd always wanted.

It Takes Three
(Silhouette Special Edition #1631)

*Available August 2004
at your favorite retail outlet.*

COMING NEXT MONTH